11th Hour

The Women's Murder Club

A complete list of books by
James Patterson is at the back of this book.
For previews and information about the author,
visit JamesPatterson.com or find him on
Facebook or at your app store.

11th Hour

James Patterson

AND

Maxine Paetro

DOUBLEDAY LARGE PRINT HOME LIBRARY EDITION

LITTLE, BROWN AND COMPANY

NEW YORK BOSTON LONDON

Little, Brown and Company
Hachette Book Group
237 Park Avenue, New York, NY 10017

Little, Brown and Company is a division of Hachette
Book Group, Inc., and is celebrating its 175th
anniversary in 2012. The Little, Brown name and
logo are trademarks of Hachette Book Group, Inc.

ISBN 978-1-61793-372-1

Printed in the United States of America

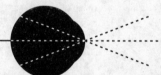

This Large Print Book carries the
Seal of Approval of N.A.V.H.

Prologue

REVENGE

One

A good-looking man in his forties sat in the back row of the auditorium at the exclusive Morton Academy of Music. He was wearing a blue suit, white shirt, and a snappy striped tie. His features were good, although not remarkable, but behind the blue tint of his glasses, he had very kind brown eyes.

He had come to the recital alone and had a passing thought about his wife and children at home, but then he refocused his attention on someone else's child.

Her name was Noelle Smith. She was

eleven, a cute little girl and a very talented young violinist who had just performed a Bach gavotte with distinction.

Noelle knew she'd done well. She took a deep bow with a flourish, grinning as two hundred parents in the audience clapped and whistled.

As the applause died down, a gray-haired man in the third row popped up from his seat, buttoned his jacket, stepped out into the aisle, and headed toward the lobby.

That man was Chaz Smith, Noelle's father.

The man in the blue suit waited several seconds, then followed Smith, staying back a few paces, walking along the cream-tiled corridor, then taking a right past the pint-size water fountain and into the short spur of a hallway that ended at the men's room.

After entering the men's room, he looked beneath the stalls and saw Chaz Smith's Italian loafers under the door at the far right. Otherwise, the room was empty. In a minute or two, the room would fill.

The man in the blue suit moved quickly, picking up the large metal trash can next to the sink and placing it so that it blocked the exit.

Then he called out, "Mr. Smith? I'm sorry to disturb you, but it's about your car."

"What? Who is that?"

"Your car, Mr. Smith. You left your lights on."

The man in the blue suit removed his semiauto .22-caliber Ruger from his jacket pocket, screwed on the suppressor. Then he took out a tan-colored plastic bag, the kind you get at the supermarket, and pulled the bag over his gun.

Smith swore. Then the toilet flushed and Smith opened the door. His gray hair was mussed, white powder rimmed his nostrils, and his face showed fierce indignation.

"You're sure it's my car?" he said. "My wife will kill me if I'm not back in my seat for the finale."

"I'm really sorry to do this to your wife and child. Noelle played beautifully."

Smith looked puzzled—then he knew.

He dropped the vial of coke, and his hand dove under his jacket. Too late.

The man in the blue suit lifted his bag-covered gun, pulled the trigger, and shot Chaz Smith twice between the eyes.

Two

A long second bloomed like a white flower in the blue-tiled room.

Smith stared at his killer, his blue eyes wide open, two bullet holes in his forehead weeping blood, a look of disbelief frozen on his face. He was still on his feet, but his heart had stopped.

Chaz Smith was dead and he knew it.

The shooter stared back at Smith, then reached out a hand and pushed him off his feet. The dead man fell into the stall, collapsing onto the seat, his head knocking once against the wall.

It was a perfect setting for the late

Chaz Smith. Dead on the toilet, a fitting last pose for this crud.

"You deserved this. You deserved *worse,* you son of a bitch."

It had been a good kill, and now he had to get out.

He put the plastic bag containing the shell casings, the GSR, and the gun back into his jacket pocket and closed the stall door.

Then he carried the trash can out of the men's room and put it down so that it blocked the door from the outside. That would hold people off for a while, make them think that the men's room was temporarily closed.

The man in the blue suit heard a rush of sound. The auditorium doors had opened for the crowd. He headed back by way of the main hallway, turning left just as people poured into the lobby, chattering and laughing. None of them noticed him, but even if they had, they would never have connected him to the dead man.

There was a fire alarm box on the wall next to a door marked TEACHERS' LOUNGE.

Using his handkerchief to glove his hand, he opened the door to the box, lifted the hammer, broke the glass, and pulled the lever; the alarm bell shrilled.

Then he walked directly into the thick of the crowd.

Children were already starting to scream and run in circles in the lobby. Parents called out to their kids, took their hands or lifted them into their arms, and moved quickly toward the front doors.

The man went with the crowd, through the glass doors and out onto California Street. He kept going, turned onto a side street, passed Chaz Smith's Ferrari, and unlocked his scarred SUV parked right behind it.

A moment later, he cruised slowly past the school. All the good people—the kids and their parents—were facing the building, staring up at the roof, watching for smoke and flames.

They didn't know it, but they were all safer now.

Chaz Smith was only one of his targets. The media had started tracking this shooter's kills—drug dealers, all of them. One of the papers had given him a nickname and it had stuck.

Now they all called him Revenge.

Fire engines approached from Thirty-Second Avenue, and the man called Revenge stepped on the gas. Not a good time to get stuck in a traffic jam.

He had shopping to do before he went home to his family.

Book One

THE HOUSE OF HEADS

Chapter 1

Yuki Castellano opened her eyes. She was in her lover's arms, in her mother's bed. If she was dreaming, it was a pretty funny dream.

She grinned to herself, almost seeing her dead mom sitting in the green slipper chair by the dresser, a look of disapproval on her face—and, as sometimes happened, her mother's voice got into her head.

Yuki-eh, you want to have husband. Not lover.

Mom. Mom, he's so great.

He so married.

Separated!

Jackson Brady stirred beside her, pulled her toward him, lifted her hair, and kissed the side of her neck.

She said, "It's . . . early . . . you can sleep for another . . ."

Yuki sighed as Brady ran his hands over her naked body, started her engine, and revved it up.

Pillows went over the side, blankets bunched up at the footboard, and he fitted himself inside her. She cried out and he said, "I've got you."

He did. He had her good.

Gasping, they bit at each other, moved together in a race that they both won. They finished entangled in bedding and each other, both of them sweating, satisfied, amazed.

"Oh my God." Yuki sighed. "That was . . . just . . . okay."

Brady laughed. "You're too much."

He kissed her again, put his fingers in the thick black curtain of her hair, watched as the strands fell through his fingers.

"I have to go," he said softly.

"Not without coffee."

He gave her bottom a smack and got out of bed. Yuki turned on her side and watched Brady walking away from her. She took in his perfect body, his pale hair hanging almost to his shoulders, the simple Celtic cross tattooed on his back.

When the bathroom door closed, Yuki got out of bed and put on a silk robe the color of watermelon, a gift from Brady.

She stepped over the clothes they'd dropped on the floor last night, took one of his clean shirts out of a drawer, put it on the green chair. She listened to the shower and thought about Brady being in it.

Tsutta sakana ni esa wa yaranai, said Keiko Castellano. *A man won't feed the fish he caught.*

Shut up, Mom. I love him.

In the kitchen, Yuki opened the cupboard, got out the coffee beans, filled the coffeemaker with water. She put bread in the toaster.

It wasn't even 6:00 a.m. She didn't have to be at her desk in the DA's office until nine. But she didn't mind getting up with Brady. She wanted to do it, because, jeez, she loved him. It was almost embarrassing how much, but God, she was happy. Maybe for the first time in her adult life.

Nah, no maybe about it. This was definitely the happiest she'd been in twenty years.

Brady came into the kitchen. His tie was knotted, shoulder holster buckled over his blue shirt, and he was shrugging into his jacket. He looked worried, and she knew he was already working on the case that had been tearing at his guts.

She poured coffee, put buttered toast on a plate.

He stirred a lot of sugar into the coffee mug, took a sip. He took another, then put the cup down.

"I can't eat, sweetie. I have to—Christ, I have a meeting in fifteen minutes. You okay? I'll call you later."

He might not call her later.

It didn't matter. They were good.

She kissed him good-bye at the door and told him she hoped that he'd be safe. That she'd see him soon, whole and well.

She hugged him a little bit hard, a little too long. He tousled her hair and said good-bye.

Chapter 2

The sun was still in bed when I parked my Explorer across the street from the Hall of Justice, home to the DA's office, the criminal court, and the southern division of the SFPD.

I badged security, went through the metal detector, and headed across the empty garnet-colored-marble lobby to the staircase and from there to the Homicide squad room on the fourth floor.

Lieutenant Jackson Brady had called us together for an early meeting but hadn't said why. I'd been working for

Brady for ten months and it still felt wrong.

Brady was a good cop. I'd seen him perform acts of bravery and maybe even heroism—but I didn't like his management style. He was rigid. He isolated himself. And when I'd been lieutenant, I'd done the job a different way.

My partner, Rich Conklin, looked up from his computer as I came through the gate. I loved Richie—he was like a little brother who looked out for *me.* He was not just a fine cop but a sterling person, and we'd had a great couple of years working Homicide together. What I appreciated about Conklin was how, in times of high stress, he always kept a steady hand on the wheel.

Our desks were pushed together at the front of the squad room so that we worked face-to-face. I hung my jacket over the back of my chair said, "What's going on?"

All he said was "I'll tell you when everyone is here."

I showed my childishness by making a lot of noise banging my chair against the desk. It took me about a minute to get it out of my system. Conklin watched me patiently.

"I haven't had coffee," I said.

Conklin offered me his. Then he threw paper clips at me until I calmed down.

At 6:30 a.m. the Homicide squad was present, all eight of us, sitting at our desks under the fluorescent lights that made us look embalmed.

Brady came out of his hundred square feet of glass-walled office and went directly to the whiteboard at the front of the room. He yanked down a screen, revealing 8 x 10s of three high-ranking bad-news drug dealers, all of them dead.

Then he stuck up photos of a fourth dead man—both his mug shot and morgue shot.

It was Chaz Smith. And his death was news.

Smith was a notorious scumbag who lived his upscale life in Noe Valley, passing as a retired businessman. He made a good living brokering the sales of millions of dollars in high-grade cocaine, delivering it to other dealers who sold on the street.

Smith had avoided capture for years because he was stealthy and smart and no one had ever caught him stopped next to another car on the shoulder of some highway transacting business through the window of his Ferrari.

Judging from the two bullet holes in his head, I figured it was safe to say he'd made his last deal.

Brady said, "Smith was at his little girl's music recital yesterday afternoon. He went to the men's room to have a snort, then took two shots through his frontal lobe. He was armed. He never got his gun into his hand."

Smith's death meant one less heinous dirtbag preying on the weak, and he'd been taken out without any taxpayer expense. I would have thought Narcotics would be dealing with this, not Homicide, but something was different about this murder. Something that had gotten to our lieutenant.

Brady took his job seriously. He didn't waste words. And yet right now he seemed to be skirting the reason he'd brought us onto the case.

I said, "Why us, Lieutenant?"

"Narcotics has requested our help," he said. "I know. We've got more than enough active cases, but here's the thing—Chaz Smith was taken out by a twenty-two that was stolen from our evidence room, one of six twenty-twos that have disappeared in the last few months. The shooter had access to SFPD floors. And the evidence log was deleted."

There was some gasping and shuffling in the room. Brady went on.

"There were no witnesses to Smith's murder, no evidence was left behind, and the fire alarm was pulled to create confusion.

"It was a professional hit, the fourth in a string of slick hits on dealers. It points to something—ah, shit," Brady said. "I'm not going to finesse it for you.

"I think the shooter is a cop."

Chapter 3

Cindy Thomas was walking down the long slope of Divisadero, with its crystal view over the rooftops all the way out to the dawn-lit bay. It was a fantastic sight that normally gave her a real rush to the heart, but Cindy wasn't sightseeing. Wasn't walking for the exercise either.

She was struggling with a conflict, a big one, and she hoped that by airing out her brain, she would get some clarity.

Her fiancé, Rich Conklin, had woken her at something like five thirty this morning when he'd gotten up to go to work. He'd been sitting on the side of the bed tying his shoelaces in the dark and he'd said, "We'll get used to this kind of thing when we have kids."

This was Rich's *third* comment about having kids in the past couple of weeks.

She'd said to him, "Hey, mister. What's the rush?"

"It's better to do it while we can still keep up with little ones, ya know?"

He'd pulled the covers over her shoulders, kissed her, said, "Go back to sleep," and she'd tried, but she'd failed, absolutely.

At six thirty she'd dressed and gone out for what she'd thought would be a short walk. She had now been walking for over an hour and was no closer to an answer than she'd been when she'd gone out the door.

An investigative reporter with the *Chronicle,* Cindy had been working the crime desk for six years. She'd earned a seat at editorial meetings and a lot of respect for her talent and her tenacity. She was well positioned for top management and a big, big future. But this job that she loved was always at risk. If she had children, she wouldn't be able to work the kind of hours she needed to; she'd never be able to compete.

Richie was handsome, sweet, and she loved him. A few months ago, he'd surprised her with his mother's diamond ring, dropped to one knee in front of the altar in Grace Cathedral, and proposed to her—like they say, in front of God and everyone.

Seriously, what more could a girl want?

As it turned out, she wanted a lot.

If she told Richie how she felt, maybe he would change his mind about her. Maybe she'd break his beautiful heart.

When Cindy got to the stop sign at the corner of Divisadero and Vallejo, she glanced at her watch and realized that if she didn't get a cab, she'd be late to work.

She got out her cell phone, and, as if taking out the phone had *caused* it, a rush of unmarked police cars and cruisers blew past her and turned onto Vallejo.

She looked down Vallejo at the impressive row of megamansions on each side of the magnolia-lined street and saw that the cop cars had stopped a few blocks away, right in front of the infamous Ellsworth compound.

Something had happened at that house. And if there really was a reason for everything, then she'd walked four miles this morning so that she would be the first reporter on the scene.

Cindy broke into a run.

Chapter 4

The Ellsworth compound was an immense and fanciful brick mansion built in the late 1800s, considered one of the most spectacular homes in Pacific Heights. A vine-covered wall fronted the house, and four attached buildings, built as servants' quarters, wrapped around the corner of Vallejo and went halfway down Ellsworth Place.

The compound had a colorful history of political intrigue and sex scandals going back over a hundred and twenty years.

But as Cindy ran along Vallejo toward

the scrum of squad cars bunched in front of the mansion, she was thinking about the *recent* history of the house.

Ten years earlier, the Oscar-winning actor and legendary womanizer Harry Chandler had bought the Ellsworth compound and moved in with his glamorous wife, fashion designer to the stars Cecily Broad Chandler.

A year later, Cece Chandler simply disappeared.

Cindy had been an editorial assistant at the paper at the time, but she followed this gripping story over the next eighteen months as Harry Chandler was investigated, then tried for his wife's murder.

Chandler had pleaded not guilty, and because his wife's body was never found, the prosecution couldn't prove its case.

No body, no crime.

Harry Chandler was exonerated.

He had kept the Ellsworth compound as an investment while he lived on a yacht at a country club marina a few miles away.

Cindy had seen Chandler a couple of

times at big social events and benefits. Looking at a man who had made so many famous films, you couldn't know if he was a killer or if he just played one on the big screen.

Now, blowing hard from her run, Cindy walked the last hundred yards to the front entrance of the Ellsworth compound, saw that it had already been cordoned off by uniformed officers. There was a crowd in front of the gate, tourists who had clearly come off a red bus marked STAR HOME TOURS.

Cindy went up to a cop she knew, Joe Sorbera, and asked him what was going on.

"You don't want to get me in trouble, Cindy. Do you? Because you know I can't tell you anything."

A young man wearing a Boston University sweatshirt came up next to Cindy and said, "Chandler thought he'd get away with it again."

Cindy introduced herself to the BU guy, said that she was a reporter, and asked the tourist to speak into her camera phone.

"The case of Cecily Chandler is a perfect example of how privileged people get over on the system," the young man said. "Harry Chandler had a famous defense attorney for a lawyer, a slick talker who probably played tennis with the judge."

Cindy shut off her phone, said, "Thanks," then muttered to herself, "for less than nothing."

A Channel Two news truck was turning onto Vallejo as two uniformed cops put out wooden barricades to block it.

Walking backward, Cindy tried again to get information from Sorbera.

"Can't you give me something, Joe, anything? I can quote you or keep you off the record, whatever you want. Please. Any detail will do."

"Stand back, Cindy. Thatta girl. Thank you."

Officer Sorbera stretched out his arms and corralled the crowd behind a barricade, letting the unmarked car Richie was driving go through.

Chapter 5

I was at my desk when the 911 call came in at 7:20 and was relayed to the squad room by dispatcher May Hess, our self-anointed Queen of the Batphone.

Hess told me, "A woman of few words called and reported two people dead at the Ellsworth compound.

"She sounded for real," Hess continued. "She said there were no intruders in the house and she was in no danger. Just 'Two people are dead.' Then she hung up. I called back twice but got an answering machine both times. I put out a call."

I listened to the 911 tape. The caller had a British accent and sounded scared. In fact, the fear in her voice and whatever she *wasn't* saying were more alarming than what she said.

Brady listened to the tape, then tagged me and my partner to take a run out to Pacific Heights.

"Just do the prelim," he said. "I'll assign a primary when you bring back a report."

Yes, sir. Forthwith, sir.

At 7:35 a.m., Conklin braked our car in front of the Ellsworth compound. Four cruisers had gotten there before us and there was also a red double-decker bus parked parallel to the curb. A gang of maybe twenty tourists were taking pictures from behind barricades across the street.

I had known the Ellsworth compound was on the historic-house tour, but I guess when Harry Chandler bought it for umpteen million dollars ten years ago, the compound went on the stargazing tour as well.

I got out of the car and approached Officer Joe Sorbera, who had been the first on the scene. He took out his note-book and said to me, "I got here at seven ten, spoke to Janet Worley, the caretaker, through the intercom. There's the box next to the gate. She said she was not in any danger and that the vic-tims, two of them, were dead. *Definitely dead* were her exact words."

The uniformed cop continued. "Lieu-tenant Brady told me to cordon off a perimeter and to wait for you, Sergeant. He told me not to go into the house."

"Has the ME been called?"

"Yes, ma'am. And CSU is on the way. I took some photos of the crowd."

"Good job, Sorbera."

I looked at the mob, saw it was thick-ening. Cars were backed up on Vallejo and were being detoured around Di-visadero. Because of the traffic, and a million Tweets and YouTube posts by tourists, the scene would be red-flagged by the press.

Death plus celebrity was a heady news combination. The media was go-ing to train its brights on this house, and any law enforcement errors would be documented for posterity.

I told Sorbera to set up a media liaison and a command post on Pierce, then I went to where Conklin was examining the front gate to the compound.

The wrought-iron gate was set into a ten-foot-high ivy-clad brick wall that gave the house total privacy from the street. The metalwork looked old enough to be original, and the lock had recently been forced. I saw fresh cuts in old iron.

"It was pried open with a metal tool, not a bolt cutter," Conklin said.

Joe Sorbera said there were two victims, *definitely dead.* Who were they? Was Harry Chandler involved?

Brady had assigned us to do the preliminary workup, meaning we had to determine where law enforcement and forensics could walk on the scene without destroying evidence. We were charged with taking pictures, making sketches, and forming an opinion.

After that, we'd turn the scene over to the primary investigator on the case.

I gloved up and pushed at the gate, which swung open on well-oiled hinges. A stone walkway crossed a mossy grass lawn and led past a couple of flower beds, one on each side of the steps, to the ornate front door.

The door showed no sign of forced entry. Conklin lifted the brass door knocker, banged it against the strike plate.

I called out, "Janet Worley, this is the police."

Chapter 6

The petite woman who opened the door was white, late forties, five three, one hundred and ten pounds, wearing leggings under a floral-print smock. Her expression was strained and her mascara was smudged under her eyes. Her nails were bitten to the finger pads.

She said her name was Janet Worley, and I told her mine, showed her my badge, and introduced my partner, who asked her, "How are you doing, Mrs. Worley?"

"Horribly, thank you."

"It's okay. We're here now," Rich said.

Conklin is good with people, especially women. In fact, he's known for it.

I wanted to learn everything at once, which was what always happened when I started working a case. I looked around the foyer as Conklin talked to Janet Worley and took notes. The entranceway was huge, with a twenty-foot-high ceiling and plaster moldings; to my right, a wide and winding staircase led to the upper floors.

Everything was tidy, not a rug fringe out of place.

Janet Worley was saying to Conklin, "My husband and I are just the caretakers, you understand. This house is thirty thousand square feet and we have a schedule. We've been cleaning the Ellsworth Place side of the house over the past three days."

Looking through the foyer, I thought the house seemed gloomy, what you would expect from a relic of the Victorian age. Had we stepped into a *Masterpiece Theatre* episode? Was Agatha Christie lurking in the wings?

Behind me, Janet Worley was still talking to Conklin and she had his attention. I wanted to hear her out, but she was going the long way around the story and I felt the pressure of time passing.

"Why did you call emergency?" Conklin asked.

Worley said, "I had better show you."

We followed behind the small woman, who took us through the foyer, past a library, and into a living area with an enormous stone fireplace and large-scale leather furniture. Sunlight passed through stained glass, painting rainbows on the marble floors. We went through a restaurant-quality kitchen and at last arrived at the back door.

Worley said, "We haven't been in this part of the house since last Friday. Yes, that's right, three days ago. I don't know how long these have been here."

She opened the door and I followed Worley's pointing finger to the chrysanthemum-lined brick patio in the backyard.

For a moment, my mind blanked, because what I saw was frankly unbelievable.

On the patio were two severed *heads*

encircled by a loose wreath of white chrysanthemum flowers.

They seemed to be looking up at me.

The sight was grisly and shocking, made for the cover of the *National Enquirer*. But this was no alien invasion story, and it was no Halloween prank.

Conklin turned to me, my shock reflected in his eyes.

"These heads are real, right?" I asked him.

"Real, and as the lady said, definitely dead."

Chapter 7

Adrenaline burned through my blood-stream like flame on a short fuse. What had happened here?

What in God's name was I looking at?

The head to the right was the most horrific because it was reasonably fresh. It had belonged to a woman in her thirties with long brown hair and a stud piercing the left side of her nose. Her eyes were too cloudy to tell their color.

There was dirt in her hair that looked like garden soil, and maggots were working on the flesh, but enough of her features remained to get a likeness and possibly an ID.

The other head was a skull, just the bare cranium with the lower jaw attached and a full set of good teeth.

Two index cards lay faceup on the bricks in front of the heads and both had numbers written on them with a ballpoint pen. The card in front of the skull read *104.* The other card, the one in front of the more recently severed head, read *613.*

What did the numbers mean?

Where had these heads come from?

Why were they placed here in plain sight?

If this was a homicide, where were the bodies?

I tore my gaze away from the heads to look into Janet Worley's face. She covered her mouth with both hands and tears sprang to her eyes.

I saw a meltdown coming. I had to question her. Now.

"Who do these remains belong to? Where are the bodies? Tell us about it, Mrs. Worley."

"Me? All I know is what I just told you. I'm the one who called the police."

"Then who did this?"

"I have no idea. None at all."

"You understand that lying would make you an accessory to the crime."

"My God. I know *nothing*."

Conklin said, "We need the names of everyone who has been inside this house since last Friday."

"Of course, but it's only been my husband, my daughter, and me."

"And Mr. Chandler?"

"Heavens, no. I haven't seen him in three months."

"Have you handled these heads or disturbed anything on the patio?"

"No, no, no. I opened the door to air out the room at about seven this morning. I saw *this*. I called my husband. Then I called nine-one-one."

Janet Worley went inside the house, and Conklin and I were left to consider the nature of "this."

Was it Satanism? Terrorism? Drug-related homicide? Who were these victims? What had happened to them?

I wanted to start looking around, but

Conklin and I had to stay on the bricks and focus on what we could see without contaminating evidence.

Brady had told us to do the prelim.

That was the job: scope out the crime and tell our lieutenant whether this was a double homicide or a freak show that should be handed off to Major Crimes.

"I don't know what the hell we're looking at," I said to Conklin.

Truly, I'd never seen anything like it in my life.

Chapter 8

The back garden was a dark, three-quarter-acre triangular plot that looked as though a slice of woodland had been dropped down in one piece behind the Ellsworth house.

The parcel was shadowed by buildings and mature trees, crossed with mulched paths, bounded by the house on one side and by two ten-foot-high brick walls that met at a toolshed at the farthest end of the garden.

Looking for entrances, I saw, in addition to the front gate with its broken lock, five doors that opened to the garden from the main house and a gate in the wall next to the toolshed.

"There's a multipurpose tool," Conklin said.

He was pointing to a shovel half hidden by a shrub, and beyond the shovel was a mound of soil and a hole dug in the dirt. The hole was about two feet across, the right size for potted chrysanthemums—and also just right for disembodied heads.

I saw a second hole, just visible from the far corner of the patio, and beside that hole was a rounded stone.

Now that I was looking for them, I saw other stones around the garden. Maybe they were decorative in a gnomish way, or maybe the stones were markers.

If the shovel had been used to break the lock, it would mean that whoever broke in knew where to look for the disembodied heads and had then exhumed them.

Did that mean that the intruder was the killer?

Or was he an accessory to whatever mayhem had taken place?

I took another look at the numbered index cards.

When a killer deliberately leaves a calling card, it's a dare. Usually means he's trying to show the cops that he's smarter than they are. It's playing a very risky game.

Here was the game board as I saw it: a large hidden garden, two severed heads wreathed with flowers, cryptic numbers on a matching pair of index cards.

Did the numbers indicate how many heads were in the garden? Could hundreds of skulls be in this place, perhaps stacked in holes, one on top of another?

Beyond the complete creepiness of the skull tableau, I didn't have a sense of the meaning or intent of any of it, but we were just getting started and hadn't yet scratched the surface.

I said to Conklin, "The quickest way is also the best."

"Ground-penetrating radar," he said, staring out into the garden.

"And cadaver dogs. We've got to dig this place up."

Chapter 9

We met Nigel Worley in the kitchen of the Ellsworth house.

At six three, he was a full foot taller than his wife and had almost a hundred and fifty bloated pounds on her too. His face was puffy. Looked to me like he was a heavy drinker, and I noticed that he had rough dark-stained hands. He answered only questions directed specifically to him, and when he spoke, it was to a place in the air between Conklin and me.

Mr. Worley had no theories about the severed heads, and his tone was hostile. But he had to make a statement on the record. We gave him no choice. The Worleys were witnesses and they were also the only suspects we had.

We put on the siren and drove the English couple from their residence back to the Hall.

While Conklin interviewed Nigel Worley, I sat across from Janet Worley in the smaller of our two interrogation rooms. Brady paced unseen behind the glass.

Brady had already told me that he was unhappy with how our day was turning out. In his opinion, the Ellsworth case was a tar pit, and Conklin and I were going to get sucked under. He needed us to work the vigilante-cop case, and he wanted us to work it now.

I understood his concerns, but I'd seen the severed head of a woman who'd been alive a week ago. She was a Jane Doe, and because we didn't know her name, she was about to get an official case number and a spot on a refrigerated shelf in the city morgue.

The camera in the corner of the interview room rolled tape as Janet Worley told me that she and Nigel had come to the United States from England ten years before and that they had been working for Harry Chandler since he bought the compound.

She said that she'd "adored" the Chandlers and were shocked and heartbroken when Mrs. Chandler disappeared. The Worleys had stayed on at the compound when Mr. Chandler went on trial, in part because their daughter loved living there and still did.

"Nicole is with Fish and Wildlife," Janet told me. "She hasn't been home all weekend. She's a biologist, you know. Off on some animal rescue mission in the wilderness, I expect. I haven't been able to reach her on the phone."

Janet Worley thought Nicole would be returning home that evening but said they never knew her movements for sure.

"She's twenty-six, you understand. She leads her own life."

"Explain to me about the buildings on Ellsworth Place, the ones that look to be part of the compound."

"They were servants' quarters originally, then over the years they became apartments. Mr. Chandler owns them all," said Janet Worley, "but he's been moving the tenants out. There are very few occupants now."

Janet Worley told me that Nicole lived in number 2 Ellsworth, that Mr. Chandler's driver lived in number 4, and that the other two buildings were vacant.

I strained Worley's statement for inconsistencies, watched her body language, and I thought she was being truthful. I asked her to write down names and phone numbers of the Chandler staff living on Ellsworth Place, and while she did that, I went out of the room and compared notes with Conklin.

Nigel Worley had told Conklin the same story Janet had told me. He'd said that no one had a grudge against him, his wife, or his daughter and that Mr. Chandler hadn't received any hate calls or letters at the compound.

Nigel Worley, like his wife, insisted that he had no idea who could have put the severed heads on the patio and that he had never before seen the victim with the long brown hair.

If we were to believe them, the Worleys had been together virtually every minute of the last ten years and could vouch for each other's whereabouts over the weekend in question.

I was frustrated but tried not to show it.

How could Brady expect me to leave our Jane Doe and that naked skull unidentified? How could I put this case down without solving it?

I couldn't.

Chapter 10

I knocked on Brady's open office door. He waved me in and told me to sit down.

I knew this office very well. It had once been mine, but I had given up the job of lieutenant so that I could do detective work full-time instead of watchdogging time sheets and writing reports.

Warren Jacobi had been my partner back then.

Ten years older than me, with many more years on the street, Jacobi had good reasons to move into this corner office when I left it. He didn't want to work the street anymore. He wanted more access to the top, less sprinting through dark alleys. He had taken over from me and gotten the squad running like a fine watch, and soon he was promoted to chief, leaving the lieutenant's job vacant again.

That was ten months ago.

Jackson Brady, who had recently transferred from Miami PD, had asked for the promotion and gotten it, along with the small glass-walled office with a window looking out on the James Lick Freeway.

Applying the whip was nasty work, but someone had to do it. Brady was doing fine.

"I need a minute," I told Brady now.

"Good. That's all the time I've got."

"I want to run the Ellsworth case as primary," I said. "It's going to be a bear, but I'm into it. I can handle both Ellsworth and the vigilante cop if I work with Conklin and another team."

Brady got up from behind the desk, closed the door, sat back down, and gave me his hard blue-eyed stare, full-bore.

"There's something you have to know about the vigilante cop, Boxer. He's not shooting just dirtbags. His last victim, Chaz Smith, was working undercover."

"I'm sorry. Say that again."

"Chaz Smith was a cop."

Brady told me his theory: a cop who worked in the Hall of Justice had gotten fed up with due process and decided to go it alone, but he had screwed up more than he knew when he took out Chaz Smith.

"Smith was running a big operation for Narcotics," Brady told me. "And he had other cops working for him down the line. We have to protect those cops, and we have to bring this vigilante down. No room for failure. No excuses."

"I have to tell Conklin."

"Where is he?"

"Driving Harry Chandler's caretakers to a hotel."

"You can tell him," Brady said, "and I'm willing to give you a shot working both cases, Boxer. But if one of them has to take a backseat, I'll tell you right now, it's going to be your house of heads."

"I hear you."

"Make sure you do. This vigilante is not only a cop, he's a cop *killer.* He murdered one of us."

Chapter 11

I spent the day working both cases.

I'd ransacked the missing-persons databases for a match to our long-haired Jane Doe. After that, Brady and I checked names of cops who had access to the property-room floor and compared those cops' time sheets with the times drug dealers had been killed with one of our vouchered-and-stolen .22s.

The list of cops was very long and Brady was still working on the project when I left him.

I got back to the Ellsworth compound

as the sun was setting, flying pink flags over the bay. TV satellite vans were double-parked along Vallejo, their engines running and their lights on. Talking heads were using the compound as a backdrop for their on-air reports.

Reporters shouted my name as I went through a gap in the barricade. A lot of our local media knew me. One of them was my close friend Cindy Thomas, who called me on my phone.

I didn't pick up. I couldn't talk to Cindy right now.

Conklin came toward me, then walked me back through the front gate.

"It's been crazy," he said. "I've become the go-to person. The press is barking and I don't have a bone to throw them. Brian Williams called me. How'd he get my number?"

"No kidding. *NBC Nightly News* Brian Williams? What did you tell him?"

"Ongoing case. No comment at this time. Call Media Relations."

"Exactly."

"Oh, and 'I love your work.'"

I laughed.

Conklin said, "But seriously, Lindsay,

if we don't give Cindy something news-worthy, my home life is going to suck. She was on the scene before we were, you know?"

"Hey, here's news: Brady gave us the green light. This is officially our case now."

The Ellsworth garden had been trans-formed while I was out. An evidence tent had been set up just off the patio, rolls of brown paper had been unfurled over pathways, and a grid of crime scene tape had been stretched across the gar-den.

I saw several new holes. Soil had been piled on tarps, and halogen lights were on. But even with the halogens, there wouldn't be enough light to work the scene once the sun had set; the foren-sics team would have to quit for the night so that evidence didn't get lost or trampled.

God help us if it rained.

Chapter 12

I found my best friend, chief medical examiner Dr. Claire Washburn, inside the tent wearing a size 16 bunny suit and booties, what she called a full-body condom with a zipper.

She greeted me, said, "Fine mess we have here, girlfriend. No, don't hug me. And don't touch anything. We're trying to hermetically seal whatever kind of crime scene this freaking obscenity is."

She kissed the air next to my cheek, then stepped aside so I could see her worktable.

Four heads were lined up, three of

them as clean as the proverbial whistle, and as the head numbered 104.

The fourth skull showed some traces of scalp.

"The hounds just got another hit," Claire told me. "Another skull. Of the six I've examined so far, all were severed with a ripsaw."

The tent flap opened and Charlie Clapper came inside. Man, I was glad to see the chief of the Crime Scene Unit. Clapper is a former homicide cop, my friend, and SFPD's own Gil Grissom. He was as dapper as anyone could possibly be in a bunny suit, and I could see comb marks in his hair.

Clapper was carrying a heavy brown paper bag that he handed to Claire, and he held a small glassine bag in his gloved fist.

"Hey, Lindsay. I hear Brady tossed you this hot potato."

"I self-tossed it. It's either work the case or lie awake wishing I were working it."

"I feel the same way. Don't try to take this once-in-a-lifetime mind-bender away from me. It's *mine*. Hey, I've got something here for us to ponder."

"Hit me with it."

"I found blood in one of the holes, made me think that was our fresh Jane Doe's grave. If I'm right, this necklace was probably hers."

He held the baggie up to the light.

"A trinket," he said. "A necklace. But no neck to hang it on."

The necklace was made of glass beads on a waxed string with a cheap metal clasp, the kind of costume jewelry commonly found at street fairs. What made this one special was that Jane Doe had handled it. There was a slim chance we might be able to lift her fingerprints from the beads.

Maybe her killer had left DNA on them too.

Charlie Clapper was saying, "I found other doodads. This one," he said, holding up a baggie. "It's a pendant. Could be an amethyst set in a gold bezel. The rest of the artifacts have been moldering in the ground too long for me to say what they are or to get anything off them.

"But they *are* trophies, wouldn't you say?"

A lightbulb went on in my mind. I was finally getting the picture.

"What if the *heads* are the trophies?" I said to Clapper. "I think this place is a trophy garden."

Chapter 13

That night we all met in Claire's domain, the Medical Examiner's Office, which is right behind the Hall of Justice.

All four of us—Claire, Cindy, Yuki, and me—sat around the large round table Claire used as a desk, ready for a four-way brainstorming meeting of what Cindy had dubbed the Women's Murder Club.

Normally when we meet to talk about a case, we worry about Cindy reporting something she isn't supposed to know. If you forget to say "Off the record," your words could be tomorrow's headline.

But tonight I was more worried about Yuki.

Yuki is an assistant DA and I knew anything we said was off the record—but was it off the pillow?

Yuki was dating Jackson Brady.

Yuki was sleeping with my *boss*.

I said, "Don't tell Lieutenant Wonderful, okay? He wouldn't like this."

"I hear you," Yuki said, grinning at me. She patted my arm. She promised nothing.

Claire turned up the lights, passed out bottles of water, told us that the six skulls were in paper bags to prevent condensation and that the long-haired Jane Doe's remains were in the cooler so that the soft tissue didn't decompose further.

Claire said, "I'm going to give all seven heads a thorough exam in the morning, but I also hired a forensic anthropologist to consult. Dr. Ann Perlmutter from UC Santa Cruz. You've heard of her. She was a special consultant identifying bodies in mass graves in Afghanistan. If anyone can work up identifiable faces on bald skulls, Ann can."

"How long will that take?" I asked.

Claire shrugged. "Days or weeks. Meanwhile we'll work with Jane Doe's face. Photoshop her a little bit. Put her on our website."

"I can create a Facebook page for her," said Cindy.

"Not yet," I said, trying to rein in Cindy's racehorse tendencies. "Give us a chance to ID her in real life, keep her parents from finding out that she's dead by seeing her page on the Web."

I told Cindy and Yuki about the numbers 104 and 613, showed them a photocopy of the index cards we'd found with the first two heads. No numbers had been found with the other heads.

"So, two numbers only. Maybe it's a game," said Yuki.

"So you think the killer is into Sudoku?" I said.

"You're funny," Yuki said, giving me a soft punch in the arm.

"But you said there were no numbers with any of the other remains," Claire said.

"To me that means whoever dug up the heads left the numbers," I said.

"These are two distinct acts—burying and exhuming. They may have been done by different people."

Cindy had been tapping keys on her laptop.

"I just ran the numbers through Google. Came up with a lot of stuff that doesn't seem related to backyard burials. For instance, I've got numbers of committees on radiation, department numbers at European universities."

"Gotta be some kind of code," Yuki said.

"Maybe it's an archive number," I offered. "The head-and-flower tableau was set up almost like an exhibit."

"Let me run with this part of the puzzle," Cindy said. "I'll let you know what I find, and what do you say, Linds? I have first dibs on the story if I find out what the numbers mean?"

"If you actually find something we can use."

"Right."

"I'll have to clear it before you run it."

"Of course. My usual penalty for being friends with you guys."

"Okay," I said to Cindy. "The numbers are yours."

"Biggest issue for me," Claire said, "is that we have no bodies. Without bodies, we may never be able to determine causes of death."

"Well, at least it's seven bodies we need to find, not six hundred and thirteen," Yuki said.

"Not six hundred and thirteen *so far,*" said Claire. "There are many more backyards in Pacific Heights."

We groaned as one.

It was raining when I ran out the back door of Claire's office to my car. Reporters were in the parking lot waiting for me, calling my name.

I got into my car, started up the engine, turned on the lights and the sirens, and pulled out onto Harriet Street.

No bones, ladies and gentlemen of the press. I have no bones to throw you at all.

Chapter 14

I was still thinking about the six skulls in sealed paper bags and the young Jane Doe's head in the cooler when I opened the door to our apartment on Lake Street. Martha, my border collie and pal of many years, whimpered and tore across the floor, then threw her full weight against me, almost knocking me down.

"Yes, I *do* love you," I said, bending to let her wash my chin, giving her a big hug.

I called out, "Joe. Your elderly primigravida has arrived."

Claire had told me that *elderly primigravida* meant "a woman over thirty-five who is pregnant for the first time," and it was a quaint and unflattering term that I usually found just hilarious.

Joe called back, and when I rounded the corner, I saw him standing between piles of books and papers, wearing pajama bottoms, a phone pressed to his ear.

He dialed down the volume on the eleven o'clock news and gave me a one-armed hug, then said into the phone, "Sorry. I'm here. Okay, sure. Tomorrow works for me."

He clicked off, kissed me, asked, "Did you eat dinner?"

"Not really."

"Come to the kitchen. I'm going to heat up some soup for my baby. And for my old lady too."

"Har-har. Who were you talking to on the phone?"

"Old boys' network. Top secret," he said melodramatically. "I have to fly to DC tomorrow for a few days. Cash flow for the Molinari family."

"Okayyy. Yay for cash flow. What kind of soup?"

It was tortellini en brodo with baby peas served up in a heavy white bowl. I went to work on the soup and after a minute, I held up the bowl and said, "More, please."

Between bites, I told my husband about the house of heads, which was what the Ellsworth compound would inevitably be called from that day forward.

"It was indescribable, Joe. Heads, two of them set up on the back patio. A display of some sort, like an art installation, but no bodies. There was no sign of mayhem. No disturbance in the garden except for the two holes the heads had been in. Then CSU exhumed five more heads, just clean skulls. Honestly, I don't know what the hell we're looking at."

I told Joe about the numbers *104* and *613* handwritten on a pair of index cards.

"Cindy is running the numbers. So far we know that six-one-three is an area code in Ottawa. Lots of radio stations start with one hundred and four. Put the two numbers together and you get a real estate listing for a three-bedroom house in Colorado. What a lead, hmmm?"

"Ten-four," he said. "Radio call signal meaning 'I acknowledge you. Copy that.'"

"Hmmm. And six-thirteen?"

"June thirteenth?"

"Uh-huh. The ides of June. Very helpful."

Joe brought a big bowl of pralines and ice cream to the counter. We faced off with clashing spoons, then had a race to the bottom. I captured the last bite, put down my spoon, held up my arms in victory, and said, "Yessss."

"I let you win, big mama."

"Sure you did."

I winked at him, took the bowl and the spoons to the sink, and asked Joe, "So, what's your gut take on my case?"

"Apart from the obvious conclusion that a psycho did it," said my blue-eyed, dark-haired husband, "here are my top three questions: What's the connection between the skulls and the Ellsworth place? What do the victims have in common? And does Harry Chandler have anything to do with those heads?"

"And the numbers? A tally? A score-card?"

"It's a mystery to me."

"One of our Jane Does is relatively fresh. If we can ID her, maybe the numbers won't matter."

Four hours later, I woke up in bed next to Joe with the remains of a nightmare in my mind, something Wes Craven could have created. There had been a pyramid of skulls heaped up in a dark garden, hundreds of them, and they were surrounded by a garland of flowers.

What did it mean?

I still didn't have a clue.

Chapter 15

By seven, I was awake for good, this time with a mug of milky coffee and my open laptop. I zipped through my e-mail fast but stopped deleting junk when I saw two Google alerts for SFPD.

The alerts were linked to the *San Francisco Post,* and the front-page story was headlined "Revenge vs. the SFPD."

My stomach clenched when I saw the byline.

Writer Jason Blayney was the *Post*'s crime desk pit bull, well known for his snarky rhetoric and his hate-on for cops.

The *Post* didn't mind if Blayney stretched the facts into a lie—and often, he did.

I started reading Blayney's account of Chaz Smith's murder.

Chaz Smith, a known top-tier drug dealer, was assassinated Sunday afternoon in the men's room at the Morton Academy of Music during their annual spring recital. The academy, located on California Street, was packed with parents and students during the shooting.

Smith has been under investigation by the SFPD for the past three years but because of the closing of the city's corrupt drug lab, he has never gone on trial. According to a source who spoke to the *Post* on condition of anonymity, Chaz Smith's assassin "demonstrated professional skills in the killing of this drug dealer. It was a very slick hit."

Smith is the fourth high-level drug dealer who has been executed in this manner. In the opinion of this reporter, a professional do-good hit man is cleaning up the mess that the SFPD can't rub out. That's why I call this killer Revenge—and given the size of the mess that needs to be cleaned, he could just be getting started . . .

He'd said it himself: "In the opinion of this reporter." It was a phrase that meant "I'm not actually reporting. I'm telling a story."

And his "story" was a slam against the SFPD.

The Delete button was right under my index finger, but instead of sending the article to the recycle bin, I opened the link to the second story, headlined "Death at the Ellsworth Compound?"

Right under the headline was a photo showing Conklin and me going in through the compound's tall front gate.

My heart rate kicked up as I read Blayney's report; he said that Homicide had been called to a disturbance at the famous Ellsworth compound, owned by Harry Chandler.

Blayney gave the context of the story

by telling his readers about the SFPD's dismal rate of unsolved homicides.

Then my name jumped out at me.

Our sources tell us that the Southern Division's Sergeant Lindsay Boxer is lead investigator on the Ellsworth case. Boxer, rumored to have lost her edge since stepping down from the Homicide squad lieutenant's job several years ago . . .

It was an unfair jab and I wasn't prepared for it. I felt a shock of anger, and then tears welled up. This guy was knocking a decorated elderly primigravida with a dozen years on the force and a pretty decent record of solved crimes.

Not 100 percent, but high!

I sat on the kitchen stool long enough for my coffee to get cold and my hormones to give me a break.

Blayney had attached himself to both of my cases, but so far he didn't know that Chaz Smith was an undercover cop and that seven heads had been dug up at Harry Chandler's house.

We had no leads, no suspects for either crime.

How long would it be before "anonymous sources" leaked *that* to Jason Blayney?

Boxer, rumored to have lost her edge . . .

The government was broke. Jobs were being eliminated. Blayney's cutting remarks could color the top-floor bosses' perception of me.

For the first time in a dozen years, I worried about keeping my job.

Chapter 16

I drove my husband to the airport through the maddening morning rush. Traffic was congested, gridlocked at the stop-lights, and Joe's flight would be leaving without him if we didn't get clear road-way soon.

Still, I was glad for the drive time with Joe's sharp, former-FBI-agent brain.

I buzzed up the car windows and beat the steering wheel for emphasis as I filled Joe in on the well-planned execu-tions of *four*—yes, *four*—notorious drug dealers and told him that Narcotics was now asking Homicide for help.

Joe asked, "And why is Brady sure that Revenge is a cop?"

"The slugs that killed Chaz Smith match to a gun stolen from the property room, and all of the hits were so smoothly executed that the shooter had to know the dealers' whereabouts. It's like he had inside knowledge. Maybe it came from inside the Hall."

I told Joe that all of the executed drug dealers were big-time and that Chaz Smith's death had been a blow to the top floor of the SFPD.

"Smith's real identity had been a very well-guarded secret, Joe. He headed up a large undercover operation that can't be blown. Cops' lives are on the line."

Joe said, "Lindsay, this is a nasty case, and dangerous. Did your shooter know Smith was a cop? Maybe he did."

It was a possibility, maybe a good one. I said, "Hang on," then hit the departure ramp at fifty and pulled the car up to United Airlines' curbside-check-in, no-waiting zone.

I shut off the engine, looked at my husband, and said, "Don't go."

"And you. Keep your head down.

Don't work more than one shift a day. Get some sleep tonight. Okay?"

We both grinned at the impossible demands, then got out of the car. I gave Joe a full-body hug and sprinkled tears on his neck.

We kissed, then Joe bent down and kissed my baby bump, making me giggle at the looks we got from two commuters and a luggage handler.

"Goofball," I said, loving that Joe was *my* goofball.

"Don't forget to eat. I already miss you."

I kissed him, waved good-bye, watched him disappear into the terminal. Then I drove to the Hall.

Brady was waiting for me and Conklin inside his office. He closed the door, put the *Post* on his desk, and turned it so we could read Jason Blayney's headline: "Revenge vs. the SFPD."

Conklin hadn't yet seen the story. He pushed his hair out of his eyes and began reading as I started talking.

"How does Blayney know so much about the Chaz Smith shooting?" I asked Brady. "Is a cop tipping him off?"

"Absolutely," Brady said.

"Don't look at me," said Conklin. "My in-house crime reporter didn't have either one of those stories. What does that tell you?"

"I'm the unnamed source on this one," Brady said. "It was me."

Conklin and I said, "What?" in unison.

"Blayney waylaid me. I told him that Chaz Smith's killer was a pro. That's all I gave him, but I like it. It puts this Revenge guy on notice. Gives him something to worry about."

Chapter 17

After Jason Blayney's story about Chaz Smith's murder appeared, the phone lines lit up with calls from tipsters, hoaxers, and reporters from all corners of the Inter-Web. People were afraid and they were also titillated. A professional shooter had killed a drug dealer inside a school.

Whose side was the shooter on? Would he kill again?

Was it safe to send your kid to school?

While Brady fielded phone calls in his office, Conklin and I sat across from each other in the squad room, pecking at our keyboards.

If Revenge was a cop, the clues were in the paperwork. Conklin and I worked a page at a time, comparing hundreds of time sheets with the four drug dealers' times of death, stamping our feet at square one.

Up to a point, the premise was valid— separate out the cops who were off duty when all four shootings went down and check their alibis.

But the flaw in the premise was obvious. A cop's being off duty when a dealer was killed was not a smoking gun. We were using a very large-holed sieve. It was all we had.

Conklin said, "This guy Jenkins fits the time frame."

"I know Roddy Jenkins," I said. "He's a crack shot."

"He's a candidate."

By noon, Conklin and I had a list of a dozen cops whose time sheets showed that they were off duty when the four drug dealers were killed. Three of those cops had worked in Narcotics at one time in their careers. Stick a gold star on each of them.

I forwarded our list of cops to Brady, who wrote back saying he would have their personnel jackets pulled. Just then, my intercom buzzed.

It was Clapper, calling from the compound. I put his call on speakerphone.

"What's new, Charlie?"

"We're still sifting the dirt in the yard, but we're done with the main house," he told me. "We found nothing in there. No blood or decapitated bodies, no additional index cards. Prints are the Worleys'. I told Janet that they could go home."

"How'd she seem to you?"

"Wired. Chatty," Charlie said. "Her daughter is back from the wilderness. They're going to do some housecleaning. And Janet is in a swivet about the mess we left. Another citizen complaint."

Chapter 18

Janet Worley was flustered when she came to the door.

"Yes? Oh. Right. Come in. I expect you want to speak with Nicole."

Conklin and I went with Janet through the front rooms to the kitchen, where Nigel Worley was cleaning fingerprint powder off the stove.

Janet said, "I can tell you Nicole knows nothing. She wasn't even here."

"We understand," Conklin said. "We want her impressions and so forth."

"She's in her flat. Nigel, ring her up, will you?"

I said, "Mrs. Worley, what can you tell us about Harry Chandler?"

"Would you like tea?"

"No, thanks," I said.

We took seats at a kitchen table with a view of the evidence tent in the garden. Water from last night's rain dripped from the canopy onto the bricks.

Janet said stiffly, "What do you wish to know about Mr. Harry?"

I told Janet Worley to tell me about his personality, his character, and she did. He was honest, she told me. He was rich, of course, but according to Janet, Harry Chandler was very normal for such a famous person.

Normal?

Harry Chandler was to the movies what O. J. Simpson was to football.

Janet said, "After Mrs. Chandler disappeared, during the year and a half when Mr. Chandler was indisposed, we became almost like his family. We moved from our flat in number two into the main house so that the place wouldn't go cold.

"Mr. Chandler appreciated that. He has always been very generous," Janet said. "He paid for Nicole's education. He gave us things. Gave us a car one year, didn't he, Nigel?"

"His dead wife's car."

"Yes. It was secondhand, but we still have it."

I asked, "When did you see Mr. Chandler last?"

"Three months ago. Yes. He came for dinner on Christmas. I always find Mr. Chandler charming, although maybe a little distracted. Always rehearsing something in his mind, I expect."

Something crashed against the stove behind us.

I turned. Nigel Worley's face looked like a furrowed field.

He said, "Rehearsing? Distracted? Yes, he was distracted. He's a bloody womanizer," Nigel Worley said. "Well, it was in all the papers, Jan. Don't look at me like I drowned the baby in the bath."

"He was a ladies' man," Janet conceded.

"Harry Chandler is what you might call an equal-opportunity ladies' man. He liked all types," Nigel went on. "Actresses mostly, but he fancied the odd waitress or even women of a certain age."

Janet's stiff expression tightened.

"I don't think he ever met a woman he didn't like," said Nigel Worley, turning his eyes directly to me for the first time. "Harry Chandler would like *you*."

His stare was chilling. It was as if he had put his hands around my neck and squeezed.

Chapter 19

A young woman burst into the room, the sound breaking her father's double-fisted lock on my eyes.

Janet Worley said, "Nicole, these people are from the police." To me, she said, "I'll be in the parlor," and she left the room.

Nicole Worley was midtwenties, pretty, with a heart-shaped face, dark hair, green eyes, flushed cheeks. She wore jeans and a green sweatshirt with the U.S. Fish and Wildlife logo on the front.

Nicole asked her father, "What's going on with you?"

"Your mother. She drives me round the bend."

"I wish you wouldn't fight."

"The way she goes on about that self-important prick—"

"Stop that."

"You women are crazy."

"All right. All *right*," Nicole said to her father. To me, she said, "I'm Nicole. You wanted to see me?"

Nigel started cleaning the burners on the stove, and Nicole joined us at the table.

I said, "We need some basic information, Nicole. Where were you over the last few days?"

"I was off on a rescue," she said. "Pronghorn antelope get panicked at headlights, or at anything really. This one was hung up in a fence."

"And when did you leave for this rescue?"

"Friday morning."

"Were you alone?"

"Yes. I drove up north to Mendocino County by myself. What is it that you want to know? Did I kill some people and then dig up their heads? Leave them on the back step to scare my parents?"

"You tell me, Nicole. Did you have anything to do with the remains found here yesterday morning?"

"Absolutely not, and I cannot imagine how something like this could ever have happened."

"Can you tell me how it's possible that the three of you live in this house and are completely unaware of a series of crimes that happened over time outside the back door?"

Behind us, Nigel Worley said angrily, "Bloody cheek, these questions."

"Dad, don't you have something else you could be doing?" said Nicole.

Nigel Worley was a big, angry man with large hands. I could picture him turning violent. But if he'd killed these seven people, his exhuming their heads made no logical sense. And putting a garland of chrysanthemum blossoms around them seemed a little dainty for him.

I said, "Mr. Worley. Do you think Mr. Chandler could have been involved in what has happened here?"

"Killing and digging would require actual labor, wouldn't it? I don't picture Mr. Chandler getting his hands dirty."

I didn't know about Harry Chandler, but Nigel Worley looked like he got his hands dirty every day.

Chapter 20

Nigel Worley slammed around behind us, crashing the last of the iron trivets against the stove.

When Nigel had left the room, Conklin put a picture of the recently decapitated woman's head in front of Nicole. Her eyes widened at the sight of that decomposing face and she pushed back from the table.

"Do you know this woman?" Conklin asked her.

"I've never seen her in my life."

"This is one of the two heads your

parents discovered yesterday morning," I said.

"It's revolting. It's horrible."

"She was walking around last week, Nicole. Then her head was cut off with a saw."

"I find this unfathomable."

"What is your relationship with Harry Chandler?"

"I'm his caretakers' daughter. That's all. Do you want my opinion of him?"

"Please."

"He's been accused of horrible things before, but I know him to be a good man. He has been very kind to my family. We've been good to him too."

"Your father seems to dislike him."

"Oh, all that growling means nothing. He thinks my mother is starstruck and he hates that."

"You were sixteen when you came to live here?"

"That's right."

"And the reason you moved from London?"

"My parents had a romantic notion about America. As soon as we arrived, I fell in love with this city and this house.

I'm kind of an expert on the Ellsworth family. Harry lets me live in number two at no charge," Nicole explained, "and so I give lectures about the house to the tourists in exchange for free rent."

I said, "So you know everything about this house, Nicole. Everything except that the backyard was basically a cemetery."

The young woman's face colored.

The direct approach wasn't working, or maybe Nicole knew as little as she said she did.

Before I could fire off another question, my phone rang.

I glanced at the caller ID, got up, and took the call in the pantry.

Claire said, "I spoke with Dr. Perlmutter. She said looks like all the skulls are female. We've got a little multicultural mix going on here. Two of the skulls plus the head of our Jane Doe makes three white women. We also have one female of African background, one Asian, and two undetermined."

"Their ages?"

"Approximately twenties to forties."

"How long have the heads been in the ground?"

"It's hard to be precise, Lindsay. But yes, they could all have been buried in the last ten years."

Since Chandler bought the Ellsworth compound.

I hung up and called out to Conklin, asked him to join me in the pantry.

Conklin can read me like a map.

He knew that I felt pressure from Brady to work on Revenge and that at the same time, I was committed to the Ellsworth case. I wanted to do both.

I told him about my conversation with Claire.

He said to me, "I'll work on Nicole."

I nodded, said, "Good. While you do that, I'm going to use my famous charm on the movie star."

Chapter 21

Conklin held the back door open for Nicole, then followed her out to the patio. They ducked into the tent and Conklin said hello to a tech who was labeling bags of dirt.

"Got booties?" Conklin asked.

The tech handed him a carton of disposable shoe covers and Conklin took two pairs, then handed one pair to Nicole.

A brick path skirted the base of the wall, and once their feet were swaddled in plastic, Nicole and Conklin walked around the shadowy patch of garden.

Conklin focused his attention on Nicole Worley, watched her body language as she told him that she was a biologist and was hoping a teaching job would open in one of the schools within commuting distance of the Ellsworth place.

"My parents are getting older, and it's better for them if I'm around. I keep them from killing each other—oh, I didn't mean that literally."

Conklin smiled, said, "I knew what you meant."

Nicole slipped into her tour-guide role, talked about Bryce Ellsworth, his five wives and fourteen children, how the house survived the great fire of 1906. She had anecdotes about Prohibition and about Billie Holiday, the famous chanteuse, who'd sung for the Ellsworth family in their own parlor.

As Nicole and Conklin rounded the corner of the lot, Nicole indicated the four six-story houses beyond the wall.

Nicole said, "These houses are high for this area, but Bryce Ellsworth wanted them to balance the height of the main house. He liked symmetry. Notice that there are no windows facing the back garden. This is one of the interesting things about this place. I can't even see the garden from my flat in number two."

"What was the point of not having back-facing windows?"

"The first Mrs. Ellsworth was very private. I think it was her idea to keep the help from spying on her when she walked in the garden."

Conklin looked up at the brick buildings, built at the same time as the Ellsworth house. As Nicole had said, the windows were false, brick outlines with no glass, which made the one real window in the next-to-last building stand out.

"There's a window on the top floor of number six."

"Number six has been boarded up for years," Nicole told him. "I'm pretty sure that window opens onto a stairwell."

Conklin had gotten what he could from Nicole Worley's running on about the history of the house and San Francisco. Now he wanted answers.

"Who does the gardening?"

"Ricky someone. I can find out."

"Do you have a boyfriend?"

"Pardon?"

"Do you have a boyfriend?"

"Not currently. Not seriously. No one I've brought here."

"Have any of your friends been hanging out here recently?"

"Inspector Conklin, I'm starting to feel that you're harassing me."

"Nicole, would you rather come to the police station and spend a few hours with me and Sergeant Boxer? We can hold you as a material witness."

Her eyes welled up. "I don't bring my friends here."

Conklin pressed on.

"Have you seen anyone on or near the grounds who struck you as out of place?"

"No. I don't think so."

"What about those star tours? Do the tourists come into the garden?"

"No, and they don't come into the house either. It's strictly an outside-the-front-gate lecture series."

"Thank you, Nicole. I need your contact information."

Conklin smiled, gave her a pad and a

pen. Watched her write, took back the notepad, and handed her his card.

"I'll need the gardener's name and number, and if you think of anything, *anything,* call me anytime."

"I will certainly do that."

Conklin nodded at the tech who was photographing one of the grave markers.

"We'll be here for a while. Until we know who those seven victims are and the circumstances of their deaths, we'll be turning over every stone."

Chapter 22

I'd grown up seeing Harry Chandler's face in both huge Hollywood productions and tight, well-produced independent films. He was sexy, had terrific range, and was convincing as a hero and as a villain.

I'd checked out Chandler's bio before getting on the road to South Beach Harbor, and as I'd expected, his story was now colored by the disappearance of his high-society wife, presumed dead. Much had been written about Chandler's trial and acquittal, a story as dramatic as any film since *Citizen Kane*.

Popular opinion had it that even though the evidence wasn't there, Chandler had nonetheless been involved in the crime. He had made a few pictures since he'd been found not guilty of murder, including the iconic *Time to Reap,* a cynical look at the meltdown of the global economy.

Chandler had won an Oscar for that performance. His second. I have to admit, I was eager to see him in real life.

It was only a four-mile drive from Vallejo Street to South Beach Harbor and the yacht club, both of which were part of the gentrification of the industrial area that had started in the 1980s.

I took Pierce to Broadway, then took a right to the Embarcadero. To my left was the bay. I saw sailboat masts showing above the yachts filling the harbor.

I parked my car in the lot, then found the security guard inside the harbor office at the entrance to the South Beach Yacht Club. He wrote down my name and badge number, made a call, and I went through a gate and found Chandler's boat, the *Cecily,* at the end of a pier. It was a sleek, eighty-foot-long modern yacht, Italian make, a top-of-the-line Ferretti, so impressive it actually made me imagine a life in a super-luxury craft on the bay.

I walked down the pier and found Harry Chandler waiting for me, sitting in a folding chair at the foot of his slip. He saw me at the same moment I saw him; he put down his newspaper, stood up, and came toward me.

Harry Chandler looked to me like an aging lion. He was bearded and his face was lined, but he was still handsome, still the star who'd made female movie-goers all over the world fall in love with him.

"Sergeant Boxer? Welcome aboard."

I shook his hand, then felt a little charge when he put his hand on my back and guided me to the gangway. I climbed the steps to a covered outdoor cabin on the main deck that was furnished in white sofas, sea-green-glass tables, and teak appointments all around.

Chandler told me to make myself comfortable. I took a seat while he went to the refrigerator under the bar and poured out bottles of water into two chunky crystal glasses of ice.

When he was sitting across a coffee table from me, he said, "I read about this—what would you call it? This *horror* that happened yesterday. And Janet called, nearly hysterical. If you hadn't phoned I was going to call the police myself. I'm at a loss to understand this."

I kept my eyes on the actor as he spoke. I'd seen his handsome face so many times, I felt as if I knew him.

Was he telling the truth or giving a performance? I hoped I could tell the difference.

I showed Chandler Jane Doe's picture and he half turned away, then dragged his eyes back to the photo.

"I don't know her. I am wondering, of course, about Cecily. We still don't know what became of her. Could she be one of those victims in the garden? That would be a hell of a thing."

"Wondering, Mr. Chandler?"

"Yes. I want to know what happened to her."

If Cecily Chandler's remains were recovered, Harry Chandler wouldn't be charged, not for her death anyway. He'd been found innocent of her murder and couldn't be tried for it again. But if Cecily Chandler's remains had been buried on his doorstep, Harry would be the number one suspect in six other deaths.

Could Chandler have killed women over time and buried them in the dark of his garden, trusting that they would never be found? Had he kept the house he no longer used so as to protect his private trophy garden?

Did Nigel Worley have a better reason than his wife's crush on a movie star for the anger he expressed on hearing Harry Chandler's name?

Harry Chandler was sitting so that the San Francisco Bay was at his back.

I thought about convicted murderer Scott Peterson, recalled that his dead wife and unborn child were found washed up across the bay. It seemed very possible that a lot of bodies had been dumped in the water here. That they didn't all wash up onshore, and that some were never discovered because they floated out to sea.

I smiled at the movie star and tried that charm I'd joked about to Conklin.

"Can you tell me your movements over the last week, Mr. Chandler?"

"Call me Harry. Please. Of course. You need my alibi."

He walked to an intercom panel in the kitchen, pressed a button, and said in his memorable, resonant voice, "Kaye, the police want to talk to you."

Chapter 23

I liked Kaye Hunsinger on sight.

She was about forty, had a wide, toothy smile, and owned a small bike shop in North Beach. I made note of her massive diamond ring of the engagement kind.

Kaye, Harry Chandler, and I sat on semicircular sofas at the stern with little multigrain sandwiches on a plate in front of us. We caught some afternoon breezes, and everything was chatty and casual, but all the while, I was checking the couple for tells.

Could they have been players in the

nightmare on Vallejo Street? Was Harry Chandler a murderer? Was Kaye Hunsinger, knowingly or not, covering for him?

Kaye told me that she and Harry had been down the coast for the past week, returning to the South Beach Yacht Club only last night.

"It was a brilliant week," she said. "Zipping down to Monterey, docking at the marina there. Kicking off the boat shoes, putting on heels and a witchy black dress—oh my. Dancing with Harry."

Pause for an exchange of moony grins and hand-clasping. Okay. They were believably in love.

"We signed in with the harbormasters at stopovers, of course," Chandler said to me. "And lots of people saw us. If you still need more of an alibi."

I was thinking about Chandler's remarks of a few minutes before, that he'd been "wondering" if his wife's remains were among those that had been dug up in his garden. I wondered too, and I was equally interested in the woman whose head had been separated from her shoulders with a ripsaw about a week ago.

Had a body dump been part of the Chandler coastal cruise?

I had no warrant and no probable cause to search Chandler's yacht, so an eyeball search of the premises might be my only opportunity to check out the floating home as a possible crime scene.

"I'll take that list of stopovers," I said. "And I'm really dying to see the rest of this yacht."

Harry and Kaye showed me around the four-cabin luxury craft. It was *House Beautiful* marine style, everything enviably top of the line, and not a throw pillow out of place.

The boat was fast, and the alibis could have been manufactured, but I strained to find a reason why Harry Chandler would come back to San Francisco during his cruise, dig up a couple of skulls, and then leave them with a cryptic message in his backyard.

It would be crazy, and I didn't see any crazy in Harry Chandler.

I complimented the couple on the boat, and before the conversation could devolve into chitchat, I said that I'd be going and gave Chandler my card.

Chandler said, "I'll walk you out."

I started down the gangway and this time Chandler's hand on my back was firmer, more forceful. I stepped away and turned to give Chandler a questioning look.

"You're like a butterfly," Harry Chandler told me, fixing his gray searchlight eyes on mine, "with steel wings."

I was taken aback for three or four reasons I could have spat out right away. Had Harry Chandler's crazy just surfaced?

What had Nigel Worley told me?

Harry Chandler would like you.

I said, "I hope you're not coming on to me, Mr. Chandler. Because when a suspect in a murder investigation hits on a cop, you know what I think? He's desperate. And he's trying to hide something."

Chandler said, "You actually think of me as a suspect, Sergeant?"

"You haven't been excluded."

"Well, I'm sorry. I didn't mean to offend."

I said sharply, "Stay anchored. If I were you, I wouldn't draw attention to myself by leaving town."

Chapter 24

Jason Blayney moved purposefully through the large open space with the supersize bar and the high ceiling, the main room of the yacht club.

The reporter was twenty-seven years old, an average-to-nice-looking guy, and, along with his more intellectual talents, he had a trick left arm. When he was a kid, he had learned how to pop his shoulder so that it looked deformed, and this little sleight of arm gave him an edge in certain situations.

Right now, for instance, the arm made the security guy decide not to confront him. Blayney said, "How ya doing? I'm with the O'Briens. Mind if I use the bathroom?"

Guard said, "Sure," and pointed the way.

Blayney went to the men's room, washed his hands, finger-combed his hair, and straightened the camera hanging from his neck.

Then he left the club through the back door that opened onto the wide deck fronting the marina. He was imagining the smoking interview he was about to have with Harry Chandler.

Blayney had grown up in Chicago, and after graduating from the Medill School of Journalism at Northwestern, he had gotten off to a fast start at the LA bureau of the *New York Times*. Six months ago, he got the offer from the *San Francisco Post* to aggressively report on crime, and he'd moved up the coast and into a job that fit him like the cover of darkness.

Now he had a prominent platform to do whatever it took to crush the *Chronicle*'s dominance in crime reportage and establish himself as a player on the national stage.

Today, Blayney was as stoked as he'd ever been in his life. Yesterday's ruckus at the Chandler house was the start of a monster story that had legs up to the moon. He'd flattered a traffic cop and gotten a tip, and as far as he knew, he was the first journalist to learn that several heads had been dug up at the Ellsworth compound.

By itself, this information was tremendous on every level, and he was just getting started.

A half hour ago, Blayney had followed Lindsay Boxer from the Ellsworth compound. As soon as she got into her car, he'd been sure that she was going to the yacht club to interview Harry Chandler.

He took his time, and as he headed into the marina, Blayney saw Boxer leaving the slip where Chandler's boat was docked. Her head was down, her blond hair hanging in front of her eyes as she talked on her phone. Blayney thought of Lindsay Boxer as a character in his story; she was a good cop, but what really got him going was that she was emotional. If he dogged her, she would react and probably lead him into the heart of the story. She could be the heroine or the screwup on both of her active cases. He really didn't care which.

Either way, Lindsay Boxer had taken him to Harry Chandler.

He took a couple of pictures, but she didn't notice him.

"Nice one, Sergeant," he said quietly. "I think you made the front page."

Chapter 25

Blayney immediately recognized the man heading up the gangway to his yacht wearing denim and walking with a swagger. It was a thrill to actually put his eyes on the actor in real time, real size, the man whose face had been ubiquitous on Court TV for almost two years, a guy who possibly had killed his wife and gotten away with it.

Blayney wanted an interview with Chandler as much as he had ever wanted anything in his life. He pointed his camera and took another couple of shots, then called out, "Mr. Chandler."

Chandler turned to face him, taking a solid stance on the dock. His hands were curled into fists.

"Yes?"

Blayney opened the unlocked metal gate, said, "Mr. Chandler, I'm Jason Blayney, with the *San Francisco Post*. I'd like to talk to you."

"You're a reporter?"

"How do you do, sir? Mr. Chandler, I'm wondering if you can tell me what's going on at your house on Vallejo? I'd like to be your advocate, Mr. Chandler. Help you get your side of the story out—"

"Get off this dock. This is private property."

Chandler pulled his phone out of his hip pocket, called a number, and said, "This is Harry Chandler. I need security."

"What I've heard is that a number of human skulls have been exhumed from your backyard, Mr. Chandler. Would you care to make a comment?"

Chandler said, "Don't point that camera at me. I have no comment on or off the record, you get me?"

Blayney moved closer to show that

he wasn't backing down. "Did you kill your wife ten years ago, Mr. Chandler? Did you bury her in your garden? Are any of your past girlfriends buried there too, sir?"

Chandler reached out and grabbed Blayney by the front of his shirt and back-walked him to the edge of the dock. Holding the reporter, Chandler almost pushed Blayney off, then jerked him back to safety, looked down at the collapsed shoulder, and said, "Don't ever come here again."

"You're acting like you have something to hide, Mr. Chandler," Blayney said, stumbling and pressing forward at the same time.

Chandler said, "Wow, are you stupid."

The actor shoved the reporter toward the edge again, still holding on to the front of his shirt.

"Don't do it, Mr. Chandler. My camera. It cost me two thousand dollars."

Chandler snatched the camera off Blayney's neck, then pushed the reporter into the water.

The water was shocking, but Blayney was loving this encounter. He spat water, then started laughing. He popped his shoulder back in, then swam to one of the davits and wrapped both arms around it. A life preserver splashed into the water and Blayney grabbed it.

He was still laughing when he called out, "I like how you express yourself, Mr. Chandler. Illegal actions are *better* than a quote."

Blayney found a rung of a rope ladder and hauled himself out of the bay, thinking, *Oh man, how great is this?* Harry Chandler had *assaulted* him.

He would have given a year's salary for a picture or a witness. But anyway, the entire incident confirmed the monster quotient of this story.

He picked his camera up off the dock, snapped off some shots of Harry Chandler's back. Life was good.

Chapter 26

Bec Rollins, a PR biggie from the mayor's office, was waiting for me when I got back to the Hall. She was sitting in Conklin's chair.

Bec was intense, fierce, and she didn't waste time.

"Hi, Bec, what the hell is wrong? And don't say *everything,* because that's *my* line."

She gave me a fleeting grin, said, "Sit down, Lindsay. I think you want to see this."

She showed me her iPad, and I saw

a picture of me on the dock walking away from the camera.

"Wait. Where did that come from? This was taken today."

Rollins scrolled down, showed me the headline on Jason Blayney's article: "Heads Unearthed at Harry Chandler's Pad; Boxer Investigates."

I said, "What?" and began to read. My case was all over the Web. "Bec, Blayney knows what I know. Heads unearthed. Chandler's house. Chandler's boat. Someone leaked. But it wasn't me."

"I know, I know," Rollins said. She took back her gizmo, said, "Here's the thing, Lindsay. Blayney is a juvenile viper. He's got a license to harass and nothing to lose. I don't need to tell you how he can spin this story, poison any potential jury pool. He can make things hard for sources to come forward."

"I'm not cooperating with him, Bec. I didn't see him."

"Gotcha. But be aware of him. Here's what he looks like."

She showed me the picture of a man

in his twenties, dark hair, narrow eyes, a lot of teeth. He looked like a wolverine.

"He's going to confront you, count on it. When he does, you've got to be wise and cool and act as if you're approachable—but don't tell him anything unless Brady says okay first."

"Brady has talked to Blayney. Did you know that?"

"Yes. I knew. Let Brady do the talking for you on both of your cases. And here's the other thing. Your friend Cindy."

At the mention of Cindy's name, my partner left the break room and came toward our desks. Bec Rollins leaned in and finished what she was saying.

"Cindy Thomas is an investigative reporter."

"Don't you think I know that?"

"Inevitably she's going to want an inside track on this story."

"For God's sake. Are we done?"

"Lindsay, please keep in mind that whatever the press writes is worldwide and forever. Oh, hi, Rich," Bec said to Conklin. "I'll call you," she said to me.

Conklin sat down and said, "What's this about? Don't tell Cindy anything?"

"Something like that," I said.

Cindy Thomas is an honest, dedicated, and talented writer, and she has helped me solve crimes. That's how good she is. The kind of bureaucratic bull Bec Rollins had brought into the squad room like a lame pony is exactly why I'd eventually said "No, thanks" to the corner office.

I'd committed to being a career homicide detective. I had to be better than good. I had to be excellent.

Chapter 27

Conklin and I sat in the observation room, our hands cupped around containers of cold coffee, as Lieutenant Lawrence Meile and Captain Jonah Penny, from Vice and Narcotics, respectively, interviewed each of the three Narcotics cops whose names we'd tagged four hours before.

It was uncomfortable, yeah, and painful to see men I'd known for years being grilled about their whereabouts at the time Chaz Smith had been shot. In fact, no one was happy in that interrogation room, not the men asking the questions and especially not Sergeant Roddy Jenkins.

Jenkins kept his voice even, but I thought he was a picture of contained fury as Meile asked him to produce an alibi for Chaz Smith's time of death—and he didn't have one.

"I was just driving around. That's what I like to do when I'm off duty."

Meile said, "Come on, Roddy. It was two days ago. Where were you in the afternoon?"

"I was screwing your wife, Meile. Ask her. It was pretty good."

Meile boiled out of his chair and went for him. Penny pulled Meile off Jenkins, and Conklin got into the room in time to stop Jenkins from throwing a punch.

"Roddy. Roddy. Settle down."

Jenkins acted like Conklin wasn't there. He shouted at Meile, "I said I was driving around. What? Are you fuckin' kidding me? You accusing me of taking out that douche bag? I'm not saying another fuckin' word until my fuckin' lawyer is sitting next to me."

Roddy's name was still on the short list when he threw down his badge and gun and stormed out of the interview room shouting, "Fuck you. Fuck all a' you."

Conklin returned to the observation room, said, "That could've gone better."

I said, "I don't mind seeing his temper. He's organized. He's got a lot of years on the force. He's smart enough to have waited in the bathroom for Smith, and if he was mad, I don't doubt he would have pulled the trigger. And get two shots dead center too."

"He's worked in the department long enough to get a hate-on for dealers."

"Yeah."

I crumpled my coffee container, dunked it into the trash, answered my ringing phone.

I hoped the call was from Joe; it wasn't, but it was almost as good. Claire was calling.

"Got a couple of minutes for me, girlfriend?"

Chapter 28

I said to Conklin, "Claire wants to see me. If she had nothing on the heads, she would've said so on the phone, right?"

"We've got an interview in a few minutes, Linds."

"I'll be right back."

I jogged down the stairs to the lobby, stiff-armed the back door, and trotted along the breezeway to the ME's office.

I found my BFF in the chill of the morgue. Her lab coat with the butterfly appliqué on the breast pocket was buttoned up to her neck and she was wearing sweatpants under that.

"Summertime" was playing loudly on the radio, the San Francisco Symphony's version. Claire's husband, Edmund, plays cello in the orchestra.

"Dr. Perlmutter just sent me a status report," Claire shouted. She turned down the volume.

"Uh-huh, uh-huh, what'd she say?"

"Here's what you want to know," Claire said. "None of those skulls belonged to Cecily Chandler."

"Not that I'm doubting you, but what did she say exactly?"

"Cecily Chandler had A-one perfect teeth," Claire told me. "And not all of them were homegrown. Her dental records do not match the dentistry in any of the skulls."

I felt let down.

I hadn't been as certain as the supermarket tabloids were that Harry Chandler murdered his wife, but if Cecily Chandler's head had been discovered in Chandler's garden, I would have been more convinced that he was our killer.

I said to Claire, "Well, it only means

that Chandler didn't bury his wife's head in the garden. Doesn't mean he's off the hook for the others, right? Any other news from the doctor?"

"There was no trauma to any of the skulls."

"So you still don't know causes of death."

"That's correct."

My best friend held up a finger and said, "So, I've been working on the head of our Jane Doe in the cooler. I made a maggot milk shake."

"Wonderful. I hope you'll give me your recipe."

"Maggots, like all animals, are what they eat. If Jane here was poisoned or drugged, the tox screen on the milk shake would reveal that. So I put some squirmers into the blender and sent that out to the lab. Hoping for something, Linds. I was hoping for arsenic. Instead, we found benzoylecgonine, a metabolite of cocaine."

"So you're saying Jane Doe was a drug user."

"Yep, but there wasn't so much that it would've been fatal, so—"

"So all we know is that Jane Doe did drugs."

"We're not done yet. Dr. Perlmutter is working up those skulls for facial identification. We'll have something soon."

"When?"

"Soon."

"Good. Because right now we have nada, nothing, goose egg," I said. "I need help."

Chapter 29

I was thinking about the seven unidentified heads as I retraced my steps back upstairs to the squad room. I came through the gate, saw Conklin at his desk with a thin, lank-haired man of about forty sitting in a side chair talking to him.

Conklin introduced me to Richard Beadle, the headmaster of the Morton Academy. I shook his damp hand, took my desk chair, and joined the interview already in progress.

"I gave out my home number," Beadle said. "I felt that I should do that, but now my phone rings constantly and at all hours. Parents are distraught. Kids are having nightmares, and I don't know how to comfort them.

"Here's the latest," Beadle went on. "This is the prizewinner. Chaz Smith's family is speaking to the school through *lawyers*. They're suing *us*. Please tell me you've got something on that killer. Anything will do, anything I can tell the board and the parents."

"We're working this case hard," Conklin said. "It's our number one priority. Let's look at pictures, okay?"

Beadle had printed out sixteen photos that had been taken at the spring recital. Most of them were impromptu family portraits that had been shot in the school lobby before the fire alarm had rung.

I scrutinized each shot, and as I looked at cute kids and proud folks, I asked myself if I could be wrong about an angry cop called Roddy Jenkins. Could he really have taken a stolen .22 to the Morton Academy and put two rounds into Chaz Smith's forehead?

I didn't see it. And I didn't see Jenkins. Not in the foreground and not in the background, and I didn't see anyone who looked out of place.

The headmaster put a name to every man, woman, and child in each picture. We tagged partial sleeves and collars and hairlines to the identified pictures, and every piece of clothing matched to a known person.

Except for one.

I stared at an unfocused picture of the back of a blue suit jacket worn by someone we couldn't identify, and my throat tightened.

Was I looking at the only recorded image of the shooter?

I was pawing through photos in search of that blue jacket when Brady's shadow crossed my desk. We all looked up.

Brady was menacing even when he wasn't trying to be, like a linebacker primed to unload.

The lieutenant said hello to Beadle, then banged six photographs down in front of him, every one of them a picture of a cop who worked for the SFPD.

I knew all six of those men. Knew them *well*.

"Give them all a thorough inspection, Mr. Beadle," Brady said, looking like he was going to shake the guy until he picked out the shooter.

What if, in his panic, Beadle picked someone out?

What if he fingered a good and innocent cop?

Beadle's eyes bored in on each of the six photographs; he took Brady's advice and didn't rush.

"I don't recognize anyone," Beadle said, finally. "Is one of these men the killer?"

Brady's relief was apparent.

"No," he said. "You did fine."

We wrapped up the interview and I said good night to the office. Or I tried to.

Reporters were waiting for me outside the Hall, a bunch of them surging up from Bryant Street, stampeding toward me as I stood on the top of the Hall's front steps.

Now that I knew what Jason Blayney looked like, it was easy to pick him out of the crowd.

Chapter 30

Blayney was at the leading edge of the pack of reporters, some of whom I'd known for years. Others had to be out-of-towners who'd just blown into the Bay Area for a big, banging story that would be making headlines indefinitely: murder at the Ellsworth compound.

The reporters were on the move, sticking elbows into ribs, treading on toes, jostling video equipment as they angled for position on the Hall's front steps.

Microphones advanced.

Cameras fired in a 180-degree arc around my face.

I'd been mobbed by the press hundreds of times before, but today, I'd been told to keep my mouth shut and let Brady do the talking.

Jason Blayney called out to me, "Sergeant Boxer. What does Harry Chandler have to do with the bodies at his house? Is he a suspect?"

Overlapping questions came at me like flights of arrows: How many bodies had been found? Had the victims been identified? Had the SFPD arrested anyone?

"Is Harry Chandler a suspect, Sergeant?"

"Lindsay, please give us something, okay?"

I looked for a way out, but the crowd was dense and shifting, too thick to bull through. I reminded myself to adopt the wise and cool mind-set Bec Rollins had advised.

Suddenly, that seemed like a good idea.

I took a breath, said, "Sorry, everyone. You know the drill. I have nothing

to tell you at this point. I have to protect
the integrity of the investigation. That's
all I've got, so if you'll please excuse me,
I'll see you some other time."

The reporters weren't taking *no way*
for an answer. I looked around for anyone leaving the Hall of Justice who could
step in and take the cameras off me. I
was hoping to see the DA or Jackson
Brady.

But that wasn't happening, and Jason
Blayney was still in my face.

"Sergeant Boxer, the public has a
right to know *something*. If there's a
murderer on the loose—"

"Mr. Blayney? We can't give out infor-
mation about an ongoing investigation.
You know that, or you *should* know that.
You want a statement, contact Media
Relations in the morning. Thank you."

I ignored the renewed flight of questions and parted the throng by lowering
my head and making gravity my friend.
I'd gotten down the steps and across
Bryant, all the way to my car in the lot,
when I heard footsteps, someone running up behind me. It was Jason Blayney,
damn it, and he was calling my name.

I kept my back to him, got into the Explorer, had the door half closed behind me when Blayney put his hand on the door handle and pulled.

Was he *kidding?* This was over the freaking *top.*

I whipped around and faced him down.

"Blayney, are you crazy? The answer is no. No statement. No nothing. Now back the hell off."

Grinning, he took my picture, then shut off his tape recorder and said, "Thanks for your nothing statement, Sergeant."

I knew I was going to see my picture on the *Post*'s front page and that I was going to look insane.

So much for wise and cool.

I was steaming as I drove out of the lot. Blayney was a cockroach, but frankly, he and I both had the same questions.

Who were the victims?

Why had heads been dug up at Harry Chandler's mansion?

And why didn't we have a single bloody clue?

Chapter 31

Cindy not only dubbed our gang of four the Women's Murder Club but also branded Susie's Café our clubhouse. It was a small miracle to have this big hug of a hangout where we could get lost in a cheerful crowd and one another's company.

I was checking my rearview mirror to see if that a-hole Jason Blayney was following me, and at the same time I was looking for a parking spot on Jackson.

I was about to go around the block again when a car pulled out from the curb, leaving me a space right outside Susie's front door.

I got out of the Explorer, my legs wobbling with exhaustion, and then I was inside Susie's, enveloped by calypso music, laughing people, golden-yellow sponge-painted walls, and the smells of coconut shrimp and curried chicken.

Cindy was at the bar in the front room. She was wearing pink with a sparkling barrette in her hair and was putting down a cold one.

She waggled her fingers and at the same time gave me the evil eye. She was unhappy with me. I knew why, and I didn't blame her.

I ordered a root beer and when the bottle was in my hand, I took a swallow, and then I tried to make peace with my friend.

"I know you're pissed at me."

"I'm pissed at Richie too, so go ahead, both of you can take it personally."

"I brought you something," I said.

I opened my bag, took out a printout, handed it to Cindy, and watched her expression change.

"Oh. No. I mean. This is one of the

Ellsworth house victims?" She was staring at the artist's sketch of Jane Doe,
the woman whose head was in Claire's
cooler.

"We need the public's help in identifying this woman."

"What else can I say?"

"She may be the victim of a crime."

"And what about Ellsworth?"

"I'll tell you what I can, but don't say
that she was found at Ellsworth yet,
okay? We're not ready to officially open
the story to the press."

"And what about unofficially? The
Post has the damned story, Linds,"
Cindy said. "Everyone does."

She was mad, but she was clutching
the drawing and not letting it go.

"I'll tell you officially when I can. But
we can go off the record now."

"Okay. Shoot."

"Seven heads were exhumed. All of
them are female, buried over the course
of a number of years. We can't identify
any of them. We don't have a clue what
happened to them, how they were killed.
We don't know anything."

"If I write that, I'm going to have to apply for a job at the post office."

I guess my frustration was showing, and maybe some panic too, because Cindy was saying, "Okay, okay, Linds. Calm down. Take it easy," as Yuki and Claire came in together.

Cindy settled the tab. About forty-two seconds later, the four of us were at our booth in the back room and had ordered jerked pork and pitchers of beer. Yuki was off to the races about how in love she was with Jackson Brady.

And speak of the devil: Brady picked that minute to call me and tell me he needed my butt back at the Hall.

Chapter 32

That night, revenge sat in his Hyundai SUV, engine running, under a shot-out streetlight on Sunnydale Avenue, an ugly and dangerous artery that wound through the decrepit heart of the Sunnydale Projects. All around him, packed tight and wall to wall for a square mile, were squalid housing units on streets dominated by two violent and warring bands of thugs, the DBG and Towerside gangs.

A four-dimensional map of these badlands and its occupants was engraved on his mind—every unit and alley in the projects, every felon, juvenile offender, innocent citizen.

Revenge was watching both vehicular and pedestrian traffic centered on the Little Village Market up ahead at the intersection of Sunnydale and Hahn, and he was also focused on a block of tan stucco housing units to his right: two stories high with bars on the lower windows and burned-out grass between the footings and the street.

A shadow emerged from between two units.

It was Traye, a slouching young man wearing a ball cap and baggy gangsta clothes that swallowed his slight build.

Accompanied by the pulsing music pounding out of cars and windows, Traye made his way across the avenue, slipped into the passenger side of Revenge's car, and slumped below the line of sight.

He was nineteen and had burn scars on his neck and arms from a meth-lab explosion that had occurred inside his housing unit while he was playing outside, almost out of harm's way.

The boy had survived, but he had

never had much of a chance until a year ago, when Revenge took him on as a confidential informant.

Revenge said, "I spoke to the arresting officer. He's not going to show up in court."

"You for sure?"

"I said I'd get the charges dropped."

"You say so."

Revenge gave the boy a paper bag. Inside were three meat-loaf sandwiches his wife had made for Traye, a bottle of chocolate milk, a bag of Chips Ahoy, twenty dollars, and a pack of smokes.

The boy opened the bag, unwrapped a sandwich with shaking hands, and said between bites, "I don't got nothing for you."

"It's okay. Take your time."

Revenge dialed up the volume on the radio. Car accident on Mansell. Domestic violence on Persia. Backup requested at the Stop 'n Save. It was a slow night.

The boy chugged down the milk, put the twenty inside his shoe, rolled up the mouth of the bag, and then put it under his shirt. He looked at Revenge.

It was thank-you enough.

"I gotta go."

"Another time."

Traye got out of the vehicle, crossed the street to the alley between the buildings, and went from there to a basement hole, where whatever was left in the bag would be commandeered or the kid would get hurt—or both.

The man known as Revenge worried about Traye, wondered how long he would survive. Another year? Another week?

Deafening so-called music grabbed Revenge's attention, coming from a car heading up the avenue behind him. He checked the mirror, saw the black BMW with the death's-head stencils on the chassis.

Okay.

Now things were getting interesting.

Revenge put the SUV in drive and when the BMW passed him, he pulled out into traffic behind it.

Chapter 33

Revenge knew who was driving the BMW and who was going along for the ride.

Jace Winter, Bam Cox, and Little T Jackson were small-time drug dealers with long sheets for heavy crimes. They forced children into theft and females into prostitution; they broke down families; they caused destruction and desperation; and they sent young kids toward certain death.

They were, in a word, scum.

Revenge took a Boost phone from his glove compartment. He'd confiscated it during a bust and it couldn't be traced to him. He dialed 911 as he drove up Sunnydale, the BMW's taillights in view right up ahead.

The 911 operator asked him what his emergency was, and he put on a ghetto accent stained with panic.

"They's a shooting going down right now. Oh God. They's shooting at cops. They shot a cop!"

He gave an address three miles south of his current location, then clicked off and tossed the phone out the car window.

Revenge followed the BMW east on Sunnydale, and as the gangsters sped up, he followed them through the thick of the ghetto and out the other side to where the housing was single-family homes, flat fronts with garages and driveways on the street level.

The BMW took a right onto Sawyer and when it hit Velasco Avenue, Revenge put on his siren and his grille lights. Stuff started flying out of the windows of the BMW. Small glassine packets, a couple of guns.

He spoke into the bullhorn. "Pull over. Pull the car over. Now."

The BMW did slow, went from sixty to forty down Velasco, took a right onto Schwerin, and stopped next to an abandoned lot fenced with broken chain link and filled with garbage.

Revenge braked behind the BMW.

He left the engine running as he screwed the suppressor onto the muzzle, grabbed his flashlight, and got out of his car. He approached the driver's-side window of the BMW, shone his light in the driver's face.

The smell of weed coming from the BMW was so strong, one good inhale could produce a profound contact high.

The driver, Jace Winter, said, "Wus up, Officer?" He was smirking. Laughing with his homeys. Unafraid. Stoned out of his mind.

"Cox. Jackson. Put your hands on the ceiling," Revenge said.

"Man, how'm I going to show you license and registration with my damned hands—"

"Winter, keep your right hand on the wheel and open your jacket."

"Yo, what was I going? Twenty-eight in a twenty-five zone?"

"Good night, you piece of crap."

Revenge pointed the gun into the interior of the car. He shot Winter first, two shots in the chest, another round in the neck. Jackson and Cox went crazy trying to get out of the car, and then the last man they would see in this world sent several shots into various parts of their upper bodies until no one moved.

Revenge stripped off his jacket, balled it up with the gun, and dumped the bundle into Winter's lap.

A car went by fast, didn't stop, didn't even slow. Revenge went back to his vehicle, took out the plastic liter bottle filled with gasoline, and returned to the BMW. He poured gas inside the car, front and back, made a good job of dousing the dead men.

Then he lit a match and tossed it inside the drug-mobile.

There was a loud puff as the flame caught, then the car started to burn, and within a few seconds, the whole of it was engulfed in fire.

Keeping his head down, Revenge returned to his SUV. He watched the BMW explode as he backed out, then he made a U-turn and drove through the projects again.

He felt cleansed and almost high.

Like he was younger, and lighter, the very best version of himself, and since he would never get credit, he thought it was okay to give himself a pat on the back for a very clean shooting. Three heinous sewer rats were dead.

In twenty minutes, Revenge would be sitting in front of the TV watching the game, but he'd be thinking of Jace Winter's smug face and then his expression when he realized he was going to die.

Revenge listened to the police band, learned that cops were still investigating a report of a cop down but hadn't yet determined who had been shot or where. He turned off the police band, found a rock station on the radio. He was whistling as he drove home.

Book Two

MEDIA CIRCUS

Chapter 34

I paced around a garbage-strewn vacant lot off Schwerin Street, a potholed one-laner that ran between the Sunnydale Projects and through Visitacion Valley.

Normally desolate, tonight Schwerin was impassable in both directions, cordoned off and hemmed in by twenty-odd police cars, three fire rigs, two ambulances, the fire investigator's truck, the scene-mobile, and the coroner's van.

Outside the lot, between the broken chain-link fence and the street, an incinerated car was turning the night sky opaque with smoke.

I coughed into my sleeve, kept a good twelve yards between myself and the smoldering car as Chuck Hanni, our chief fire investigator, processed the scene with his crew. One of his key associates was Lacy, an ignitable-liquid-detecting K-9, a black Labrador with an excellent nose.

The last time I saw Hanni, a meth lab disguised as a school bus had exploded on Market Street during morning rush hour. There had been casualties, but none of them, thank God, were children. Hanni had detailed that horror show with his first-rate expertise, as he was doing now with the remains of a fatal fire that looked to be a triple homicide.

As I watched, the K-9 alerted Hanni. The fire investigator pulled something out of the car, shone his Maglite on it, then sealed it in a paper bag. Claire and Charlie Clapper walked over to Hanni and had a powwow with him, and then they took over the scene.

Techs were taking bodies out of the

vehicle as Hanni came over to brief me on what he'd learned so far.

He massaged his scarred right hand as he crossed the lot, the result of an injury he'd gotten in a fire. He wore his everyday chinos and white shirt under a sports jacket, and although Hanni was the first to get his hands dirty metaphorically, I'd never seen him with so much as a smudge of soot on his clothing.

"I've got a lot to tell you," Hanni said.

I wanted to know everything.

He couldn't tell me fast enough.

Chapter 35

"The fire started in the passenger compartment," Chuck Hanni said. "See, the engine compartment is in relatively good shape. Flames probably vented through the open window."

"The windows were open?"

"Just the driver's window."

"License and registration, please," I said. "Could have been a traffic stop. Go ahead, Chuck. I interrupted you."

"Not a problem. So, this is what I see happening. As the interior burned, the windshield failed and the rear seats were consumed. Then the fire entered the trunk and destroyed the back of the car."

"Yeah, the rear tires are melted," I said. "So what caused the fire?"

"Lacy alerted on what was left of a plastic bottle that had rolled under the front seat. I think gas was inside that bottle, but anyway, some kind of accelerant. It looks to me like the passenger compartment was doused, and the fire was started with a match or a lighter.

"I doubt the lab is going to get prints or DNA off that bottle," Hanni continued. "But they can try. Maybe you'll get lucky."

I was taking it all in, trying to picture it.

I said, "Someone pulls the car over, throws gas inside the vehicle, sets the fire. So why are the victims still inside? When the fire started, why didn't they get out? Were they already dead?"

"Claire is swabbing their nasal cavities now. She'll be able to tell you in about five seconds if the victims breathed smoke in or not."

"Okay. What else?"

Hanni grinned at me and said, "Patience, Lindsay. I'm getting there. I removed all of the debris that fell from the dashboard, headliner, and door panels, and I found a spent round for you. Twenty-two caliber."

I got a little chill. The good kind you get when your hunches pay off. Doesn't happen every day. There are a million .22-caliber guns on the street, and our cop shooter had used one of them on Chaz Smith. Maybe he'd used the same gun to take out a few drug dealers from the projects.

I thanked Hanni and started to call Claire to find out if she'd found soot inside the victims' nostrils but got distracted by the loud *whoop-whoop* of a siren announcing that another cop car was arriving at the scene.

It was Conklin and he came toward me at a trot. He was hyperventilating and it wasn't because of the thirty-yard sprint.

"She's here," he said. "We've got our witness."

It felt like Christmas and my birthday and Mother's Day all wrapped up together and tied with a bow.

A witness had seen a cop pull a car over on Schwerin just moments before that car had become a fireball.

The witness had given her name and number to the 911 operator. She wanted to talk.

Chapter 36

Anna Watson sat across from us at the fold-down Formica table inside the RV that served as our command post. She was sixty-four, black, small, chain-smoking Marlboros and stubbing out the butts in a tinfoil ashtray.

I tried to keep my expectations in check but failed. Anna Watson knew the victims and she'd seen them just before they were shot and their car burned to a turn.

"I was driving along Schwerin," Watson told us. "I was going to my daughter's house over in Daly City? I was a ways back from Jace's BMW," she said, hooking a thumb in the direction of the crime scene. "But I recognized it easy from the decals, and I know the boys driving that car. I've known them since they were small. I used to babysit two of them."

I pushed a pad and pen over to Watson's side of the table and asked her to write down the names. As she did it, I saw her eyes tear up and her lips quiver.

Reality was hitting her. Three people she knew were dead. She passed the list over to me and as Conklin continued to question her, I ran the names through the computer: Jace Winter, Marvin "Bam" Cox, Turell "Little T" Jackson.

Winter, the oldest of the three, was nineteen.

All three were gangbangers and had been arrested many, many times while they were still juveniles: possession of illegal substances, possession with intent to sell, attempted murder. Robbery, multiple counts.

They had gotten off because all their cases had been thrown out. Witnesses had failed to show up in court. Evidence got lost. Nobody wanted to go against these young hoods and have their homes shot up, their kids ambushed on the way to school. No one wanted to get murdered.

Anna Watson was saying to Conklin, "I was feeding my grandkids in front of the TV and I saw the news chopper, you know? And it's taking video of that car burning up. God Almighty."

Her hands were shaking. Another cigarette came out of the pack.

"Could I have some water, please?"

"Sure," Conklin said; he got up, pulled a bottle of water out of the minifridge, handed it to Watson.

"So I called nine-one-one," Watson said, "because I saw that car right after it was stopped by the police. I drove right past it on my way to Malika's house."

"Let me get this straight," Conklin said. "At about six o'clock, give or take a few minutes, you were behind that BMW and then you passed it on the side of the road because the driver had been pulled over by a cop."

"That's right."

"The car was speeding?" Conklin asked.

"No, Jace wasn't speeding. He probably had a warrant or something. That's what I thought when I saw him stopped by this cop car with all the lights a-blinking."

"Did you get a good look at the cop?"

Watson shook her head no.

"His back was to me and he had a flashlight in his hand and was pointing it at Jace. I was looking at the flashing lights and I was looking at Jace."

"You got a look at the cop's vehicle though?"

"I wasn't paying attention to that car. I slowed down so I didn't get stopped myself, and then I just kept going."

"Was it a cruiser? A black-and-white?"

"No, it was one of those SUVs."

"Was there any kind of insignia on the car?"

She shook her head no.

"Can you describe the flashers?"

"Front headlights were blinking, first one, then the other."

"Wigwags," said Conklin.

"And there was blue and red lights, I

don't know if they came from the grille or the dashboard . . ."

"That's very good, Mrs. Watson."

"Oh Jesus. Do you think that cop set Jace's car on fire?"

"We'd just be speculating at this point," Conklin said. "We're going to have to check out the names you gave us, and we'd like you to come down to the Hall and look at some photographs. Vehicles and people. Is that okay with you?"

Watson said, "What if I had stopped? Maybe those boys would be alive."

I said, "If you had stopped, you might have been killed, Mrs. Watson. This isn't your fault. You're helping us to find who killed those kids."

And then she started crying. Anna Watson was maybe the only person in the world who felt bad that those gang-bangers were dead.

And then she said to Conklin, "I don't know who's going to take care of me now."

"I don't understand."

"Jace is gone. How'm I going to get my—"

Conklin held up his hand and said, "Mrs. Watson, I'm sorry you lost your dealer. I can't help you with that."

Watson nodded. She said to my partner, "If you drop me off at my house for a minute, after that I can come with you to look at pictures."

Chapter 37

It was after eleven when I got home. I was hoping for some quiet time with a half-pint of ice cream, just me and Martha and Baby made three.

I put my key in the lock, but the front door was open. I went inside, saw lights on in the living room. The TV was on too. Heyyy. Joe wasn't supposed to be home for a day or two.

How great was this?

"Joe?" I called out.

Martha galloped into the foyer, and a person in loose clothing came up behind my dog. The figure was backlit, in silhouette, and was definitely *not* my husband. I started and had my hand on my gun before it clicked.

The woman with the long red hair and cute glasses was Karen Triebel, Martha's "nanny," and as far as I knew, she wasn't even a little bit dangerous. Still, my heart was pounding as if I'd walked in on an armed robbery in progress.

My fear reaction was quickly followed by mortification.

I'd forgotten to call Karen to say I was going to be late. I apologized now, thanked her for hanging in.

"We watched a movie," Karen said, then added to Martha, "Didn't we, big girl? And I baked a potato," she said to me. "And finished off the ice cream. I hope that's okay."

"Sure," I said. "Of course. I'm sorry that I lost track of the time."

"Martha has a real crush on Tom Cruise," she said.

I walked Karen out to her car, stood on the sidewalk until I couldn't see her taillights anymore, then I went back upstairs to my dog.

The phone was ringing when I got inside.

I looked at the caller ID and saw it was my sister, Catherine, who lives a little way down the coast in Half Moon Bay.

I'm four years older than Cat; we've both been divorced, and she has two girls. She's been coaching me on the care of my child onboard, name to be determined, sex unknown to me and Joe.

I grabbed the receiver off the hook, took Joe's big chair in the living room, and put my hand on my tummy; Martha circled, then collapsed onto my feet.

"Linds, why don't you call me back? I get worried."

"I just walked in," I told her.

"Joe is still out of town?"

"He'll be back tomorrow, I think."

"You sound like the walking dead."

"Thank you. That's how I feel, if the walking dead feel anything."

"Yeah, well, pregnancy does that. It also makes you feel like you've lost about fifty IQ points, as I recall."

I laughed, and my sister prodded me
to tell her about my two active cases. I
held a few things back, but I gave her
the basic rundown on the heads found
at the Ellsworth compound. And I told
Cat about the triple homicide that had
kept me working late tonight, first at the
scene, then at the Hall, then at the
morgue, and finally at the forensics lab
until a half hour ago.

"The guy is some kinda vigilante," I
told Cat. "I guess he doesn't trust the
cops will bring in the bad guys so he
figures he's the man to do the job."

"Lindsay. You're saying he's armed
and dangerous. And you're trying to
bring him down. Why won't he go after
you?"

"I'll be fine, Cat, really."

"Bull. You can't know that."

Cat was now beginning her lectures
on the value of rest, on how I could burn
out, on how my workload wasn't good
for the baby. I couldn't argue with her. I
just had to take it.

Then a call-waiting signal beeped in
my ear. I checked the caller ID, and if I
hadn't been trying to get away from my

sister, I never would have taken the call from Jason Blayney.

I told Cat I had an urgent call, said good-bye, and then put on a frosty voice for the crime reporter from the *San Francisco Post*.

Chapter 38

"It's late, Mr. Blayney. And listen, don't call me again. The person you want to talk to is Bec Rollins in Media Relations. She'll be happy to speak with you. Use my name."

Blayney ignored me, pressed on. "We got off to a bad start, Sergeant, and I know it was my fault. I get a little carried away. Does that ever happen to you?"

"Does *what* ever happen to me?"

"Do you ever get a little carried away when you're really into a case? In my situation, when I'm on a story, I want to live it, breathe it, dream it."

Blayney was trying to bait me into saying *Yes, I sometimes get carried away.* Did he think I was stupid?

"I understand that sometimes reporters who are living, breathing, and dreaming their stories get carried away. They should take care that what they consider enthusiasm isn't actually stalking or assault."

Blayney laughed. "Okay, okay, you win, Sergeant. But I still have an offer for you."

"Oh, really."

I was tired. Unlike the dealers who'd died tonight, I had inhaled smoke. And unlike Chuck Hanni, I'd gotten soot all over me. I looked charred. I *felt* charred.

"Good night, Mr. Blayney."

"Listen, I don't think you'll go to hell if you call me Jason. And here's my offer."

I sighed loudly.

"Have lunch with me. I want to tell you what I'm trying to do at the *Post.* I think you'll see that I'm not a bad guy. I'm on your side. I could be even more on your side if we work together."

I laughed at him. It was a genuine laugh. The guy was actually funny. I recognized a journalist's trick of the trade: make friends with your subject and gain trust—then betray that trust.

"I want to give you my number," he said. "I sleep with my phone next to my pillow."

I said, "Who doesn't?"

"I never miss a call."

"Sweet dreams," I said. I heard him calling my name as I moved the receiver toward the hook.

I said, "What is it?"

"Just take my number, okay? You may change your mind about talking to me."

I said, "Uh-huh, uh-huh," pretending to write down his number, then I hung up. I was dying for a Corona, but instead I had a big glass of full-fat milk, got into bed with Martha, and put my feet up on some pillows.

Martha put her head on my belly, about where I thought the baby's little butt might be. I talked to them both for a few minutes, laughed at myself, and then turned on the news.

I fell asleep with all the lights on. I hadn't set the alarm. I hadn't even brushed my teeth. And then came the call from the crime lab, from Charlie Clapper, who was pulling a double, maybe a triple shift.

Clapper said, "We found a gun inside the car. Thought you'd want to be the first to know."

"What kind of gun?"

"A twenty-two. The number had been filed off, but we recovered it with acid and traced it. We already know all about that gun."

"It was one of the guns stolen from our evidence room."

"Well, you took all the fun out of that," said Clapper.

"Brady is going to want to know."

"He's next on my call list."

I thanked Charlie, said good night.

I stared at the ceiling until six, then got dressed and took Martha for a run. The killer Jason Blayney had nicknamed Revenge had taken out seven people, one of them an undercover narc.

Revenge was on a spree, and he was stepping up his timeline, doing multiple homicides. He was growing into his job as an executioner and he was becoming fearless.

These days, I couldn't walk through the Hall of Justice without looking at every cop and wondering, *Did you do it? Are you the one who's gone rogue?* I had the sense that I knew Revenge, that he was a regular cop, hiding in plain sight.

Chapter 39

At 8:00 a.m. we were in an unmarked Chevy Malibu, Conklin at the wheel.

"I slept on the couch again last night," he told me. "If this keeps up, I've got to upgrade to a king-size couch. Or cut my feet off."

"Cindy's upset, you're saying?"

"She said it was because I stunk and whatnot, but it wasn't the smoke in my hair, Linds. She's pissed."

"I know. I know. What should we do? Tell her we're looking for a cop who's taking out drug dealers? Then she'll get the scoop, and we'll be whistling and wearing white gloves directing traffic."

Conklin laughed. "That's not funny."

"She'll get over this."

"When?"

"Sorry I can't do more to help your love life," I said. "She's mad at me too, you know."

Conklin laughed again, said, "Yeah, but you're sleeping in your bed, am I right?"

He made the turn onto the wide and beautiful stretch of Vallejo Street, now barricaded and three reporters deep on the sidewalks. I saw the local guys as well as some press displaying decals of various countries' flags on their satellite vans.

There was nothing like severed heads at the home of a movie star who'd once been tried for murder to bring out inquiring minds from all nations.

I was recognized and a small mob stampeded toward our car even as a uniformed cop pivoted a sawhorse to let the car through.

"There's your friend," Conklin said to me, indicating the young guy at the front of the barricade who was taking pictures and looking very pleased with life. It seemed like Jason Blayney didn't ever have bad days.

"Yeah. My friend." I snorted. "Wants to have lunch with me."

"You going to do it?"

"Be serious."

We drove up to a space in front of the mansion, left the car under the protection of the men and women of the SFPD, then went through the gate.

Ricky Perez, Harry Chandler's gardener, was sitting on the front steps of the Ellsworth house waiting for us. He was in his twenties, and his massive upper-body musculature showed under his sweatshirt and plaid flannel jacket.

He also had a great smile.

This kid was in charge of the trophy garden. He was too young to have been caretaking the Ellsworth garden when the heads were first buried there. But I hoped he could lead us to a killer with the sensibility of a department-store window dresser and the bloodlust of Jeffrey Dahmer.

Chapter 40

I introduced myself and my partner to Ricardo "Ricky" Perez, then asked him what he knew about the heads that had been presented on the back patio of the house, garnished with chrysanthemums.

Perez said, "All I know is what I read and what Janet Worley told me. She grilled me, for God's sake. You ought to consider hiring her for your rubber-hose-and-third-degree department."

He looked for a laugh, didn't get one. He appeared surprised. Big, good-looking kid, worked for a movie star. He was probably used to adoration and he seemed to like attention.

I asked Perez where he'd been over the last week, and he had no trouble re- membering. He'd been out with three different girls over the weekend and had slept in with Miss Early Monday Morn- ing in his flat.

He was awoken by a call from Janet Worley, who'd filled him in on the shock- ing events. According to Perez, the whole story was from "the planet Weird, man," and he had no idea how these heads could have been buried right un- der his feet without him knowing it.

He was either genuinely perplexed or a pathological liar. I asked, "When was the last time you were in the back gar- den?"

"Last Friday. I work Tuesdays and Fri- days. There were absolutely no heads lying around when I weeded the flower beds. And I didn't see any sign of dig- ging. Nothing. At all. When do you think I can get in there and get the place cleaned up?"

"You work exclusively for Mr. Chan- dler?"

"No, but he's my main job."

The three of us took a stroll along the outer path of the garden. The tape was still up, and so was the main tent just off the patio. The piles of dirt were casting shadows over the pachysandra.

The kid told us that he'd had this job for only three years, but he was attached to the place. He got agitated when he saw what the forensics team had done to the garden.

"Look at this mess. Just look. I'm pretty freaked out, if you want to know the truth. Whoever did this knows this garden. He could be someone I *know*."

I said, "Who, Ricky? Who do you know who could have done this?"

"Look, I want to tell you something, but not officially."

"Okay," Conklin said, playing along.

"Nigel Worley doesn't like Mr. Chandler. And I know why, because Janet confided in me. She had a thing with Mr. Chandler when the Worleys first moved in, like ten years ago."

"A 'thing'?" Conklin said.

"Janet told me it was just a fling and that she didn't hold that against Mr.

Chandler. She was married. He was married. It went on for a couple of months.

"She said that she still loves him in a funny way."

"That's the word she used? *Funny*?"

"She said *odd.* Do I think that she killed people and dug up their heads? Honestly, I don't see it."

"And Nigel?"

"Nigel has a temper and he's not subtle. If he was going to kill someone, he would just freakin' kill him. And I think first up would have been Mr. Chandler."

Perez showed us the gate that opened onto a narrow concrete walkway on Ellsworth Place and he showed us the lock for the gate. He said that he had the only key.

It was a simple lock, could have been picked, but there was no evidence to show that it had been tampered with.

I took out the sketch of Jane Doe.

"Do you know this woman?"

Perez took the drawing, looked at it for a long few seconds.

"Is she one of the victims?"

"Yes."

"Her head was cut off?"

"Do you recognize her?"

"She looks familiar, but I don't know her. It's like, maybe I saw her in a coffee shop or something like that."

He handed the drawing back to me, then said, "You know who you should talk to? Tom Oliver, Mr. Chandler's driver. He's been with Mr. Chandler for about twenty years. He's gonna be your expert on Harry Chandler. And maybe he'll recognize this woman."

Chapter 41

I pressed the bell marked T. L. OLIVER at number 4, one of the four identical six-story brick houses on Ellsworth Place that bounded the mansion on its west side.

"Mr. Oliver?" Conklin said into the intercom. "This is the police."

T. Lawrence Oliver buzzed us in and we climbed the flights of stairs up to the top floor and found Harry Chandler's driver waiting for us at his front door.

He was forty-something, white, looked like he could bench-press three hundred pounds. He wore jeans and a print shirt, earring in his left ear, which in the nineties would have meant he was straight. Now it only meant that he liked earrings.

We took seats in the run-down apartment with no view of the back garden, and Conklin started asking the questions. Oliver answered, but he was edgy. He fidgeted with a watch; it looked like a gold Rolex.

"I take time off when Mr. Harry is away," he told us. "So I dropped him and Kaye off at the boat on Thursday afternoon, then I drove to Vegas. I was gone the whole weekend."

"Where'd you stay?" Conklin asked.

"The Mandalay Bay. I played a lot of blackjack. I didn't win and I didn't lose, but I did get lucky," he said.

"Write down the name of that lucky person for me, will you?" Conklin said.

"Aw, jeez. Her name was Judy Lemon or Lennon, something like that. She's a cocktail waitress at the casino. Oh. Wait. I have her phone number."

He wrote down the number for Conklin, then said, "Anything else?"

"Relax, Mr. Oliver. We've got a lot of questions."

"Can I get you a beer? Mind if I have one?"

Oliver was drinking at nine in the morning. What did he know? What had he done? He dragged a kitchen chair into the living room, and Conklin and I took turns throwing questions at him.

He told us that he had worked for Chandler since long before the trial. While Chandler was in the system, Oliver had taken a job in LA driving for a friend of Chandler, a TV producer. He'd come back to the Ellsworth compound when Chandler was acquitted.

He said he knew nothing about the severed heads except that it was creepy, and his vote for Most Likely to Commit Murder was Nigel Worley, although he couldn't come up with a motive.

He also didn't recognize our Jane Doe.

Oliver said good things about Chandler, how generous he was, how there was no way the movie star had ever killed anyone. He said Chandler's only vices were women and nice things.

"He gave me this watch when he got tired of it," Oliver said, showing off the seven-thousand-dollar Rolex.

I didn't like Oliver, but was he a killer? I told him we'd be checking out his alibi and I gave him my card. He wanted us to leave so badly that I pushed back one more time.

"Mr. Oliver, if you had anything to do with this crime, you should tell us now, before it goes any further. My partner and I can help you. We can say that you came to us voluntarily."

"No, no. I haven't done anything like that. I came back from Vegas and saw all the cop cars outside the main house and thought, *Aw, shit.*

"Listen, I drove Mr. Chandler's Bentley to Vegas. I'm not allowed to. I don't want to get fired. Please don't tell him. Check it out with the garage at the hotel. There's a time-stamped record of the Bentley going in and out all weekend."

I told Oliver we'd check out his story and that I wasn't making any promises about what I would say to Chandler. I told him that if he had any thoughts about what happened inside the walled garden to call me any time.

"I have a thought right now. Do you know LaMetta Wynn?"

Chapter 42

Lametta Wynn was Harry Chandler's personal assistant. She lived in a small Victorian house in Golden Gate Heights, a residential neighborhood where everyone had his or her own patch of lawn and a porch overlooking the street.

Ms. Wynn was fifty or so, white, a fading redhead with sharp, pale eyes.

She asked us to come in, and we sat down in her living room. There were watercolor landscapes on the wall and a shotgun in a rack over the sofa. She answered our questions about her whereabouts, saying that she'd been alone all weekend.

"I got some sleep, caught up on e-mail, and was in touch with Harry Chandler. You know, he pays me a lot. He expects me to answer the phone when he calls."

"Did he call you over the weekend?"

"In fact, he did. He was in Monterey. Wanted to get the names of some restaurants where he could take Kaye."

"I understand that Mr. Chandler has an active social life."

"I'm not going to tell you the names of Harry's old girlfriends," Wynn said. "Take it from me, there have been a lot of women, but Harry will be happy to give you names and dates, if you just ask him. I want to help you if I can. But I don't know who could have done this— whatever *this* is."

"All of the heads that were exhumed from the garden were female," I said.

LaMetta Wynn sat back in her seat. She seemed to be thinking about that, then she said, "You're the homicide detectives, so help me to understand. If Harry Chandler is the killer, why would he bury his victims' heads in his own backyard?"

"I guess you're assuming that killers are logical," I said. I pulled out the drawing of Jane Doe, a drawing that was getting rumpled from handling.

Wynn got a glimpse, then seized the drawing from my hand.

"I know her," she said. "I *know* this woman. Is she one of the people who was killed?"

"Yes. Who is she?"

"Her name is Marilyn. Varick, I think. She lives on the streets. Occasionally she sleeps in a doorway.

"I've given her spare change. She comes from Oregon," said LaMetta Wynn. "I didn't get into any long conversations with her. I mostly brought her soup."

"Did Harry Chandler know her?"

"Impossible. He couldn't have. And I want to be perfectly clear. I know Harry Chandler well. He isn't a violent man. He's a scamp, but, apart from breaking hearts, he'd never hurt anyone."

Chapter 43

Conklin and I took the fifteen-minute drive to the yacht club. I wanted my partner's opinion of Harry Chandler. And I wanted to see Chandler's face when I showed him the drawing of the girl whose head had been unearthed from his garden.

As before, Chandler was sitting in a deck chair at the foot of his gangway when we arrived. He had a big smile for me, shook Conklin's hand, and said, "I hope you have some news for me."

"We do, Mr. Chandler."

"Come aboard," he said.

I think Conklin's jaw dropped a little bit when Chandler showed us to the sitting room on the aft deck. I guess my jaw had dropped the same way when I saw it the day before.

I said, "Mr. Chandler, the remains found in your garden were all examined, and none of them are a match to Cecily Chandler."

"Oh, thank you, Sergeant," he said, his expression full of relief. "I don't think I was ready to hear that she'd been buried in the backyard all these years."

"But this woman *was* buried in your garden," I said. I unfolded the drawing of Marilyn Varick and showed it to Chandler.

He took the paper, looked it over. I stopped breathing for the time it took him to scan that drawing. Then Chandler looked up at me.

"She was killed and her head was buried in the garden?"

"That's right. Do you recognize her?"

"Not at all. I'm sorry. Sorry that she's dead. Sorry I can't help."

I returned the drawing to the inside pocket of my blazer. I had seen nothing in his face that told me Chandler was lying.

"There's something else," I said. "Are you involved with Janet Worley?"

"Now? No, and not for at least ten years. Why would you ask me that?"

"But at one time, you were intimately involved."

"We had a couple of trysts, that's all," Chandler told us. "She was very pretty and delightful, and we both knew it was just for fun. I was in love with my wife."

I didn't like a definition of *love* that included trysts with someone else while you were living with your beloved spouse.

I thought about how Worley had spoken disparagingly of Chandler's womanizing while crashing stove parts in the kitchen. He had made his accusations sound personal. In fact, Janet had left the room.

The people we had spoken with said that Nigel was brutish, that he didn't have a flair for fine details. But if he was involved in the murder and in digging up those heads, maybe he hadn't been working alone.

Chandler was saying, "Janet is a fine person. I care about her. I don't love her, but I really do care about her. Until I met Kaye, I hadn't been in love since Cecily disappeared.

"You know why I still live in San Francisco when I could live anywhere in the world? Because maybe Cece *wasn't* murdered. Maybe she was abducted. Or maybe she just wanted to get away from me. Maybe she'll come home, and if she does, I'll be waiting for her."

Conklin and I left Chandler on the *Cecily*. As we walked across the dock toward the parking lot, my partner said to me, "Janet Worley has been holding out on us."

"Just spitballing now, but try this on for size," I said. "Say Nigel Worley does the killings because he's angry that his wife had an affair, plus he's crazy. Janet goes along with it. And she's the one who does the decorating with numbers and flowers."

"And they put the heads on the back step? Why?"

"Because it makes Harry Chandler a suspect. If he gets accused of murder again, then maybe this time, he doesn't get off."

"All because of a fling ten years ago."

"Maybe neither Janet nor Nigel got over the insult," I said. "Maybe hatred of Harry Chandler is what keeps those two together."

Chapter 44

"I've got her," I said to Conklin.

He looked up from his computer.

"Marilyn Varick," I said. "Google shows a dozen pages on her. She was something special about five years ago."

Our former Jane Doe had saturated the local surfer news and blogs. Many of the articles about her had photos of her in a Speedo standing next to her surfboard, and there were links to YouTube. I clicked on one, played a video of Marilyn riding enormous waves at Pillar Point.

I turned the monitor so Rich could see.

"Jane Doe was a surfer," I said. "A champion."

Rich had been doing his own research as I looked up Marilyn Varick on the Web. He said, "She's got priors for possession, loitering, panhandling, all in the last two years. She was always picked up in Pacific Heights. I guess that was her home base."

"LaMetta Wynn said that she was sleeping in doorways. LaMetta gave her money. Maybe other people did too," I said to Rich. "Our drawing doesn't look much like these younger pictures of her in real life. It's like comparing a plum to a prune."

I did a search for Marilyn Varick on Facebook, found more beauty shots of a graceful young woman daring the waves off Ocean Beach, but she hadn't updated her page in two years.

"Something happened to her a couple of years ago," I said. "She dropped out."

Rich said, "Wynn said there was no way Harry Chandler knew Marilyn Varick. Chandler also said that he didn't know her. But then we have Nigel Worley saying Chandler had a wide range of types. Maybe a pretty surfer girl would have been one of those types."

"Speculating now," I said. "Say Chandler meets her, dates her, breaks her heart. Marilyn goes downhill. Starts living on the street near Chandler's house."

"She's not in missing persons," Richie said. "But she's got parents living in San Rafael."

"Someone's got to do the notification," I said.

"It's my turn," said Rich.

"I'll do it," I said. "I want to."

Chapter 45

I sat by the indoor swimming pool in a lovely modern house in San Rafael, nineteen miles north of San Francisco. The walls were glass and the morning sun made beautiful swirling patterns in the water. An English springer spaniel slept in a dog bed, his legs running in a dream.

Richard and Virginia Varick were a handsome couple in their sixties, dressed in tennis shorts and sweaters. Mrs. Varick couldn't sit still. Her husband leaned back in a metal-frame webbed chair and looked at me suspiciously.

I thought he knew why I had come.

When I first saw Jane Doe's remains, I thought that once we knew who she was, the rest of the puzzle would fall into place; we'd learn the nature of the crimes and the motive, and from there we'd have a good shot at figuring out who had killed her and the others.

Now, as I sat with the Varicks, my only thought was that I was about to shatter the final happy moment in their lives.

"When was the last time you spoke with your daughter?"

"Is Marilyn in trouble?" Virginia Varick asked me.

"I'm not sure, Mrs. Varick. Could you look at this drawing?"

I had printed out a clean copy of the sketch that had been drawn from the partially decomposed head of Jane Doe. I handed it to Mrs. Varick.

"Who is this person?" she asked me.

"Does she resemble your daughter?" I asked.

"She doesn't look anything like my daughter. Why? Who is she? I thought you had news of Marilyn. Don't you? Dick? I don't understand."

She handed the sketch to her husband, who held it with both hands, then drew back from it, turned it over, and put it facedown on the table in front of him.

"Mrs. Varick, this is a drawing of an unidentified woman whose remains were found a few days ago in San Francisco. I'm sorry to have to bring this sad news to you—"

"Don't worry, it's not my daughter," Mrs. Varick said, her voice getting high. "Wait here. I'll show you my daughter."

Virginia Varick left the room, and I said to her husband, "When was the last time you saw Marilyn?"

"We haven't seen her in two years."

"And why is that?"

"She didn't want to see us," Dick Varick told me. He was clasping his hands tightly together. His knuckles were white, his complexion gray. "I think she was doing drugs. She called from time to time and my wife and I would talk to her for ten or fifteen minutes, although Ginny and I did most of the talking.

"Marilyn said she was fine. And she asked us not to try to find her. We looked for her anyway, but she'd gone underground. None of her old friends had seen her or knew where she lived."

I said, "Did something happen at about the time she stopped seeing you? An incident or trauma?"

"Nothing that I know of," Varick said to me.

"I need something of hers that might contain her DNA. Hairbrush, toothbrush. Maybe a hat."

"We don't have anything like that. She never lived here."

Virginia Varick returned to the room carrying an enormous blue-leather-bound scrapbook. She sat on a footstool, opened the book, and turned it so that I could see the pages.

I recognized many of the photos, but others were new to me; family photos with her parents, her dog, boyfriends, all of which made me wonder how it was that no one had identified her when the *Chronicle* had run the sketch.

Had Marilyn changed so much?

Was the sketch a poor likeness of Marilyn Varick?

Or had Harry Chandler's assistant been wrong when she identified the person in this sketch as Marilyn Varick?

I scrutinized the photos Ginny Varick showed me, and I was convinced they were of the same person as the one in the drawing. Virginia Varick just didn't want to face the truth.

"She was a beautiful young woman," I said.

The anguished woman stood up and snarled at me, "Don't say *was*. She *is* a beautiful woman. I told you, whoever this person is, she's not my Marilyn."

Chapter 46

Dick Varick reached out for his wife, but she drew away. He said, "Ginny, you haven't seen Marilyn in a long time. Listen, I brought her some money about eight months ago. She didn't want me to tell you."

"You saw her? And you didn't tell me?"

"She was in bad shape, dear. She was high and talking crazy. She wouldn't come home. I pleaded with her, but she wouldn't let me get her any help. She said all she needed was a loan. I gave her a thousand bucks. She called us twice after that, so I knew she was okay."

Ginny Varick put her hands to her mouth and then ran from the room.

Dick Varick stood, jammed his hands into his pants pockets, and walked to one of the glass walls. He looked out at the Japanese maples and the sharp shadows they cast across the back lawn. Then he turned to face me.

"I'm sorry I lied to you about not having seen her. I didn't want to tell Ginny. And now I have, in the worst possible way."

"So this drawing *is* of Marilyn?" I asked.

"Yes," he said. "How did she die?"

"We don't know, not yet."

"You have to tell me what you know."

"Come sit down," I said.

Dick Varick returned to his chair and leaned forward with his hands pressing hard on his knees, his eyes on mine.

I had been dreading this moment. How do you tell parents that their daughter's head had been removed from her body—and that you don't know how she was killed, by whom, or even the physical location of her body?

"Some human remains were disinterred at the Ellsworth compound."

As soon as I mentioned the Ellsworth compound, Varick became agitated. He interrupted me to tell me what he'd read in the papers and to ask if Marilyn was one of the victims of that crime.

I told him what little I knew.

I asked, "Did Marilyn ever mention Harry Chandler?"

"No. Is he responsible? Did that miserable bastard—"

"I'm asking because her remains were found on his property. That's all. Did Marilyn tell you or give you a sense that someone wanted to hurt her?"

"No, she said she was living with friends. Sergeant, I hardly knew my daughter when I saw her. All traces of the young woman I'd known and loved was gone. She was an addict. She wanted money for drugs. She didn't even ask about her mother."

"I'm sorry," I said. "I'd like the names of the friends you spoke with when you were looking for her."

"She was thirty-three," Varick said, typing names and contact information into his iPhone. I gave him my e-mail address and he sent the list to me. "She wasn't a teenager," Varick said. "I couldn't call the police and have her brought home."

"I understand."

"Do you want me to come and identify her?"

"Contact the medical examiner," I said. I wrote down the phone number on the back of my card, and then Dick Varick walked me to his front door.

He looked years older than he had only half an hour before, shaken, hopeless, the father of a murdered child.

I got into my car and tried to contain my own feelings—but I couldn't do it. I drove down the block and halfway up the next one before I pulled over, put my head down on the steering wheel, and sobbed.

Chapter 47

There were two newspapers outside my front door the next morning: the *Chronicle,* with its headlines about the G8 meeting and the San Francisco city budget, and the *Post,* with its sixty-four-point headline in thick black ink:

BODY COUNT AT THE HOUSE OF HEADS: 613 DEAD; 613 VICTIMS!

Story by Jason Blayney, of course.

I read the first couple of paragraphs despite the bile backing up in my throat and going all the way up to my eyes.

The *Post* has learned that the heads unearthed at the Ellsworth compound were accompanied by an index card with the number 613 written by hand.

As of six this morning, the SFPD crime lab is still working the site, and if the number is indicative of the total death toll, the disinterred heads retrieved so far are just the first of a large number of victims that could make this crime the work of the worst mass killer in history.

What crap! What total flaming bull-crap!

Sergeant Lindsay Boxer, who is the lead detective on this case, has not returned our calls . . .

I called Brady, left him a voicemail, and he called back while I was in the shower, naturally. He left a message saying he was heading into a meeting and that he'd see me at the press conference.

"City Hall, room two hundred," his voice told me. "Don't be late."

I dressed a little above my pay grade, buffed my shoes, and even put on lipstick. I kissed my dog good-bye and when I got into my car, I called Cindy and told her to meet me outside City Hall.

I drove to Van Ness, parked in an underground lot on McAllister, then walked across Civic Center Plaza. I knew I was putting myself at risk. But I owed Cindy a break.

I saw her standing under a linden tree thumbing on her BlackBerry. I called out to her and she put her phone away and came toward me, her blue eyes frisking my expression for clues.

I gave her a hug and she hugged me back.

We walked together through the park toward the formidable and impressive beaux arts building where the mayor's office was located and where much of the city's business was conducted.

"Here's the deal. I'm an anonymous source," I said. "Seven heads were disinterred from the Ellsworth garden. All were female, buried at different times over approximately a ten-year span. Those numbers that were written on index cards—"

"One hundred and four and six thirteen. I can say that?"

"Yes."

"What about the identity of that Jane Doe whose picture we ran yesterday?"

"Her name was Marilyn Varick, age thirty-three, unemployed, former surfing champion. Good enough?"

"Excellent. Thank you, Linds."

We went up the steps to the imposing entrance to City Hall. I squeezed Cindy's arm, then stepped away from her and headed into the rotunda.

The press conference was about to start.

Chapter 48

Room 200 at City Hall is arranged like a courtroom. There's the dais and the built-in wooden chairs, then a railing that sets the audience apart from the main action. The walls are painted cream, and there are video screens so that even those in the back of the room can see you sweat.

I stood on the dais and watched the gallery fill with press. Cindy took a seat in the third row and immediately bent her head over her laptop.

When the rear doors closed, the mayor stepped forward, adjusted the mike, greeted the press. Then he filled them in on an OIS, an officer involved in a shooting, that had happened last night in the Mission.

He played a 911 tape, then showed a dash-cam video of a man running at the cops with a sword, refusing to back away until he was finally, fatally, gunned down.

There was a brief silence in room 200, then hands shot up. The mayor fielded questions about the shooting, then took questions about the SFPD, specifically about the crime rate and why so many crimes were unsolved.

When the mayor had had enough, he introduced Lieutenant Jackson Brady and left the stage.

Brady advanced to the podium with his crib sheet and, holding it rigidly in front of him, began his prepared remarks.

"Three known drug dealers were shot last night on Schwerin Street and their car was set on fire. The men were dead when the fire started and the blaze pretty much obliterated all forensic evidence."

Brady listed the victims' names and said that the police were looking for the shooter; he said that the preliminary ballistics tests of the slugs found in the dead men's bodies showed they were a match to the ones removed from the body of drug dealer Chaz Smith.

"We still have no leads to the shooter's identity, but he does have a pattern. His victims are all drug dealers. The investigation is on the front burner. And that's all I have for you now."

Hands went up like an acre of beans sprouting in time-lapse photography, but Brady ignored them and said, "Sergeant Boxer will brief you on the case involving the remains at the Ellsworth place. Sergeant?"

And then he took a place to my right and all I could do was step forward.

Chapter 49

I can give a speech when I have to, but I'd rather be on slops for a week than face the media in a formal setting. Fifty or sixty pairs of eyes focused on me as I took the microphone.

I said, "Good morning," then got into it.

"Monday morning, two skulls were discovered at the back door of the main house in the Ellsworth compound. These skulls were unearthed by a person or persons unknown who dug them out of the back garden and may have gotten onto the property by breaking the lock on the front gate. Along with the two skulls were two index cards with the hand-printed numbers one hundred and four and six thirteen."

Someone shouted, "That's for the number of heads that were buried, right?"

"No," I said. "We have no reason to believe that there are hundreds of heads. CSU has disinterred seven heads from the Ellsworth compound, all female, all unidentified, but we are working with forensics on attaching names to these victims and should have news later this week."

"What about the identity of the Jane Doe whose picture ran in the *Chronicle*?"

"We're withholding her name until we have a positive ID. We expect to have that information for you shortly."

"What about Harry Chandler? Is he a suspect?"

"Mr. Chandler is cooperating fully with the police and he is not charged with any crimes."

I felt like I was in a batting cage facing an automated pitching machine set on kill. Sweat beaded at my hairline. My voice caught in my throat as overlapping comments and questions came flying at me.

"But the heads were buried in Chandler's backyard."

"Where are the bodies?"

"Is it true that you have witnesses?"

"What happened to the bodies?"

"How were the victims killed?"

I avoided a few more inside fastballs, then Brady came to my rescue. He waved his hands and said, "Thank you, that's all for today."

I left the room through the back door. I went along the hallway, took the stairs down, then exited into the astonishingly beautiful rotunda.

I was glad to get into the sunshine, and the farther I got from room 200 the better. I was heading toward the garage when my phone buzzed. I looked to see—it was a text from Cindy.

You did good.☺

I smiled and put my phone back in my jacket pocket, then heard a man's voice call my name.

Naturally, Jason Blayney had followed

me. I should have made a bet, because I would have won money on it.

"No comment," I said to Blayney. "I'm done commenting for the day."

"Have lunch with me," he said. "Please."

Chapter 50

I wanted to straighten Blayney out, on or off the record—and I wanted to know why he was on my case.

He saw me hesitate and set the hook. "How about St. Francis Fountain? They have a fabulous breakfast menu."

He was talking about a classic old-timey eatery on the corner of Twenty-Fourth and York, built almost a hundred years ago.

I said, "Okay, okay, *okay*."

I followed Blayney to the Fountain, parked my car where I'd be able to see it through the plate-glass window, and went inside.

The diner had a soda fountain on one side of the room, straight-backed wooden booths on the other side, and tables and chairs in the window apse. Blayney called out to me from the window table and I slid into a chair across from him.

The waitress came with the laminated menus listing your standard diner fare: burgers, club sandwiches, malts, and shakes.

I ordered decaf and toast. Blayney went for the big man's breakfast: pancakes, chorizo hash, fried potatoes, high-octane java.

While we waited for the food, Blayney told me all about himself: his education, his job with the *Times,* his opportunity at the *Post,* and his determination to rule crime journalism.

The food came, and he talked while he ate, kept talking until there was nothing on his plate but a smear of syrup.

Then he placed his utensils on the upper right rim of the plate and told me that he believed in supporting the police department. And that he also believed that people have a right to know how the police department does its job.

"It's my duty to tell them the truth," he said earnestly.

"What were you doing when you told your readers that six hundred and thirteen people had been killed?"

"Okay, that was my editor who did that," Blayney said. "If I go a couple of days on a story without news, he'll boost what I do have. So the number six thirteen becomes six hundred and thirteen victims. You can't tell me otherwise, can you? Let me ask that another way— what does the number mean exactly?"

"Jason, that number is exactly the kind of detail we don't release, and if it wasn't for your story, I would not have mentioned it today. When the nutjobs start confessing to crimes they didn't commit, details, like handwritten index cards, are how we exclude them. Do you understand? So, by putting six hundred and thirteen out there, you made our job much harder. Maybe six hundred and thirteen times harder."

"Well, I'm sorry. I really am. I had to

run with something. Give me something now. I can make you the heroine of this story," Blayney said.

"I'm not looking for that, Jason. I'm not a hero. I'm not superhuman. My partner and I, all of the SFPD, we're doing our best, working as hard as humanly possible. Print that, will you?"

I dug a five out of my pocket and put it down on the table.

I left the diner thinking it had been a mistake to go there. I'd wanted him to give the good guys a break, but that wouldn't give him the brazen headlines that sold papers.

I could almost see his next story: a photo of my back as I went to my car and a quote, "Sergeant Boxer tells this reporter, 'I'm doing the best I can.'"

Chapter 51

By the time I got back to my desk, Cindy's featured story about the press conference was the front page of the *Chronicle* online.

Cindy's headline:

ONE ELLSWORTH VICTIM IDENTIFIED; SFPD STILL SCRAMBLING.

I scanned the article.

Cindy's lede was about Marilyn Varick, her background, her triumphs. The second paragraph detailed her more recent decline. There was a picture of Marilyn coming out of the ocean with her surfboard, and then Marilyn Varick was left behind as the article steamed ahead.

> Although Marilyn Varick has been identified, six victims remain un-named. Sergeant Lindsay Boxer of Homicide admitted this morning that the SFPD still has no suspects and no leads to solving the crimes committed at the Ellsworth com-pound.

I finished reading Cindy's irritating story and wondered if I was paranoid.

I said to Conklin, "I'm starting to pick up a bash-Boxer trend in the media. Do I look like a piñata to you?"

He glanced up, said, "A little bit. Your bangs, maybe. Why do you ask?"

He laughed. I stuck out my tongue and said, "Well then, I'm going to be the best piñata I can be."

Just then, Brady's door opened. He stood there and stared across the bull-pen, then called the two of us into his office.

Brady looked like he'd been sleeping facedown on his desk. His skin was ashen and he had swollen bags under his eyes. Whatever was on his mind, I could tell it was bad.

Brady said, "I just got a heads-up that Chaz Smith's society wife is going public. Big-time. Prime time. Her interview with Katie Couric is going to air tonight."

I grabbed the one side chair and Conklin leaned his tailbone against the credenza. He asked, "What's the gist of the story?"

"Mrs. Smith says that her husband was an undercover cop. That the SFPD screwed up, of course. Narcotics is going to take the heat for Smith, but his murder is going to get connected to the ones last night in the hood, and therefore, Homicide will also take a beating."

I looked at the stacks of personnel folders on his desk. Brady saw me looking and went on. "I asked for a rundown of all police personnel who have been suspended or canned. Or who have had some sort of major meltdown due to either a one-off incident or the cumulative wear and tear of being a cop.

"I went over every cop's file in every department."

He dragged his chair out from behind his desk and dropped into it. He sighed, then looked at me and Conklin. "It makes me sick to have to say it, but the person on the top of my list is your old partner, Boxer. Yours too, Conklin. Warren Jacobi."

I almost had a meltdown myself.

Spots blinked on and off in front of my eyes and I thought for a minute that I was going to faint.

Jacobi was on medical leave. He hadn't punched a time clock in months. He was tough, but he was not a vigilante. I refused to believe otherwise.

I finally managed to say, "Boss, that's not possible. With all due respect, you don't know Warren Jacobi. At all."

Chapter 52

My relationship with Jacobi went back ten years. He was my partner for most of that time, and we were nothing short of great together. We averaged fourteen hours a day sitting side by side in a car or face-to-face across our desks.

I laughed at his crude jokes and he told me I was brilliant, since I thought he was funny. We solved some terrible crimes together and became the closest of friends. It got so that we moved as though we were operating with the same brain.

Then something happened that brought

us even closer together. In fact, it bonded us with blood.

We'd been watching a late-model Mercedes parked in a bad neighborhood. When it took off at seventy miles an hour, we followed. It was a chase that ended when the top-of-the-line luxury sedan crashed and flipped in a dark and desolate alley.

Two kids were in the car, both sky-high on meth. The older was a fifteen-year-old girl with a pixie haircut, a pink sweater, and I think some kind of sparkly makeup on her cheeks. Her brother was two years younger and he was injured.

Both of them were crying and bloody and afraid we would tell their father that they had taken his car. Jacobi and I put one and one together, got two scared teens, called for medics, and put our weapons down.

It was a mutual lapse of judgment and could have been the biggest mistake of our lives.

The girl went for her learner's permit and pulled out a gun. She got off five shots, hitting me twice, and her brother put three rounds into Jacobi before I managed to take them down. Then we lay on the deserted street and almost bled to death before the ambulance came.

Jacobi's injuries that night had slowed him down. He couldn't run. He put on weight. He was in constant pain, and about ten months ago, Jacobi had been promoted to chief.

The pain got to him though, and recently, Jacobi had taken medical leave to have his damaged hip replaced.

"He's been out for three months," Brady said to me now. "Jacobi was either off duty or on leave when the first three shootings occurred. He was off the radar when Chaz Smith was taken out and when those three shits were wasted on Schwerin."

Brady talked over my objections. Told me to hear him out.

"Jacobi can use his radio two ways: to gather intel and to create a distraction. He has street sources. He could go into the property room at any time. He's chief of police, Boxer. Who's gonna suspect him? He can hide in plain sight the way only a fifty-five-year-old white guy with a limp can."

"He's not a killer."

"Let's say you're wrong," Brady said.

"He's like family to me," I said.

"I don't buy it either," Conklin said. "He's a great cop. He just wouldn't go off the deep end and become a vigilante."

Brady waved our comments away.

"I need you both to work closely with me. We're not going to say anything to Jacobi or to anyone else. We're just going to watch him."

My mind drifted.

I hadn't been in touch with Jacobi in months. I'd gone to the hospital after his operation. I'd brought flowers, but I'd called him only a couple of times after that. It was embarrassing to think about it. I wondered now how was he doing.

Was he depressed?

Was he angry?

Did getting shot on Larkin Street by a drug user constitute motive to go on a killing spree?

According to Brady, it did.

"Are you listening to me, Boxer?"

"I'm sorry. No. What did you say?"

"I said, if anyone can talk him in, it's the two of you. I'll tell you where to be and when. That's all."

Chapter 53

At just after 6:00 p.m. Revenge was standing at the counter at Peet's waiting for take-out coffee for his drive home.

Someone had left the *Post* behind and he read the front-page story about the shooting outside the projects. Despite the overheated writing about the deaths of the three dirtbag drug dealers, it was clear that the cops had nothing on the shooter except the gun he'd tossed into the car, the gun that had been used to take out Chaz Smith.

There were no prints on that gun, and

there was no way to link it or anything else to him.

The primary on the case was Lindsay Boxer. He had met Boxer a couple of times back in the day. She was a hands-on homicide cop, maybe gifted, and certainly tenacious. But smart and dogged could only help you so much when you didn't have a clue.

Martina, the girl behind the counter, took cash from an old man with a limp, said, "Thank you. Come back soon."

She closed the cash drawer, dropped the small change into a cup, and exhaled a long sigh.

Revenge knew that Martina was depressed about her pending divorce. Although she laughed it off, called it "losing a hundred and seventy-five pounds," Martina was obviously heartsick.

She put on a brave face for him and said of the front-page story, "That's something, isn't it?"

She poured hot coffee into a cardboard coffee cup, leaving two inches at the top for milk, the way he liked it. "Some kind of vigilante is killing drug dealers. Have you heard about him? He's called Revenge."

"Just reading about it now," he said. "I don't read the paper all that often."

"But you do watch TV, right? One of the guys Revenge killed was a big-deal undercover cop, and his wife is going to be on TV tonight. With Katie Couric."

"No kidding. Well, maybe I'll watch it then."

He smiled at the waitress, poured milk into the cup, and capped it. He left four dollars on the counter, told Martina to take care, and went out into the strip mall.

He got into his vehicle and called his wife, told her he'd be home in half an hour; did she need him to pick up anything?

"No, thanks. We're good, sweetie," she said.

Revenge hung up and had just started the engine when he saw something that almost snapped his head back. It was Raoul Fernandez, a scumbag drug dealer who was moving up in his world from small-timer selling teenths in the hood to distributor with young kids doing the dealing for him.

While Revenge was with the DEA task force, he'd looked for evidence against this ugly piece of work. Fernandez was cagey and elusive, and after serving two years for dealing, he had been released.

That should never have happened. Now Revenge watched Fernandez lock up his sporty little Mercedes and head across the parking lot toward the Safeway.

The strip mall was busy. Revenge had just been seen by Martina and everyone who'd been in Peet's. He knew he ought to let Fernandez go. He should drive home to his family, just drive away.

But fuck it. He might not get this chance again.

Revenge got his gun out of the glove box and stepped out of his car. He walked past the Mercedes and followed a dozen yards behind the drug dealer, his gun pressed against his leg.

Fernandez might have heard something, or maybe he just had a sixth sense; the dealer turned toward Revenge, and he had a gun in his hand.

Revenge felt his heart rate spike.

The voice inside his head was saying, *This was a mistake. This is where I go down. I guess I want it to happen. Today.*

Chapter 54

Conklin and I stood with Charlie Clapper on the bricks behind the Ellsworth compound watching CSU pack up their gear. The garden was pocked with holes and heaped with mounds of dirt; it looked as if a hundred woodchucks on crack had run amok there.

Still, no additional heads or any other body parts had been found. There was no new evidence of any kind.

I was struck again by how twisted this case was, how unusual in every way.

Ninety-nine percent of the time, a homicide investigation revolves around a body and a scene where the crime actually took place.

You've got an assortment of material to work with: clothing, blood, fingerprints, hard evidence that can tell you who the victim was, what caused his death, and possibly when the victim died. You can even compare a photograph of the victim with the DMV's database and most of the time can come up with a name.

Or you start with a missing-person report and you work the case from the other side. You start with dental records, maybe DNA, a list of friends, coworkers, phone numbers, the time the missing person was last seen.

All we had were holes, piles of dirt, unidentified remains, and a list of suspects that barely made the needle jump.

We couldn't even say for sure that the seven victims had died from homicidal violence. Maybe they had all died of natural causes and their heads were brought to the site for burial.

All we knew for certain was that whoever buried those heads had access to the garden behind the Ellsworth compound over a period of perhaps ten years or more.

As we waited for the forensic anthropologist to complete her measurements and run the data through software that could put virtual features on bare skulls, we could do nothing but hope for a lucky break or—please, God—a confession.

Now Clapper unzipped his coveralls, stripped off his gloves, and sighed.

"We've sifted every square foot of this place. We've got everything there is to get. Those artifacts we pulled out of the graves were clean. No prints. No DNA. Just doodads."

"If we identify the victims, the doodads may mean something to the families," I said.

Clapper said, "Okay, then. I gotta get out of here. My wife is expecting me home for dinner, first time this week."

I felt deflated and frustrated. I was about to suggest to Conklin that we go to the firing range and put a lot of holes in some paper targets when Brady's phone reached out and connected with mine.

"Boxer, there's been a shooting. Looks like another one of these freaking Revenge killings. That son of a *bitch*. Is Conklin with you? Good. You two go to Potrero Center. I'll meet you there as soon as I can."

Chapter 55

Potrero Center was on Sixteenth and Bryant, a modern strip mall of wall-to-wall retail stores: Office Depot, Safeway, Jamba Juice, and more. A stone wall with a metal rail on top enclosed the vast parking lot that was nearly always packed.

The sun was going down when we drove between the stone pillars on Sixteenth and identified ourselves to the uniformed cops at the entrance. I asked for the name of the first officer, then Conklin parked our car near the dozen or so squad cars right inside the gates.

We headed toward the yellow tape at the perimeter, and as we worked our way through the shifting crowd, I saw fear and anger on the faces of shoppers. Clearly, they'd been told that no one could leave the lot without giving a statement, and the handful of officers on the scene were just starting a process that could go long into the night.

The first officer was Mike Degano, a young guy who had been a block away when the call came over his radio. He wanted to help, had the look of a patrolman who aspired to work homicide.

Degano pointed to a late-model black Mercedes XL, said to us, "That's probably the DB's car. He had a Mercedes key ring in his hand when he went down. Car is registered to Raoul Fernandez. I ran his name. He has a record for assault and for possession with intent. Spent a couple of years at Folsom, released in 2010. Wait'll you see this."

Conklin and I walked with Degano to where the body of a heavily tattooed twenty-something man was splayed on the asphalt. His arms were flung out like wings, his legs were twisted. It looked to me as if he'd been walking toward the shopping center, had turned toward his killer, and had been blown off his feet by the four bullets he'd taken to his face.

It took a steady hand and an automatic gun to throw four shots in such a tight pattern. I'm a good shot, and I couldn't have done it.

I took another look around the lot as lights came on. Shopping carts were adrift, like dinghies on a blacktop sea. Broken paper bags spilled groceries where they'd fallen. I saw surveillance cameras on light poles, but the shooting had taken place a good hundred yards from the closest camera.

"Were there any witnesses?" I asked Degano.

"Yes, ma'am, we have one sort of witness. Mr. Jonathan Nathan, over there. Old white dude. Red shirt. He heard the shots."

Chapter 56

Jonathan Nathan was in his seventies, stooped, glasses balanced on the lower slope of his nose, red-and-white aloha shirt under a windbreaker, khaki pants. Flip-flops. His eyes switched between us and the parking lot, as though anything could happen, as though he didn't feel safe.

I said, "Can you tell us what you know?"

"Sure. Happy to. I was putting my groceries into the trunk of my car when I heard the shots. I looked around, but I didn't know where the shots came from,"

Nathan told us. "My head was inside the trunk when the gun went off, you know? Plus a lot of cars were coming and going. It was crazy noisy."

"What happened then, Mr. Nathan?" I asked.

"Then I saw the body," Nathan said, spreading his fingers, framing his face with his hands. "I ran over to him, but the guy wasn't breathing. He was absolutely dead. I didn't touch him, okay? There was no point."

"Sure, I understand. Please go on."

"My phone was also dead, so I waved down this guy in an SUV and asked him to call the cops. He did it, and then he drove off."

Conklin and I had the same thought at the same moment. The so-called cop who had stopped the drug dealers on Schwerin had been driving an SUV.

Conklin launched into his trademark rapid-fire interrogation with a smile.

"The guy in the SUV," Conklin said. "What did he look like?"

"What did he look like? Jeez. I don't know. Regular guy."

"Black? White? Hispanic?"

"White."

"Young? Old? Fat? Skinny?"

"I don't know. I don't *know*."

"Hair color?"

"I was on the far side of the car. He was in shadow."

"Okay, Mr. Nathan. What about the SUV?"

"It was black, I think. No, it was definitely black."

"American make? Foreign?"

"I have no idea. Look," Nathan said, getting steamed. "There were bullets flying around. I'm supposed to notice what kind of car the guy with the phone was driving? Listen, I've gotta get home. My wife is sick with worry. Plus we got people coming over. I just ran out for some groceries."

I took Nathan's contact information, gave him my card.

My partner and I went back to view the body, stood off to the side as the CSU van rolled up and techs piled out onto the parking lot.

I said to Conklin, "Look at how close the shooter gets to the vics. Chaz Smith. Those guys in the BMW the other night.

Now Mr. Fernandez, dope dealer to Potrero Hill. This shooter knows these guys. He's organized. He's a perfectionist."

"And most of all, he's *insane*," said Conklin. "He's taken out five people this week, for a total of eight, Lindsay.

"And Brady thinks Warren Jacobi is capable of this?"

"Here comes Brady now."

Chapter 57

Brady's car braked with a squeal only yards from the barrier tape. Lieutenants Brady and Meile boiled out of the vehicle, both of them agitated and demanding to be briefed.

Brady said, "What have we got?"

"Raoul Fernandez," I said, pointing to the deceased. "Meth dealer, former convict. He was dead before he hit the ground."

"Witnesses?"

"One so far. He maybe saw our shooter, a generic white male driving a black SUV. Our witness asked the driver to call nine-one-one, and he apparently did it. Dispatch is pulling the tape now."

I went on to say that uniforms were taking down the name and number of everyone who'd been in the lot when the police showed up. Other uniforms were canvassing the shops.

"Plate readers have been down the rows," I said, "and it was a decent sweep. Two stolen cars, two other drivers with outstanding warrants, but none stand out as our shooter.

"I asked the ME to give us an hour with the scene. Meanwhile, we've got surveillance tapes on the way from the security chief."

"Let's hope we got that black SUV on tape . . ."

Brady let his words trail off but I knew where he was going. Digital forensics was getting so refined that even a partial shot of the vehicle's fender could yield enough information to identify the make and type of car.

I stood with Brady and Conklin and watched the light trucks come in. CSU was working fast and well, photographing scrapes on car doors, marking blood spatter, bagging found objects on the asphalt.

Soon the ME would remove the body, and CSU would take the car back to the lab on a flatbed truck. By tomorrow morning, the shopping center would be open again, like the shooting had never even happened.

But it had happened.

A spree killer was running the table.

I told Conklin I'd be back in a couple of minutes. I ducked under the tape, turned my back to the crime scene, and called Jacobi.

His voice sounded so real to me that I actually said, "Jacobi, it's me, Lindsay."

The voice kept talking, said, "Leave me a message."

I told my old partner's voicemail that I missed him, wanted to get together with him, asked him to call me.

I really did miss him.

I wanted to tell him about this spree killer, hear what he had to say. Maybe he had an idea we hadn't thought of and maybe in the course of the conversation, he'd tell me something that would establish his innocence. I was sure that Brady was delusional. My old friend wasn't the killer.

It just *couldn't* be Jacobi.

Chapter 58

Cindy wasn't the only person working after close of business, not even close. A dozen offices in her line of sight had the lights on; loud laughter came in bursts from the corner office; and down the hall, the copy machine in the hallway chugged out copies.

These days, no one left work early.

Everyone wanted to be sure of a chair if the music stopped.

Cindy turned on her desk lamp and read Richie's text message again. *Caught a homicide. Cya later. XXX.* She texted back: *Copy that. Ttys.*

She put her phone down and asked herself why she'd let Richie's message go unanswered for so many minutes, why she'd withheld returning the XXXs, wondered again if she was becoming like her parents.

Her mom was a shrink, her dad was a math teacher, and when she was a kid, she had called them Robo-Mom and Robo-Pop because they both over-analyzed absolutely everything. Every. Little. Thing.

This was what she was doing with her relationship with Richie: *Yes, no, maybe.* Repeat.

She was also obsessed with her story, treating the numbers found with the Ellsworth heads as if they were the da Vinci code.

She justified her obsession like this: If she didn't decode those numbers, someone else would. Jason Blayney would. And so, partially because of him, partially because she would have done it anyway, Cindy had been flipping the flipping numbers every which way, forward, backward, inside out.

First she'd tried to connect the numbers to Harry Chandler. He'd notched his bedpost innumerable times during his long life as a star. He'd been named *People* magazine's sexiest man in the world three times and had been the tabloids' favorite cover boy for decades because of the many famous girlfriends he had squired to black-tie events.

Had Harry Chandler had 613 lovers? Was that what the number meant? If so, how did the 104 figure in? Not his address, not his birth date, not his license-plate number.

So Cindy had abandoned that line of inquiry and moved on. She had plugged the numbers into her search engine and found that if she put a colon between the *6* and the *13,* Google kicked out an interesting passage from the Bible.

Romans 6:13: "Do not offer any part of yourself to sin as an instrument of wickedness, but rather offer yourselves to God as those who have been brought from death."

It was interesting and, in the context of the buried heads, very creepy. "Do not offer any part of yourself to sin . . ."

Was the person who dug up the heads

at the Ellsworth compound saying the dead had been guilty of sin? Adding the colon to the other number didn't help— biblically speaking, 1:04 meant nothing.

Moving on, there was 1:04; 6:13. Time of day, time of death, day of the year?

Cindy reviewed the lists she'd cut and pasted from Wikipedia into her research file, the tens of dozens of names of people who had been born on January 4 and died on June 13, and absolutely none of them rang bells when it came to the skulls at the house of heads.

Cindy grabbed her phone and texted Lindsay: *Any IDs yet on skulls?*

Still waiting, Lindsay texted back.

Thx.

Crap. Cindy got up from her desk, walked down the hall, and found three people who would share a pizza with her. She ordered out, and while she waited, she ran the numbers again.

Chapter 59

It was Groundhog Day all over again.

I came home at 11:00 p.m. with swollen feet and a growling stomach; was greeted at the door by my manic border collie and her tranquil nanny. I walked Karen out to the street, watched the taillights of her old Volvo disappear into the distance. Then I returned to an apartment that was devoid of Joe.

I had spoken to Joe twice a day since he'd left town, but swapping conversational tidbits by phone was way short of being in my husband's real live presence.

I nuked a he-man-style TV dinner of Salisbury steak and green beans and brought it into the living room. I got into Joe's big chair, put my feet up on a footstool, and rested my tray on my bambino's rump.

"You don't mind, do you, darling?" I asked him or her.

Not a problem, Mom.

The national news was wrapping up as I tucked into my fancy steak burger, and then the local headlines came on. First up was the report on the 6:15 shooting at the Potrero Center.

The on-site reporter described the latest drug-dealer execution in fairly accurate and gruesome detail, saying that this victim was the fifth dealer to be murdered in the past five days.

The reporter said, "In an interview with KTVU earlier today, crime analyst Ben Markey said that these killings probably are not gang related but are an indictment of the SFPD. Quoting Mr. Markey, 'The cops can't put the bite on drug crime, so a vigilante has stepped in to do the job.'

"Channel Two has learned this evening that the DEA has assembled a task force to investigate this rash of killings. Joseph Molinari, formerly a senior agent with the FBI and more recently deputy to the director of Homeland Security, has been hired to consult. Molinari is now based in San Francisco.

"And so, Tracey, back to you."

I stared at the TV for quite a long moment, trying to absorb what I'd just heard, especially the part where my husband was on a DEA task force and I didn't know a thing about it.

I gathered up my tray and myself, got out of the chair, and found my phone. I called Joe, who answered three time zones away at two thirty in the morning.

I scared him half to death.

"What's wrong, Lindsay?"

"I'm fine. We're fine," I said. "I just heard about this task force from Channel Two News."

"You didn't get my message?"

"No. *No*."

"Well, I left one for you."

I glanced at the phone, saw the blinking message light; it must've come in while I was taking witness statements at the strip mall.

"I'm sorry, Joe. I missed it."

"I'm coming back tomorrow night. I'm investigating Chaz Smith's death for the DEA."

"But why?"

"Because Chaz Smith wasn't just a narc. He was a federal agent."

Book Three

FRIENDS AND LOVERS

Chapter 60

It was 7:00 p.m., forty degrees outside the gray Crown Vic where Conklin and I sat parked across the street from Restaurant LuLu, Warren Jacobi's favorite eatery. LuLu's was a homey place with a wood-fire oven, a sunken dining room, a five-star wine list, and a memorable menu of Provençal dishes.

The last time we all ate at LuLu's, Jacobi picked up the tab because Conklin and I had brought down a long-sought psycho killer—except I was sure we had nailed the wrong man.

Now Conklin gave me a poke in the ribs and said, "What are you thinking?"

"About that time Jacobi took us here."

"You were wearing a dress, as I remember. One of the few times in your life."

"That's what you remember?"

"I had the roasted mussels. Oh. And Jacobi told you to lighten up. Give yourself a break for an hour, something like that."

We both grinned at the memory, but tonight we weren't celebrating. In fact, we were on a surveillance detail; we had followed Jacobi from his house on Ivy Street in Hayes Valley to LuLu's, where my old friend was dining alone. He did that a lot. Even at the best of times, Jacobi's life seemed almost unbearably lonely and sad, which made my neglecting our friendship all the more inexcusable.

I said, "I might as well get this over with."

I took my phone out of my pocket, punched in Jacobi's number. He picked up.

"It's Lindsay," I said.

"Hey. How are things going, Boxer?"

"Not so great. I'm working a couple of cases that are driving me crazy."

"I've been following your exploits in my morning e-mail. Seen a couple of hot stories on the news too."

"Yeah. Well then, you know. I've got twisted, bloody murders on the one hand, mysterious decapitated heads on the other. I'd love to kick this stuff around with you."

"What are you doing now?" he asked me.

"Just sitting around," I said. It was true. More or less.

"I'm at LuLu's," Jacobi said. "Just got here. You hungry?"

I told Jacobi I could be there in about ten minutes. Then I hung up, said to Conklin, "I'd say I feel like a dog but most dogs are pretty straightforward."

"Lindsay, you want to exclude him as a suspect, right?"

"Yes, I do."

"So talk to him. If you don't like what he tells you, if you get suspicious, we'll figure out how to handle it."

"Okay, Richie."

"I'm going to stay out here until you leave the restaurant."

"Aw, jeez. That's not necessary. But thanks."

"I'm waiting."

We sat together in the dark for eight minutes, then I got out of the car and went into LuLu's.

Chapter 61

I opened the front door to our apartment on Lake Street and heard *La Traviata,* saw a leather jacket hanging on the coatrack in the hall. Joe called out to me, and Martha did her amazingly fast twenty-yard dash from the living room to the foyer, concluding with a four-point leap against my body. And then there was Joe, big, adorable, his arms open.

Tears jumped into my eyes.

I was so glad to see my husband that I was mad—you could say irrationally pissed off—that he had been away for so long when I wanted him at home.

Joe put his arms around me. I gave him a peck and struggled to get out of his embrace, but he wouldn't let me escape.

"Hey, hey, it's me, Linds. I'm here."

"Damn it. My hormones are *mad* at you. And they're mad at me too."

"I know, I know."

I gave in and hugged him so hard, Joe gasped dramatically, then laughed at me, said, "Air. I need air."

He put an arm around my shoulder and walked me to the couch, sat down beside me, untied my shoes. He pulled my feet into his lap and began giving me a foot massage from heaven.

"Can I get you anything to eat?" he asked me.

"I had dinner."

"How's our kid?"

"We're both just fabulous."

"You were going to work less, sleep more."

"Joe. I'm lead investigator on two black-hole cases. What do you expect me to do?"

"Talk to me."

"When did you get home?"

"An hour ago. Talk to me, Linds."

"I'm so frustrated I cannot express it."

"Give it a shot."

My husband gave me a gorgeous smile, and finally I gave it up. I told Joe about the cop killer, everything that had happened since Chaz Smith, undercover federal agent, had been killed in the men's room of the music academy.

I told him about the three drug dealers and our working hypothesis that they had been pulled over by a cop-like man with wigwag lights and probably grille lights too who had almost certainly shot them and torched the car. That he'd used the gun that had killed Chaz Smith, which had been stolen from the property room at the Hall.

Hardly taking a breath, I filled Joe in on the shooting of Raoul Fernandez in the mall last night. "Four shots to the face in a nice tight pattern, like the guy's mug was a target and the shooter was standing five feet away."

I told my husband about Brady's theory, that Jacobi was the killer.

"Jacobi? Our Jacobi? Warren Jacobi?"

"He says that Jacobi is still holding a grudge about those drugged-up kids shooting us on Larkin Street. That what he's heard is that Jacobi has never been the same. Brady says, and I have to agree, that Jacobi could have gotten the weapons out of the property room without anyone noticing.

"And then Brady says that while Jacobi was on leave getting his hip replaced, he had the time and opportunity to take out about eight dealers—that we know about. Oh yeah, and Jacobi had a meltdown last year when some kids OD'd because of some bad horse."

"He threw a chair, as I remember."

"Right. Big deal. I've thrown chairs."

"Have you thrown a chair at a *person* during an interrogation? Have you?"

I sighed. "No."

"When was the last time you saw Jacobi?"

"About a half an hour ago. I just had dinner with him."

Joe said, "If Brady is right—I said *if*—and Jacobi has gone off the rails, he could be dangerous if he thinks you're onto him, Lindsay. Dangerous to you."

Chapter 62

"Here's why I think you're wrong," I said. We were in bed now. I rested my cheek on Joe's chest and kept talking. "Jacobi believes in the law, and going vigilante is not just unlawful but criminal. It carries the death penalty.

"Jacobi just wouldn't put himself into that kind of hole, not ever. By the way, he seemed fine to me," I said. "Relaxed. Looked good. Lost some weight. He's doing PT. He had a good appetite."

Joe got a couple of words in.

"You asked him what he thought about this Revenge shooter?"

"I did. He said that Revenge is smart and has access to real-time information about where his victims are. That he might have a police-band radio. Maybe he has informants."

"Good points," said Joe.

"Jacobi said he thinks the shooter is on a mission, maybe a suicide mission."

"That also makes sense. But it doesn't rule Jacobi out."

"I took a chance, Joe. I said that there was talk that the shooter could be a cop. Jacobi said, 'Could be a cop. Could be a hired gun. Could be a rival drug dealer who is taking out the competition.'"

"So you didn't get the feeling he was trying to steer you away? That he was hiding something?"

"No. But if Jacobi wanted to keep something from me, I think he could do it. I stopped short of asking him to account for his time last night, Joe. I just couldn't do that."

"Good. I'm glad. Keep your head down, blondie."

He kissed my forehead. I hugged him tighter. I was scared, frightened about

Jacobi, the shooter, and when there'd be another killing. But I felt safe in my husband's arms. There was nowhere I'd rather be.

"I talked to Jacobi about the house of heads."

"What did he think?"

"That the typical victim in a situation like this one would be a young street-walker. You remember that case in Albuquerque?"

"Those young working girls who were buried in the desert?"

"That's the one. I think there were about eighteen of them, late teens to midtwenties, buried without clothes, so they were just skeletons when they were found.

"There was no identification, no clues to their killer. There was a cop in the missing-persons division who had collected DNA, though, so some of those girls were identified."

"The killer wasn't caught, as I remember."

"No. Not yet. So, we have identified one of our Jane Does, Marilyn Varick. She wasn't a known prostitute."

"Maybe she was just never picked up for prostitution."

"Agreed," I said. "The stock profile for someone who preys on prostitutes is white male, thirty-five to fifty, has been in trouble with the law."

Joe said, "Harry Chandler is about sixty, isn't he?"

"Sixty-three. So, if he did it, he wants to be near his victims. And if that's the case, I don't see him as the one who dug them up. Someone else is leaving the message."

"It's a very frayed loose end," said Joe.

"Isn't it though?"

My mind went back to Jacobi. I saw him sitting across from me at LuLu's, every bit my partner and friend of a dozen years.

I said, "Jacobi isn't the shooter, Joe. He couldn't be. I know him so well."

"Do we ever really know anyone?" Joe said.

Chapter 63

I swung my legs out of bed at six the next morning, left Joe snoozing as I got my running clothes from the hook behind the closet door.

Martha and I took a brisk and challenging run through the Presidio and when we got back, sunlight was splashing on the bedroom floor and Joe was still snoring, exactly as I'd left him.

I closed the bedroom door, showered, put on a pot of Blue Bottle roast, and booted up my laptop.

My mailbox was flooded with e-mail and spam. I mean *flooded;* I had mail in triple digits. It took me about fifteen minutes to clear my in-box and get to the day's headlines. I clicked on the link to the *Post* and there was Jason Blayney's front-page story about the Potrero Center shooting.

I skimmed the story quickly to see if Blayney, that rat, had come up with an angle I should be pursuing or denying, and son of a gun, his story linked to a piece about Joe Molinari.

When I clicked on the link, I expected to see a follow-up on the DEA task-force story, so I was nearly blown off my seat by the filthy piece of trash Blayney had run under the heading "Fed Takes the Night Off."

Blayney was a snake and a liar, but there was no denying that the photo was real. And it was a killer.

It was a picture of Joe, my Joe, escorting a willowy brunette down a long flight of stone stairs. She was in a long, clingy black gown, her neck sparkling with diamonds, her arm threaded through the crook of Joe's arm.

The photo seemed to have caught Joe saying something very charming to this woman. Her face was turned up toward his and a very private smile lit her features.

Joe looked just as adorable as could be.

The story read:

Joseph Molinari, former deputy to the director of Homeland Security, was seen with June Freundorfer Thursday evening at a benefit for cystic fibrosis at the Phillips Collection in Dupont Circle. FBI honcho June Freundorfer has long been a bright and glittering fixture at inner-circle Washington, DC, events, and last night's fête was no exception.

I skipped down the page, found the sentence that brought it all back home.

Mr. Molinari is the husband of Sergeant Lindsay Boxer of the SFPD . . .

That was all I could take.

I slammed down the lid on my laptop,

but the afterimage of the photograph remained sharp and clear in my mind. I knew that June Freundorfer had been Joe's partner for a couple of years and thought that maybe Joe's relationship with her had been at the center of his divorce.

I understood that Joe had once been tight with June; I just hadn't known he was tight with her still.

Were they involved?

Did Joe see her when he was in Washington every month or so? Were my hormonal surges making me paranoid? I knew what I was supposed to do about the mood swings: take naps, go for walks, spend time with my spouse, not be so *hard* on myself.

But was I thinking clearly? Jason Blayney's mention that Joe was my husband was a direct and very personal message.

I went into the bathroom, threw up, took another shower, then went back to the kitchen. Joe had left his BlackBerry on the counter and it was buzzing.

I could read the faceplate from where I stood: *June Freundorfer.*

My hand hovered over the phone, my mind flashing like heat lightning; I had very little time to make this decision.

The phone rang for the third time.

Chapter 64

It was reckless, but I couldn't stop my-self.

I picked up Joe's BlackBerry, clicked to answer, and put the phone to my ear. I heard the traffic sounds of a faraway city. It was painful to do it, nearly impossible, but I waited the caller out.

"Joe?"

"No, it's Lindsay," I said. "Joe's wife." I sat down on a bar stool at the counter.

There was a long silence as the woman's mind fumbled for a moment. My head was spinning too.

"Ohhh. Lindsay. Hi. I—is Joe there?"

Her voice was softer, sweeter than I had imagined.

"Joe's sleeping off his jet lag," I said. "June, I want to know the truth. Are you and Joe having an affair?"

I suppose I could have eased into it sideways, asked about the charity event the other night, said that I'd seen the photo and that it made me wonder why Joe hadn't mentioned the black-tie dinner to me. A less direct approach would have given me room to retreat, but retreat was the last thing on my mind.

My pulse throbbed in my neck as the question hung on a virtual phone line three thousand miles long.

Are you and Joe having an affair?

Finally, the woman sighed.

She said, "Lindsay, maybe this isn't the best time to discuss this."

"So, when would be a good time, June? What works for you?"

"I didn't want it to turn out like this. We didn't want you to know, but I guess there's no point in lying anymore."

The ground seemed to open beneath me and I dropped into the void. I heard, as if from a long distance away, my voice saying to June, "You didn't want me to know that you're sleeping with my husband? You're aware that I'm pregnant?"

"Yes."

"I guess that's all I need to know."

"Wait, Lindsay. Joe loves you very much."

Her girlish voice was like a frigid wind blowing through my hair. She said, "Joe and I are close, have always *been* close, but it's not marriage, Lindsay. It's just one of those things."

I turned the phone off.

I remember steadying myself with both hands on the counter so that I didn't fall off the bar stool.

Was I losing my mind? Had my husband's mistress just told me that my husband loved me? I had had to hear that from *her?* That bitch!

And what did she mean by "just one of those things"? Something inevitable? Chemical? Ordained?

And *Joe.*

How could he have lied to me, cheated on me, made a fool of me and our marriage and everything I felt for him?

Who was he? Who was this man I had married?

Joe had said to me last night, *Do we ever really know anyone?*

What was I going to do?

What the hell was I going to do? I had a baby on the way. Our baby.

Joe's phone rang in front of me again.

I stared at June's name, picked up the phone, clicked to connect, then disconnected instantly. I didn't want to talk to her and I didn't want her to leave a message for Joe.

I grabbed the phone, went to the half bath off the kitchen, lifted the lid off the toilet tank, and dropped the phone into the water. I stared at it. It was ringing again.

And then it stopped.

What was I going to do?

As if a message had floated up from the inky depths of a Magic 8 Ball, I knew.

Chapter 65

I turned the doorknob and, using my hip and shoulder as a battering ram, shoved the door open. The racket startled Joe out of his sound sleep.

I'd wanted to scare him, but I hadn't thought he would go for his gun. His hand shot under the bed and he was bringing it up when he saw that the intruder was me, a version of me he'd rarely seen. I was so angry.

"Lindsay. What's wrong?"

The shouting began.

"What's *wrong* is you and June Freundorfer. How could you do this to me, Joe?"

He was sitting up in bed now, looking at me with stark bewilderment.

"I don't know what you're talking about."

"Don't bother to lie. She told me everything."

"Told you what? Lindsay, we went to a benefit. I didn't get a chance to tell you about it, but I wasn't keeping it from you."

"A benefit. Isn't that what it's called these days? A friend with benefits?"

"I don't understand why she called you."

"She called *you*."

"I see. So you intercepted the call."

I said, "Joe, how could you do this to us?"

"Lindsay, I've done nothing wrong. *Nothing*."

I went into the room, threw open the closet doors. Joe's suitcase was right there, and as luck would have it, he hadn't yet unpacked.

I hauled the bag out of the closet and chucked it onto the floor at Joe's feet.

He stood up and came toward me, his arms open. He was saying stuff, but I had closed myself off from him. I didn't comprehend him anymore, not what he'd done, not what he was saying. I took pants and a jacket out of the closet, got underwear out of a drawer.

I wanted to get away from him before I cried.

"Lindsay. Stop. Just stop. I'm not having an affair with June or anyone else."

I whipped around to face him. Adrenaline made me almost blind with rage. I could barely look at him.

"Why would June lie? She said, 'It's just one of those things.'"

"Our friendship, maybe."

"I wish I could believe you, Joe, but you're a terrific liar. I can't stand the sound of your voice, so please, just leave. I'll send your things—wherever you say. Just don't be here when I get home."

I dressed in the bathroom and left the house without saying another word to Joe.

I felt hollow and sick. I'd never been so betrayed in my life.

Chapter 66

We were in the parking lot off Harriet Street, just behind the Hall. I told Conklin that I wanted to drive.

"What's wrong?" he asked me. He was looking at me like I was wearing a live fish on my head.

"I like to drive."

"Okay. When you want to tell me what's eating you, I'm here."

He tossed me the keys and a minute later I headed the squad car south into clotted morning traffic, toward Parnassus Heights, an affluent neighborhood near the Haight.

Beside me, Conklin filled me in on the tip he'd gotten, that Harry Chandler and his son from his first marriage, Todd, did not get along.

Conklin had done some research and learned that when Todd was quite young, he had changed his last name to Waterson, his mother's maiden name, and although Todd had never lived at the Ellsworth compound, he had had access to the place while Chandler was living there with his second wife, Cecily, and for a few years after.

"Todd Waterson? The TV guy? I had no idea he was Harry Chandler's son."

"Little-known fact."

"Well, news to me, anyway. I've seen his show. He's pretty entertaining. What's his story?"

"Brainy, big paycheck, and a discreet personal life. I found no gossip about him on the Web."

Todd Waterson's house was on Edgewood Avenue, an unexpectedly shielded and wooded street.

At Conklin's direction, I drove through the gated entrance and up a generously landscaped private driveway. I braked in front of the detached garage, took a look at what three million could buy in this neighborhood.

Todd Waterson's house was a sprawling, three-level stucco contemporary with Craftsman influences. There were decks and terraces with panoramic views of the bay and the city. The property was secluded and quiet. Very.

The front door opened as we got to the threshold. Todd Waterson was waiting for us. He was five foot seven in his socks, wearing frayed jeans and a sweatshirt with a PBS logo. He had sandy-colored hair and a face populated by forgettable features: a thin line of a mouth and his father's gray eyes.

"I'm Sergeant Lindsay Boxer," I said. "This is my partner, Inspector Richard Conklin."

"Hello, and by the way, what's this about?"

I said, "We're investigating crimes committed at the Ellsworth compound."

"Let me have your numbers, okay? I can't do this right now."

"It can't wait, Mr. Waterson."

"All right. Come in," he said. "But let's make it fast, all right? I have to leave for the studio and I can't be late."

Chapter 67

Conklin and I followed Todd Waterson across his gleaming wooden floors under an airy cathedral ceiling. The walls were at hard angles, cut by beams and banks of floor-to-ceiling windows. Large photos of Waterson interviewing celebrities hung on the milk-white walls.

Waterson indicated where we should sit, and as we did, he said, "Just to cut to the chase, I haven't seen or spoken with my father in five years."

"Where were you last weekend?" I asked him.

"That's what you want to know?" Waterson asked. "What am I—some kind of suspect? That's really funny."

"I thought you wanted to cut to the chase," I said, not laughing.

"I was out and about. I spent all my nights here."

"Can anyone vouch for your whereabouts?"

"Wait a minute. Before I give you names and numbers, what are you getting at and what does it have to do with me?"

"Seven heads were disinterred from your father's back garden."

"So I've heard. I haven't set foot in that place in five *years*. Not since I had my final fight with my father."

"You mind if I ask about that fight?"

"I sure do."

Conklin took the baton. Conklin wasn't pregnant. He hadn't just told his spouse to vacate the premises. He wasn't even mad.

I sat back and let him drive the interview.

"We're checking out your father," Conklin said.

"Okay."

"What's he like?"

"He's narcissistic. He's a womanizer. He can be cruel."

"You say he's a womanizer. All the heads in the garden belonged to females."

"Is that right? So you're asking could my father, the man I just described as cruel, be responsible for those heads?"

"That's right," Conklin said.

Rich had on his good-natured good-cop smile. You had to love Conklin, and in a way, I did. He said to Waterson, "Do you think your father is capable of murder? He's been accused of it before."

"Honestly? I don't know. He's capable of a cutting put-down. He'd like to *fuck* every woman in the world to death, but that's all I know. I stay away from him. But now I'm repeating myself."

"Okay," Conklin said. "And where were you last weekend?"

Todd Waterson started to laugh.

"Let me get my book."

Waterson got out of the chair and went to his desk. I stared out the window at Mount Sutro Open Space Reserve, a swath of green that cut through the city. I was thinking about Joe. Thinking about what he had done. How would I ever forgive him, and if I couldn't, how could I raise our child alone?

How sad for our baby.

Todd Waterson returned to his seat, opened his iPad, tapped it, said to Conklin, "What's your e-mail address?"

Conklin gave it to him.

Waterson tapped his iPad a few more times, then shut it down. "That's a list of where I was and who I was with. Anything else?"

Conklin said, "And why don't you have any contact with your father?"

"He's a homophobe," said Waterson. "He disapproves of my lifestyle. That's where the cruelty comes in. Are we done?"

We thanked the guy for his cooperation and left his house.

"Okay," said Conklin. "So, theorizing here, Todd Waterson is what? A gay guy who hates his father, so he decides to kill women. He becomes a serial killer and corpse mutilator who sneaks into his father's backyard and buries the heads of his victims with some of their doodads. Later, he digs them up and decorates them with numbers and fluffy flowers."

It was my turn to look at him as if he had a fish on his head.

He said, "Makes no sense to me either."

I gave him the car keys and we drove back to the Hall in silence.

Chapter 68

I'd like to say that the day improved, but that would be a lie. I had nothing in my tank but vapors and I tried to put in a day's work on that.

Joe called a number of times, but I let the calls go to voicemail and I didn't call him back.

Conklin and I cleared Todd Waterson by noon and I called Claire three times in six hours asking if she had facial-reconstruction results on the heads from the Ellsworth compound.

I even paid her a personal visit, talking to her over the shot-up dead body of a gangbanger.

"Lindsay, it takes time. Dr. Perlmutter is giving us every minute she has, but she gets called in on other jobs. And the DNA cannot be rushed."

"I can't get any traction on the case."

"It's been five *days*. You're acting like it's been five *months*."

I got coffee out of the vending machine in the breezeway, climbed the back stairs, and settled in for the duration.

Conklin and I worked the tip line until nine that night. Sad to say, nothing of consequence washed up, just useless flotsam from people who had nothing better to do than screw with the police or indulge their paranoid delusions.

I shared a pizza with Conklin, went back to work, finally quit at ten. Half an hour later, I opened my door to a dark apartment and a note from Karen saying she had walked and fed Martha.

I listened to Joe's voicemails. I took a long shower. I drank warm milk. I put on some soft music. I didn't sleep that night.

I mean, I *really* didn't sleep. I lay in the big bed, stayed on my side of it, and listened to Martha's gentle snoring from her puffy bed on the floor.

At about two, I turned on the TV.

I watched infomercials—Jewelry TV, then the Coin Vault—learned a few things about numismatic proof coins in original packaging, just what to leave my grandchildren. I switched to the Zumba body, the Shark vacuum cleaner, and then the world's best bra ever!

I turned off the box, but my eyes stayed wide open and I replayed Joe's messages in my mind.

The first several times he'd called me, he'd been mad. He'd shouted, said that he'd told me the truth, that June had lied, and that my believing her showed I had a profound lack of faith in him. That it was insulting.

He said that he loved me and that I should pick up the phone. "Call me, Lindsay. I'm your husband."

Next few messages, he said was sorry for yelling. He realized why I was angry and said he wasn't mad anymore. He wanted to talk to me and he would tell me about every moment he'd spent with June in the last two years.

"There were not very many moments, Lindsay, and none of them were naked. None."

The last time he called, he sounded empty. He left me the name of the hotel where he was staying, said to call him if I wanted to talk or if I wanted to listen.

I didn't want to do either.

It was almost seven o'clock when I got up to make myself a cup of tea. When the phone rang, I picked it up, said, "Hello?"

But it wasn't Joe.

It was Conklin.

"A body washed up in Big Sur an hour ago," Conklin said. "A surfer, apparently."

"Marilyn Varick was a surfer."

"Yeah. This DB is a man. And he's got a head."

"So how does this have anything to do with our case?" I asked.

"The guy who called the police said there was a card lying in the sand next to the body. On it was the number six thirteen."

I stood flat-footed in my kitchen then adjusted my thinking about the remains at the house of heads. I guess I'd thought the killings were over.

"Richie, about Chandler and his boat. We always thought that body dumps were a possibility."

"Could he really be so dumb as to dump a body with all this attention on him?"

"Let's ask him."

Chapter 69

Conklin and I were in Interview 2, the smaller of Homicide's two no-frills interrogation rooms, sitting across the table from Harry Chandler and his lawyer, Donna Hewett.

Hewett was a good general counsel, known for her work on estates and trusts, and was reportedly a pretty good tax attorney too. But Hewett was not a criminal defense lawyer and that told me that Chandler didn't expect to get charged.

Was he bluffing?

Was Harry Chandler so bold or so

crazy that he would kill while under the laser focus of national news coverage?

Or was Chandler's conscience clean?

Donna Hewett patted her hair, put her briefcase on the floor, and asked, "Is my client under arrest?"

"Not at all," Conklin said. "Our investigation is ongoing and as new information surfaces, we follow up. We just have a couple of questions, Mr. Chandler. Where were you yesterday?"

Chandler smiled.

He was wearing a blue cashmere sweater, sleeves pushed up. I saw no cuts or bruises on his hands.

He said, "I've started taking notes so I can have seamless alibis in case you two pop up without warning."

He took his phone out of his pants pocket and tapped the face, then started listing where he'd been and at what times.

"Kaye and I left the *Cecily* at around eight yesterday morning, went to breakfast at the Just for You Café in Dogpatch. I had waffles. She had eggs Benedict. Our waitress was Shirley Gurley."

Pause for a movie-star smile.

"What were her parents thinking? After that, Kaye and I went shopping at the farmers' market and loaded up on produce because we were about to take a little cruise."

"And where did you go?" Conklin asked.

I thought about the dead surfer, seventeen years old, lying in the medical examiner's lab fifty miles up the coast, time of death still undetermined.

Hewett said, "What are you fishing for, Inspector?"

I took out the morgue shots of the unidentified teen on the autopsy table. I said, "This boy washed up in Big Sur very early this morning. He was linked to the bodies at the Ellsworth compound."

Chandler lifted his eyes, met my gaze. "I don't know this boy. I have never seen him before, alive or dead."

Against his lawyer's advice, Chandler gave us the names of shops he and Kaye had visited. He produced time-stamped digital photos of them together, and just for good measure, he said there was surveillance video at the yacht club showing that he'd taken the boat out at four in the morning and returned at nine at night.

I asked him when he'd last seen his son, Todd.

"Years and years ago," Chandler said. "And no, I don't think he killed anyone. But you should ask him yourself."

I said, "We've obtained a search warrant for your boat."

"You're kidding me."

"The Crime Scene Unit is there right now."

"They're inside my boat?"

I guess we finally pissed off Harry Chandler. He stood abruptly and said to his attorney, "I don't have to answer any more questions, do I?" And he stormed out of the interrogation room.

Charlie Clapper called me at the end of the day, said he'd found no incriminating evidence on the *Cecily*; no blood, no trace, no bleach, no nothing.

I had just hung up the phone with Clapper when it rang again. Claire calling to say, "That surfer boy who washed up on Big Sur?"

"Yes?"

"The ME in Monterey County said cause of death was blunt-force trauma to the head. The wound matched to his surfboard that also washed up. Witnesses saw him going out into the surf on that board."

"It was an accident."

"Right, Lindsay. Accidental death."

That card with the number 613 on it that some insane tipster said he'd found—it was pure fiction.

Chapter 70

I was in desperate need of a laugh or, even better, a boxcar full of them.

I called an impromptu meeting of the Women's Murder Club, and because it was only two blocks from the Hall, I convinced everyone to meet at MacBain's Beers o' the World Saloon.

An hour after sending up the flare, I climbed the wooden back steps to the small room with two tables and one window where Captain MacBain used to count out the day's cash. Cindy and Claire had already made good progress on the first pitcher of beer, and Yuki had only about an inch left of her margarita.

I could have put down a pitcher of beer all by myself, but the little bundle I was carrying under my jacket had the majority vote and that vote was no to booze.

Claire pulled out a chair and patted the seat and I dropped into it.

Yuki flashed me a grin, said, "I was telling everyone about Brian McInerny."

"The comedian? Go ahead, Yuki."

"Okay, so he's suing a transit worker for taking a punch at him. He deserved the punch, but anyway, I'm deposing him," Yuki said. "McInerny wants to give answers as both himself and his alter ego."

"I've seen his act," Cindy said. "He has an imaginary twin."

"Right," Yuki said. "And it's easier to let him do it than stop him. I'm asking him questions and he's answering as himself *and* as his character. So crazy. We have it all on tape."

I gave my order to the waitress, and Yuki continued her story.

"And you know, during a deposition,

when someone needs a break, the videographer says, 'All right, it's eleven twenty-three and we're going off the record.' And then when you're coming back on, the videographer says, 'It's eleven thirty-five and now we are back on the record.'

"So McInerny needs a lot of breaks. He doesn't like the deli food we served, so he has to order lunch from his favorite restaurant. Then he has to have a conference with his imaginary twin. As if that weren't enough to make us all crazy, now he's got a new shtick.

"When we restart the camera, McInerny pretends that he's in the middle of a conversation. The camera goes on and McInerny says to me, 'That's the filthiest joke I've ever heard in my life.'"

Yuki demonstrated the shocked look she got on her face; it was hysterical and we all laughed. Yuki said, "The second time we come back he looks directly at the videographer and says to her, 'Are you hitting on me? Are you coming on to me?'

"Then, of course, we had to take a

five-minute break because she was laughing so hard she was crying."

One minute I was laughing at the story, but the next my mind must have wandered off, because I suddenly realized that the girls were staring at me.

Yuki in particular gave me an appraising eye.

"Something's wrong, Lindsay. What is it?"

"I'm fine. It's been a really long day, but I'm okay."

"I know what you look like when you're tired, Lindsay," Yuki said. "This is different. You look like you've been running laps in hell."

Cindy said, "Yuki's right. Are you feeling sick? Are you coming down with something?"

The waitress brought over another pitcher of tap along with a bottle of Australian root beer and a frosty mug of ice, both of which she put down in front of me.

When her footsteps faded I said to my friends, "Joe is having an affair."

Chapter 71

I poured root beer into my mug with a shaking hand. For a long moment, the only sound in the room was the hiss and crackle of the soda hitting the ice. Then everyone spoke at once.

Claire shouted—actually, she *insisted*—"No. *No.* Joe would *never* cheat on you."

Cindy cut in. "This just can't be true."

But Yuki believed me.

She was back in her role of human nail gun, pinning me with her eyes, firing questions, *bam-bam-bam.*

"Who is the woman?"

"June Freundorfer. An old partner of Joe's in DC."

"How old?"

"My age."

"How did you find out, Lindsay?"

"Does it matter?"

"Did Joe tell you about the affair?"

"No. *She* did," I said.

"She called you?" Yuki pulled back, her face flattened in surprise.

"She called Joe. I picked up his phone."

Claire got up from her chair, wrapped her arms around me, squeezed the tears right out of my eyes.

Yuki went on as if I weren't crying, as if Claire weren't beaming stop signs at her with her eyes.

"Did you ask Joe about this?"

"Uh-huh."

"He admitted it?"

I shook my head no.

Cindy reached across the table and clutched my hands.

Yuki said, "So, just to make sure I've got this right, Joe denies the affair."

"He's lying about it, yes. So I kicked him out of the house."

Claire said, "Honey, what did this woman say?"

I shook my head. I couldn't talk anymore.

Cindy let go of my hands and gave me a wad of paper napkins stamped with MacBain's logo: the planet Earth whirling through a sudsy amber sky.

I sobbed into the napkins. It was disgraceful. It was pathetic. I couldn't stop crying. Yuki shook my arm like she was a terrier and my arm was a sock doll.

"Lindsay, do you think it's serious? Maybe it just happened and he can get you to forgive him."

By then Cindy had typed *Freundorfer* into her iPad and pulled up the benefit story. She held up the candid photo of Joe with his mistress looking adoringly into his face.

"Oh my God," Yuki said. "Oh, Lindsay. I'm going to be sick."

I loosed some fresh tears and then all of us were crying. It seemed a little less pathetic when we were all wet together, but still: Joe was having an affair, my baby and I were alone, and I wanted to

die. Before I could drown myself in root
beer, my blinking phone rang.

Was it Joe?

No. It was Brady. He was with Conklin.

I hugged and kissed my friends, then
fled down the stairs.

Chapter 72

I parked the Explorer behind Brady's unmarked sedan on the north side of Ivy, a one-way residential street in Hayes Valley dotted with trees and lined with ordinary single and multifamily houses built so close together there was no space between them.

Jacobi's brown, shingled house was at the far end of the block, and although he had a garage that took up the ground floor, his black Hyundai SUV was parked on the street.

Jacobi had a black SUV—like half the law enforcement officers in California.

Brady and Conklin got out of the unmarked and Conklin got into the Explorer beside me.

Brady stooped down by the window,
said, "We've had a team on him all day.
He came in about an hour ago. Lights
went on. He's probably in for the night."

"I take it you didn't catch him killing
anyone?"

Brady ignored my tone. "You and
Conklin do four hours. Narcotics will
spell you at eleven. If he leaves the
house, call me."

"Yes, *sir.*"

I watched Brady get into his car, then
I pulled out my phone, saw three messages from Joe, and ignored them. I arranged dog-sitting for Martha, then
leaned back.

I must have sighed.

"So you ready to tell me what's going
on, Linds? I'm not going to leave you
alone until you spill."

My mind was still in high gear, boosted
by my surging hormones and the whole
crappy day.

"Have you cheated on Cindy?" I asked
him.

His mouth fell open and he stared at me, a look of shock and disappointment on his face I hadn't seen in all the years I'd known him.

"Why would you ask me that? Is that what she thinks? Did Cindy say that to you?"

"No. So, have you, Rich?"

"No. Hell no. Seriously, is this what you've been thinking? Is this what's got you all jammed up?"

Conklin's gaze left me, went past me and through my window, but his shocked expression didn't change. I heard a hard rapping on the glass.

I swung my head, saw Jacobi's face right *there*. He was scowling. He knew that we weren't parked on his street by accident.

He signaled to me to roll down my window, and I did it.

All I could get out of my mouth was "Jacobi" before he lit into me, lit into us both.

"How nice of you to visit. You are visiting, right, Boxer? You too, Conklin. My old friends, stopping by to see how I'm getting along?"

"It's a stakeout," I said miserably.

"You're tailing me."

I dropped my head. I was ashamed and mortified. Jacobi gripped the window frame and shook it as if he were rattling bars on a cage.

"You think I'm that Revenge shooter? Is that it, Boxer? I don't hear from you for weeks, months, then, suddenly, 'Can you help me with my cases, Warren?'

"I don't know how many thousands of hours I worked with both of you," he spat. "Put my life in your hands and vice versa." He looked at me, then at Conklin, then turned his hooded eyes back to me.

"You turn my stomach, both of you."

"Jacobi, I'm sorry. Wait!"

"That's *Chief*. Chief Jacobi." He turned away, stalked off with his wooden gait. The silence in the car rang like a bell.

Conklin said, "I'm going after him."

"Okay. I'll be there in a minute."

I called Brady.

"Is Jacobi leaving the house?" he asked me.

"Brady, he made us. He made us and he called us out."

Chapter 73

Conklin came home to the apartment he shared with Cindy. It was completely dark except for the light in the kitchen. That meant that Cindy had been working for hours and hadn't gotten up to turn on the rest of the lights.

He put his keys in the dish on the hall table, called out, "Honey, I'm home." Heard a faint "Hey" in response.

He hung up his coat and gun, went into the kitchen, saw Cindy at the table exactly as he'd pictured her.

Her head was bent over her laptop, eyes obscured by the blond curls falling across her face, fingers dancing over the keys. She paused, turned, lifted her face for a kiss, and, after getting a peck, said, "Everything okay?"

"Had a completely terrible day is all."

Cindy said, "Did anyone die?"

"No."

"Shots fired?"

He laughed. "Has to be a shooting for it to be a bad day?"

"Then—can you tell me about it later, Richie, because I've got to get this done."

"Go ahead," he said. "I'll see you in bed."

Conklin opened the fridge, got out a couple of frozen dinners, put them in the microwave. While the microwave turned the turkey dinners into something resembling hot meals, he went into the bathroom and got in the shower.

Nothing like hydrotherapy at the end of the day. He thought about Jacobi saying if Rich didn't walk away from his front door, he was going to throw some shots through it.

That scene was followed by Brady chewing him out, chewing Lindsay out too, saying that they had royally screwed the pooch and were off the surveillance detail.

And he thought about Lindsay being a bitch and accusing him of cheating on Cindy, which was the last thing he'd ever do in his life.

Yes, it had been a crap day. All the way around.

Conklin got out of the shower, put on a pair of shorts, and went to the kitchen, where Cindy was still absorbed in whatever she was doing that left almost no time for him.

He pulled the plastic film off the dinners, asked, "What are you working on?"

"The *Chron* website. They gave me a blog."

"A blog, huh?"

"Tons of mail coming in on Revenge. Do you have anything I can use?"

"Negative," said Conklin. "Whatever is less than negative."

"Okay," Cindy said, tapping at the keys.

"Jeez, don't quote me, Cindy. I'm off duty."

"I wasn't quoting you."

"Good."

Conklin sat down at the table, cleaned his plate, guzzled half a liter of Pepsi, and then finished off a half-full container of double chocolate ice cream, scraping the bottom with his spoon.

He watched Cindy as he ate. Her attention never broke. Bomb could go off across the street, and unless there was a story in it, she wouldn't move.

He stood up, tousled her hair.

"I'm almost done," she said.

Conklin went to bed. He was dozing when Cindy finally came into the bedroom and took off her clothes in the dark. She slid under the sheets without touching him.

Her breathing slowed and then deepened.

"Cindy?"

"Mmmm-hmmm." She sighed.

Chapter 74

Cindy's phone call woke me up out of a deep sleep.

"Sorry," she said. "I know it's early, but I wanted to catch you before you left the house. Can you have coffee with Richie and me?"

I said, "Sure," agreed to the time and place. I lay in bed with Martha for twenty more minutes, first savagely missing Joe, then being flooded by thoughts of all the relationships I'd trashed in the previous twenty-four hours.

I supposed my asking Rich if he had cheated on Cindy had prompted Cindy's call and the breakfast meeting. I owed apologies to them both.

I met Rich and Cindy at Old Jerusalem Café, a coffeehouse on Irving and Fourteenth that had a wide assortment of coffees and teas and delicious Mediterranean pastries. I found Mr. Conklin and the future Mrs. Conklin sitting at a table waiting for me.

I said, "Hi," slid into the seat across from them, ordered Turkish coffee, and braced myself for a confrontation. I hoped I could handle it without snapping.

Rich brushed his hair out of his eyes with his fingers and said, "Cindy told me. About Joe."

I nodded miserably, looked down.

"You'll work it out," he said. "You will."

"I'm sorry about what I said, Rich."

"Yeah. It's okay. Cindy's got something for us."

I glanced up, wondering what he meant.

"Lookit," Cindy said.

She took her iPad out of her handbag, began to type. My coffee came and I sugared it heavily and then followed up the sugar with a triple dose of cream.

Cindy turned the tablet toward me. "It's numerology," she said. She showed me this equation.

$$1\ 0\ 4 = 5$$

"In numerology, you add the numbers together. One plus zero is one. One plus four equals five."

"Okay."

"Now," Cindy said, "let's look at six one three."

She typed:

$$6\ 1\ 3 = 10 = 1$$

"I get it," I said. "Six and one is seven, and three makes ten."

"Right. Then you reduce the ten by adding one and zero together. That equals one."

"Got it."

Cindy was typing numbers. She said,

"Now add the two reduced numbers together."

$$5 + 1 = 6$$

I waited for drums to roll. Cymbals to clash.

"What does six mean?"

"It means number six. As in number six Ellsworth Place."

I sucked in a breath. Cindy was referring to one of the four brick buildings adjacent to the main Ellsworth house, the detached houses that backed onto the garden.

"We didn't have a warrant to search number six," I said.

"Cindy spoke to Yuki," Rich said. "Yuki thinks she can make a case that the original warrant should have included those buildings. That the compound is all one property."

"I'm coming with you to the compound," said Cindy.

Rich and I turned to her and in unison said, "No."

"*Yes,*" she said. "The numbers are *mine*. Lindsay, you gave them to me and asked me to solve them, and I think I did it. If you want me to ever talk to you again, either of you, I'm coming with you. The answer is yes."

Chapter 75

Yuki and I were in her cubicle at the DA's offices in room 325, third floor of the Hall of Justice. I sat in a side chair, my white-knuckled hands clasped on her desk.

Yuki hooked her glossy black hair behind her ears, dialed the phone, and spoke to several people before she got Judge Stephen Rubenstein on the line.

Yuki explained to the judge precisely and urgently that a credible tip had come in referring to a suspicious location adjoining the Ellsworth house. She told Rubenstein that this location had not been included in the original search warrant because the authorities hadn't realized that the two properties were connected.

Yuki stopped talking and listened. She spoke, apologized for interrupting, and listened some more.

She signaled to me to bring my chair closer, which I did, then Yuki held out her phone so that I could hear the judge.

"Let me get this straight. You want me to expand the search warrant because you got an anonymous tip that there's some evidence—you can't even tell me exactly what. And based on *that,* you want to go rummaging around in this other house, which isn't even the crime scene?"

"Yes, Your Honor, but a person of interest owns the entire property. Number six is in close proximity to the crime scene, almost touching it."

"Oh, that's supposed to make a difference? Ms. Castellano, go Google the Fourth Amendment and brush up on it. Highlight the part about unreasonable search. No warrants shall be issued without a probable cause."

"Okay, Your Honor. Thanks anyway."

Yuki put down the phone and said to me, "So maybe if I'd told him about the numerology, it would've helped us," she said.

"You never know."

Yuki laughed. "I'm sorry, Linds."

If I wanted to get into 6 Ellsworth Place, and I did, I had to call Harry Chandler and ask permission.

I used Yuki's phone and got him on the first try. I stopped short of begging, but I was extra nice. At first.

Chandler said, "Why should I let you track your gumshoes through my property again?"

"Mr. Chandler, it's no accident that those heads were buried in your backyard. Someone wants you to be tried for murder again. But until we find that someone, you're our primary suspect. Do you understand?"

Chapter 76

The fog frizzed my hair as Conklin, Cindy, and I huddled together on Ellsworth Place. The street was short and narrow, kind of romantic, and unusual in that it met up with Pierce at one end, Green on the other, forming a right triangle.

The west side of Ellsworth was lined with newer houses in various styles. The houses across the street, the ones that were part of the Ellsworth compound, were all no-frills brick, built as servants' quarters in the late 1890s at the same time the main house was constructed. I could almost hear the sound of horses pulling buggies up the street.

While I gazed around, Conklin tightened the straps on Cindy's Kevlar vest, helped her into an SFPD windbreaker.

I waited until Cindy was cinched up, then gave her a summary of Harry Chandler's minor houses.

"Nicole Worley, the caretakers' daughter, lives in number two. She's in her midtwenties, works in animal rescue. Stays here to keep an eye on her folks. Harry's driver, T. Lawrence Oliver, lives in number four, rent free. It's an employment perk. Numbers six and eight had tenants at one time but are empty now."

Conklin added, "Three of these houses don't have any windows facing the garden in back; one of them has a single window facing it. Number six. When I was in the garden the first time, I noticed that window. Nicole Worley told me that the building was boarded up. If someone is squatting there, he could be our perp."

As we talked, the fine mist turned to rain.

We discussed who was going to do

what. Conklin asked Cindy to get back into the car until we could clear the scene. She reluctantly agreed, then Conklin and I went up the steps to the front door.

I knocked, Conklin called out, and then I rapped on the door with the tarnished brass knocker. When no one answered, Conklin tried turning the knob, but it was frozen solid, the door possibly bolted from the inside.

After a few words with Cindy through the car window, we headed for the backyard and bushwhacked through the waist-high weeds and thistles that had grown thickly between numbers 4 and 6.

The rear aspect of the brick houses was forbidding. Each blind, windowless wall had a back door and a set of steps descending from it, and only a few feet in front of those steps was the looming ten-foot-high brick wall that blocked the view of the garden.

The back doors of 6 and 8 were boarded up, but as I neared number 6, I noticed that weeds had been pulled from around the steps and thrown off to the side. I poked around a little more, saw that the sheet of plywood at the door wasn't nailed to the frame. It was simply leaning against it.

"Someone's been in and out of here recently," I said.

Conklin went up the steps and pulled the plywood away from the door, then banged on the door with his fist.

"Police. Open up," Conklin said. "Or we're coming in."

Chapter 77

No sooner had Conklin opened the door than I heard someone coming through the weeds behind me. I whipped around to see Cindy, her chin stuck out, rain streaming off her face.

"I need to be here. I can't cover this story from the car."

"This *story* could be *nothing*," I hissed to my bulldog friend. "Despite your breaking the da Vinci code, this could be an empty house and a dead end—"

"I know."

"—or it could be dangerous," I said.

"I'll watch my step."

"Could be a gang of crackheads living in here."

"Wouldn't be the first time I've gone into a crack house. Anyway, you're both armed."

It was futile, but I looked at my partner and said, "Please tell her, Rich."

He put up his hands. "Not me."

"If anything happens to you," I said to Cindy, "Rich and I are going to be fired. Me first, of course. And then we're both going to hate ourselves forever."

Cindy laughed. "Give me a break."

This was Cindy: no gun, no training, no official status, and yet the only way to stop her was to get a circus elephant to sit on her chest.

I wasn't kidding about the consequences of letting Cindy into the house, but I was done arguing. Conklin pulled his gun and went in through the doorway. I let Cindy follow him and I brought up the rear.

The hallway was lit by the dull light coming in through the open back door. There was a narrow wooden staircase just ahead of us, and the floor above us was dark.

Conklin and I turned on our flashlights and began to climb. The stairwell was clean, odor-free, and I didn't see graffiti, rags, needles, or any sign of squatters or druggies. In fact, it looked as though it had recently been swept.

We kept moving onward and upward, and when we got to the third-floor landing, I heard the faintest of sounds.

"What's that?" I whispered.

"Beethoven," said Cindy. "Sixth Symphony."

"How do you know that?"

"Sixth. Get it? Another six. And this particular symphony—I think it's about gardens. Don't you hate it when I'm right?" she said, grinning.

I said, "Shhh. Keep your eyes open."

We rounded the next flight, and the next, the music getting louder as we climbed. We came to the sixth-floor landing and faced the three doors on that level.

One was marked F, for *front,* I assumed. One was marked WASHROOM, and the third door had a note taped under the letter R, for *rear.*

Conklin shone his light on the door and I moved in so that I could read the handwritten notice: *Genius at Work. Do Not Disturb.*

Chapter 78

I'm not superstitious, but seriously, there were too many sixes in this deal. Number 6 Ellsworth, Beethoven's Sixth, and now the trail of sixes that ended on the sixth floor.

Six-six-six was an unlucky number, right? So what kind of nightmare was this "genius at work"?

I put Cindy behind me as Conklin knocked on the door and said, "Open up. This is the police."

The music was turned off, then heavy footsteps came toward the threshold. A dark eye stared through the peephole.

A chain rattled and the doorknob turned, and then, standing in the doorway, actually filling it, was a very tall white woman, maybe six two, apparently unarmed. She was wearing a long and well-worn black velvet skirt and a knit gray top with batwing sleeves. Her gray-blond hair was twisted up in a topknot. She smiled broadly.

"Oh, hello! I know who you are. I'm Connie Kerr. Come in."

I think maybe my mouth actually dropped open. I knew *her*. I didn't know her personally, but about twenty years ago, Constance Kerr had been a kind of celebrity on the pro tennis circuit. She'd been a lanky girl with a powerful serve and a very long stride.

Conklin said his name and mine, introduced Cindy Thomas without identifying her role in this escapade, and all three of us stepped into Constance Kerr's home.

It was a garret, a hidey-hole under the eaves of this Victorian house. The room had odd angles, and a closet and a small kitchen had been sectioned out of the ten-by-twelve-foot room. A fold-out bed was put up against the center of the longest wall, and there was a desk under the one window. A laptop computer was open on the desk and a three-foot-high stack of yellow manuscript boxes stood on the floor.

A heavy gray blanket was affixed to the top of the window frame and hung down over the glass, making a dense, light-blocking curtain.

I moved the blanket aside.

I could see the trophy garden and the back of the Ellsworth mansion, including the door that led from the kitchen and out to the brick patio where six days ago I'd seen a pair of skulls displayed like a monstrous art project.

The former tennis star was speaking to Conklin. "I watched you take charge of the crime scene, of course. I enjoyed that very much. I know you're trying to help Harry."

There was standing room only in Connie Kerr's little flat, but she had the air of a Nob Hill dowager holding a tea party.

"May I get you refreshments?" she said.

Chapter 79

We turned down the offer of refreshments and arrayed ourselves around the small room.

I leaned against the kitchenette counter, Cindy grabbed the only chair, and Conklin took up a position against the door. Connie Kerr stood like a flagpole at the center of the room.

"How can I help you?" she said.

"Harry Chandler," I said. "How do you know him?"

"Oh, well. Harry. I was his girlfriend a long time ago. He was a star and I was blinded by his light. It was just a fling," she said, laughing, "but I really had fun and I have no regrets."

"When did you see him last?"

"Don't hold me to the exact day, but I'm sure I haven't seen him in twenty years or more."

"But Harry lets you live here?"

"He doesn't know that I'm here. But he wouldn't mind. I'm no trouble. I live like a little mouse." She laughed again, a shrill, crazy kind of laugh. "I'm working on a book, you know. I've written ten novels so far and I've just started another. They're thrillers. Murder mysteries."

"Do you use your real name?" Cindy asked.

"Cindy, is it? I'll use my name when I'm published. I think the story I'm working on now has a real chance of getting into print."

Connie Kerr took us on a tour of her fairly wild imagination, showing us loosely connected plot diagrams that she'd drawn on brown butcher's paper and taped to the walls.

As she talked about her characters, she used broad gestures, did pirouettes, clasped her hands to her chest as though she were still a young girl and not a fifty-year-old squatter in someone's abandoned digs.

Had this eccentric mystery writer witnessed a crime through her window? Or had she gone beyond writing about murder and actually committed it?

"What can you tell us about the heads we found in the garden?" I asked.

"I know that they make a whopping good mystery," she said.

She was grinning and clapping her hands when my partner broke her mood.

"We don't like mysteries," Conklin said. "Ms. Kerr, here's the thing. We're going to need you to come with us down to the Hall and make a statement. Officially."

Kerr's radiant smile left her face. "Oh no. I really can't leave the house. I never do."

"You never go outside?" Conklin asked.

Kerr shook her head vigorously.

"How do you get food?"

"A friend brings me what I need and leaves it for me on the back steps."

"Who is this friend?"

"I don't have to say."

"Let me put it another way. Can this friend vouch for your whereabouts last weekend?" I asked her.

"You don't understand. I live alone. Nobody ever sees me. You're the first guests I've had here—ever."

Conklin said, "We've got seven dead people, Ms. Kerr. Not fiction. Truth. I think you know what happened to them."

"I did *nothing*. I *saw* nothing. What can I say to make you believe me? I'm the last person you should ever suspect, Mr. Conklin."

Conklin said, "Do you have a coat?"

"A coat?"

"Here," he said, taking off his jacket and putting it over her shoulders. "It's raining outside."

Chapter 80

Constance Kerr sat at the table in the interrogation room. She was tense, had her arms wrapped across her chest; she seemed like a trapped cat waiting for the door to crack open so that she could dart the hell out.

We knew very little about Kerr. She'd left the world stage long ago and could be anybody now: a certifiable dingbat, a witness, a killer, or all of the above.

I didn't believe that she knew nothing about the crimes committed at the Ellsworth compound, and we were going to

try to hold her until she told us something we could believe.

Conklin had a rapport with Kerr, so I
just sat back and watched, thinking what
a good guy he was and also that he was
a really good cop.

He said, "Connie, look at me. I know
you want to help us find out who did
this heinous stuff at the Ellsworth compound."

"If only I could. Honestly. The first
time I knew anything was wrong was
when the police showed up. But, Inspector Conklin, I read on the Internet
about the index cards and I was struck
by the number. Six hundred thirteen!"

"Did you write that number, Connie?
If you did and can tell me what it means,
that would be tremendous."

"No, no, but six hundred and thirteen
is verging on a Guinness world record
for a serial killer. Elizabeth Báthory, the
bloody lady of Cachtice, had over six
hundred girls killed in her castle in Hun-
gary. The exact number is uncertain.
Well, it happened in the early sixteen
hundreds . . ."

"Interesting. But I'm thinking four-hundred-year-old murders aren't that relevant to our current investigation."

He gave her a nice smile and she responded earnestly.

"No, really. This could be the clue you've been waiting for. Please check it out."

I couldn't get a handle on Kerr's mental state. Was she crazy? Or crazy like a fox? I needed to know.

I told Conklin that I'd be back in a minute, and when I was outside the room, I called psychologist Dr. Frank Cisco. Cisco answered his phone, said he was in the building and that he'd come upstairs. A few minutes later, we met in the stairwell.

Frank Cisco was a consultant to the SFPD, on call when a cop was in trouble, and he advised the DA's office as well. He was a big man with a lot of thick white hair. Today he was wearing a busy plaid sports jacket, gray slacks, and pink orthopedic shoes.

Frank was a sweet man, gave you the feeling you could say anything to him in confidence. He hugged me and said, "What's new, Lindsay?"

"A ton," I said, hugging him back.

A few days ago, I had called Cisco and asked him to review our short list of cops who were considered possible suspects in the vigilante-cop case. I didn't ask him to leak confidential information, just to look at the personnel files and let us know which cops, in his opinion, were likely to go on a shooting spree.

He'd said it would be unethical for him to finger suspects based on a hunch. Fine. I got it.

Now I said, "Frank, this isn't about the shooter cop. I need your help on a different case altogether."

He looked relieved, and as we walked back to the interrogation rooms, I told him what little I knew about Constance Kerr.

Chapter 81

I knocked on the door to Interview 1 and when Conklin stepped outside, I asked him to get Kerr to go through the whole story again for Frank's benefit.

Frank and I went into the observation room and watched the interview.

Connie asked Conklin, "When can I go home?"

Conklin said, "I just want to make sure I've got your story straight."

Kerr told the story again, but this time she added new details about the morning the heads were found: her routine on awakening, her rituals and habits, how she'd made up the wall bed and brewed a special Manchurian tea. Finally she got to the part where she heard the sirens and peeked through her back window.

Then, weirdly, she began telling the story from the third-person point of view.

"She saw the caretakers and the police standing outside the back door and the skulls were there and she thought, *Mercy. This is a day like no other.*"

"What are you doing, Connie?" Conklin asked her.

"I beg your pardon?"

"Who's the she who thought the day was like no other?"

"I was trying it on as if Emma had seen it—you know, Inspector, the character in my current work. Emma is very perceptive, but naturally she doesn't know any more than I do. I would love to hear *your* theory of the case. I think you could really help me with my book."

I said to Frank, "What are your thoughts? Is she playing us?"

"She's playacting for sure, but her nuttiness neither confirms nor eliminates her as the killer. I will say this. Based on my ten minutes of observation, I think she's going to great lengths to hide something. Could be related to this case, could be something else she doesn't want anyone to know."

I laughed, said, "Brilliant analysis, Frank. Thanks a lot."

He laughed too. "Yeah, what did you expect? That I can unwrap her crazy little mind in ten minutes?"

On the other side of the glass, Conklin was still trying to pry something useful out of Connie Kerr.

"Connie, your friend who brings you food. Who is it?"

"Ahhh," she said dramatically. "Is he a man with a past? Or is it a lady friend she doesn't want to expose?"

"Connie, this isn't helping you."

"I don't have to tell you all my secrets. And I won't. If I'm not under arrest, I want to go home. You can't keep me here without probable cause."

Conklin sat back and said without any malice, "You're wrong, Connie. I can book you for trespassing, for theft of services, for obstruction of justice."

"Listen," Kerr said, slapping the table

and leaning toward Conklin. "You're wrong about the trespassing and all the rest. Tommy Oliver knows that I live in number six and he's known it for years. I'm sure he has told Harry Chandler."

"Tommy Oliver? Is that T. Lawrence Oliver? Harry Chandler's driver?"

"Yes. Tommy hooked up my electricity. He fixed the locks."

"Okay. We're holding you as a material witness while we check out your story, talk to a few people, and so forth. The law gives us forty-eight hours."

"You can't *do* that."

"I can. I'm doing it. Please stand up."

"I demand to make my phone call."

"Not a problem."

"I want a lawyer."

"Of course. By the way, we don't have single-occupancy accommodations here, so you're going to be sharing a cell with some other ladies. If you remember something helpful about the boneyard underneath your window, please reach out to me, Connie. I'll be happy to talk to you anytime."

Chapter 82

While Conklin brought Connie Kerr to booking, I invited Frank Cisco to the break room for leftover cookies and stale coffee. He accepted.

We were alone for the moment, sitting across from each other at an old table, and what had started as a consultation suddenly felt like a therapy session. I guess that's because after Jacobi and I got shot on Larkin Street, I'd had to see Frank for a couple of months or lose my job.

I'd been furious that the department sent me to a shrink to determine my mental fitness, but even though I was insulted, I had gotten a lot from my sessions with Frank. Actually, he was a great therapist.

Now he asked me, "What's going on with you, Lindsay?"

"I'm pregnant," I said.

"Heyyy. Congratulations."

"Thank you."

I dipped my head. I didn't want to tell him that Joe had cheated on me, that I had thrown him out, that working nonstop meant I didn't have to concentrate on how I was going to provide for my baby without my husband.

"Oh, man. If you could see your face. I gotta ask again. What's going on, Lindsay?"

Frickin' mind reader.

"This case," I said, "is a bear. We've got seven victims, their heads buried on the property of a big movie star, and we can't find the bodies. Were they murdered? Or is this a very creepy art installation? We don't know.

"And here's what else is strange, Frank. With all the publicity this case has generated, no one is banging at our door asking, Is my daughter one of those victims?"

"That is remarkable," Frank said.

"We're going to close this case. We're determined to do it. But the real pressure inside the SFPD is about the shooter cop."

Frank sighed, ran his hands through his hair, said again, "Oh, man."

I wasn't deterred. I brought him up to date on the shooter cop's activities.

"The shooter killed three drug dealers on a back road—"

"And torched their car."

"Right. Two days after that, he killed a dealer in a shopping-center parking lot."

"I read that. You're sure it was the same shooter?"

"The ballistics matched to another of our stolen guns. What you didn't read is that Jackson Brady thinks Jacobi is the shooter."

"Come on. Brady believes *that*?"

"Conklin and I were assigned to tail Jacobi, and he caught us sitting outside his house. Now Jacobi hates me. And we're no closer to finding a killer who has probably worked himself up and is ready to kill again."

Frank told me not to put too much pressure on myself, said that stress wasn't good for the baby.

"Maybe you should take yourself off the case."

"I can't, Frank. I just can't."

He nodded, told me that I could call him day or night if I needed him. I thanked him, and then he asked if we could go to my desk so he could use my computer.

"I'm expecting a big document by e-mail," he told me. "It's waiting for me in the cloud. Do you know what that is?"

I smiled, said, "It's a public server. Do you have an access code?"

"I wrote it on the inside of my eyeglass case."

"Come with me," I said.

I gave my chair to Frank and made fresh coffee as he did his work. When he'd put his reading glasses back in his jacket pocket, I walked him out and thanked him for his help with Constance Kerr.

"Any time. Take care, Lindsay. I mean it."

I returned to my computer and went to open what I expected to be an avalanche of mail that had come in over the last few hours.

When I touched the mouse, the screen lit up, and instead of my usual desktop screen, a document I'd never seen before appeared. It took me a moment to figure out that it was the personnel file of a cop, William Randall. I knew his name, but I didn't know much about him.

Frank Cisco, either accidentally or on purpose, had left this document for me to read. Or maybe Dr. Freud had made him do it.

I saved Sergeant William Randall's file to my computer and went looking for Conklin.

Chapter 83

"Okay, let's have the whole story," Brady said to me and my partner. We were in Brady's office with the door closed and the blinds down. Brady was both aggravated with us and hopeful we'd gotten a new angle on the case. He didn't sit down.

"How'd you hear this about Randall?"

"I can't tell you my source," I said. "I just can't."

"Fine. Actually, I don't give a rat's ass about your source, Boxer. What do you have on him?"

I took a printout of Randall's file and

put it on Brady's desk, turning it around so he could read along as I pointed out the highlights.

"William Randall has been with the SFPD for twelve years. He got bumped up to Narcotics in '04 and did a stint as part of a task force for the DEA. He moved to Vice in '09. His oldest son, Lincoln Randall, almost OD'd on heroin the next year. It's possible that this was the boy's first time trying hard drugs."

"His son almost OD'd. Go on," Brady said. He sat down and began tapping the underside of his desk with his foot.

"Randall found him lying in the street, got him to a hospital. His life was saved, but the kid's brain took a bad hit. He was a bright boy, but now he has the mind of a baby."

"So are you saying the kid's overdose is Randall's motive?"

"Exactly," I said. "Randall has a good, clean record in the department and a sad personal story. Our working theory is that he's on a one-man crusade to take out dealers who sell drugs to kids."

"But here's the thing, boss," Conklin said. "Meile and Penny both interviewed Randall. He has an alibi for the Morton Academy shooting. He says he was home with his wife and family when Chaz Smith went down. Mrs. Randall vouched for her husband, said, 'Will was at home. He's always home after work.' The top cops bought it."

"And so why exactly do you like him for the shootings? Put me out of my misery, will you, Boxer?"

"He's obsessed with drug dealers. *Obsessed* with them."

"How do you know that?"

"My source says that Randall has compiled dossiers on every dealer in the Bay Area. He knows things about them that Narcotics doesn't know. He has sources on the street, both dealers and hookers. Add it up. He had access to our property room and could've stolen the guns. He's an excellent marksman. Maybe he's got a whole lot of anger because of his brain-damaged son."

Brady said, "Yeah, okay. It's plausible. What's your plan?"

"Same as before. The three of us and

two teams from Narcotics. We take shifts and we watch Randall's movements. And we stay off the radio."

"I like it," said Brady. "Set it up."

Chapter 84

Conklin and I followed William Randall, at a discreet distance, from the Hall to his home, cutting the headlights when we crossed the intersection of Elm and Scott in the Western Addition. I found a spot toward the end of the block where we could get a good three-quarter view of Randall's yellow Edwardian-era house.

It was now 11:30 p.m. and we'd been watching Randall's street for five hours. There wasn't a house or alleyway or garbage can I hadn't committed to memory, and I knew every line and plane of Randall's house by heart.

His three-level home was typical of its time and this neighborhood. There was a small garage on the lower level. The second floor was the main floor: living room, kitchen, and bedrooms. The third level, the attic, had probably been converted into two small rooms.

Lights were on in the house and Randall's midsize black SUV was parked in his driveway. It had been there since before we began our shift.

It's been said that stakeouts are as interesting as watching grass grow, paint dry, water boil. But working Homicide means you don't get neat nine-to-five shifts, and Conklin and I don't mind sitting together for long hours at a stretch. We're compatible and maybe a little more than that.

Once upon a time, before he was seeing Cindy and at a point when Joe and I had split up, the spark between us kindled and almost burned up a hotel bed in Los Angeles.

I'd called a breathless halt to what would have been a hot fling with a short duration and no future. I'd reconsidered that decision many times, but as Conklin was telling me that he loved me, I was thinking about how much I loved Joe. How much I missed Joe.

Joe and I got together again.

Conklin hooked up with Cindy and they were so perfect as a couple, you had to wonder why it had taken them so long. I put on the big diamond ring Joe had given me and we got married in a magical ceremony by the ocean. And now I was running it all through my head again.

Conklin passed me the thermos of coffee. I took a couple of sips and passed it back to him. He stowed the thermos in the door pocket and called Cindy.

"You going to bed?" he asked her.

Pause as she said either yes or no.

"I don't know when. I can nuke something. Don't worry."

Pause as Cindy said okay.

"I don't care how late it gets, I'm going to wake you when I come in."

He laughed at something she said.

"You too."

He closed the phone. Put it in his pocket.

"She's okay?" I asked.

"She's writing. Don't bother her when she's writing. Look," he said.

I looked past the sofa that had been put out at the curb for garbage pickup, and saw a man, probably Randall, moving around on the main floor of the house.

Then the lights went out.

I had been hoping that Randall would leave his house, fire up his SUV, and take off so that Conklin and I could follow him and find out where a cop- and drug-dealer-shooting executioner went at night.

But that didn't happen.

Soon the inside of the house was dark except for the attic rooms. I saw a TV jump to life in one of those rooms, and a few minutes later, I saw Randall walk between the lamp and the window shades in the second room. Then that light went out too.

"He's packing it in for the night," I said.

"Lucky guy," said Conklin.

We had three more hours before the next team took over.

Chapter 85

Will Randall had been watching the two-year-old blue Ford sedan from his rear window, had seen it pull into the empty space on Elm with its headlights off.

And the car was still there.

Will had expected to be tailed and surveilled, but his brothers in blue hadn't seen him do anything and had nothing on him; if they had, they wouldn't have been sitting outside in their car.

Will went down the hallway, stopped in each of the bedrooms, and checked on the younger kids, all of whom were sleeping. He filled the hamster's water bottle in the boys' room, then went to the den, where his father-in-law, Charlie, was sitting in an easy chair, asleep in front of the television.

The TV was on really loud, so Will lowered the sound and then the thermostat, opened the sofa bed, and helped Charlie get under the covers. From there, Will went into the hall bathroom and jiggled the handle on the toilet until the water stopped running; after that, he turned off the overhead lights on the second floor.

Then he went upstairs.

His oldest son's room was right off the staircase and next door to the room Will shared with Becky. He pulled a chair up to the hospital-type bed where his son was lying and said, "You want to watch a little TV, Link?"

"Dah," Link said.

"David Letterman it is."

Will pointed the clicker, turned on the TV, raised the angle of the bed with the other clicker, and when Link was sitting up, he put a straw into a water bottle and held it to his son's lips.

Father and son watched Letterman

for a few minutes, Will's mind drifting to the unmarked car downstairs, to what would happen to his family if he was caught. He'd had these thoughts before, and now he ran through the same questions and came up with the same answers.

He was in free fall, but he wasn't done yet.

He brought his attention back to Letterman, who had finished his monologue and gone to a break. Will put the clickers down and said, "I'll be back in a little while, okay, son?"

Will went next door to his bedroom and saw Becky sacked out, completely zonked from a day of running this asylum. He loved her, worried for her health, admired her selflessness, couldn't imagine life without her.

He sat down on the side of the bed, put his hand on her cheek. She opened her eyes.

"Coming to bed, honey?" she asked.

"In a little while."

"Okay," she said.

Will pulled down the shades, first standing for a moment in front of the window, knowing that a couple of cops down on the street were seeing his silhouette. Then he turned off the light.

He paused in the doorway and listened to Becky's breathing. Then he went downstairs to the garage, where he took his leather jacket off a hook and put it on. He took his gun out of a toolbox and tucked it inside his waistband. Then he exited through the rear door and went down the short flight of steps to the backyard.

There was enough moonlight to see by but not enough to be seen. He crossed the grass and cut around the swing set, disappeared through the gap between the two houses that backed up against his yard and faced onto Golden Gate Avenue.

He turned onto the deserted road with the grandiose name, kept his head down, walked a block past shabby Victorian homes, and found Becky's Camaro where he'd parked it. He opened the car and got in, put his gun under the front seat, then started up the engine.

A moment later, he was heading east on Golden Gate. He wanted to get this job done before Craig Ferguson started his e-mail segment on *The Late Late Show,* which would be in about an hour.

If everything went as planned, he was pretty sure he could make it.

Chapter 86

Will Randall drove through the light-industrial area in the northern part of the Potrero Hill District as if he had an open barrel of beer in the backseat. He kept an eye on the speedometer, came to full stops at traffic lights, was careful not to attract any attention; he wanted to get this over with and go back home.

He stopped for a yellow light at the intersection of Alameda and Potrero. Then he continued on for another block, turned right onto Utah, a quiet road adjacent to the Jewelry Center and during the day used mostly for local traffic.

At night the area was nearly deserted. The lots were empty, and metered parking was open as far as he could see. Will pulled into a spot half a block from Zeus, a club and restaurant that filled a three-story brick warehouse and had the best sound system in San Francisco.

From where he sat, he could see the 101 Freeway to the north, the newly planted trees up the street, a gang of laughing-out-loud kids stumbling off the wide sidewalk, crossing the street behind him, and heading for the black iron delivery doors that were the unmarked entrance to Zeus.

Will forced himself to watch and wait as he sat in his wife's car, a loaded gun under the seat. He thought about good and evil, that the purpose of evil was to overturn the world of good. How he'd operated for half his life on that principle and that the distinction between the two had been lost since Link's brain had flamed out on bad drugs.

Will turned up the volume on the police band and listened to the exchanges between radio cars and dispatch, and when enough time had passed and he was sure there was no activity in the northern part of Potrero, he took his .22 out from under the seat. He screwed the silencer onto the muzzle, stuck the gun into his waistband at his back, and exited the car.

The interior of Zeus sounded like a stack of bricks going around in a clothes dryer. There was noise, flashing lights, a mass of dancing, shifting youth high on their own chemistry and aided and abetted by alcohol, Ecstasy, coke, and whatever new drug had become novel and available.

Will made his way to the bar under a wall that was illuminated by videos of bolts of lightning flashing over an open field. He ordered a drink, paid for it with a ten, and left the change; he took his drink to the edge of the dance floor. Clubs with live bands attracted kids and night-scene lovers of all ages.

Watering holes brought in gazelles *and* lions. Where kids congregated, drug dealers followed. Will watched and classified the people in the surging crowd, the schoolkids, rogue males, and out-

of-towners, and he saw money changing hands near the bar.

As he watched, a dealer who went by
the name of Stevie Blow turned and saw
Will staring at him. Blow was one of
hundreds of drug dealers on Will's hit
list. He wasn't number one, but he was
up there in the top ten.

Will nodded his head; a signal sent, a
signal received. His pulse quickened as
the dealer made his way toward him
through the throbbing gloom.

Chapter 87

The tall kid with pink-blond hair falling over his face and wearing threadbare jeans and a glittering T-shirt came over to where Will was standing with his back to the wall. He asked Will if he wanted to get high.

Will didn't know this kid personally, but he knew a lot about him. His given name was Steven Sargent, but the name Stevie Blow had stuck. Blow was twenty-five, looked younger, and liked to patrol school neighborhoods during the day and clubs, especially Zeus, at night.

Will said that he wanted to buy some

coke, and Blow said sure, and then he wanted to tell Will about his own brand of "bath salts." This drug was highly addictive; it contained MDPV, a chemical that caused intense hallucinations and sometimes bad trips that made the user violent or even suicidal. Bath salts were generally available but Blow was pushing his own blend, Peach Bliss.

He shouted into Will's ear, "I guaran-damn-tee you, Peach is a smooth high. Only twenty bucks for a trial sample."

Stevie reached his hand into his back pocket and Will said, "Not here."

Some Other Mother was saying thank you, waving off an encore, taking in the storm of applause, and then leaving the stage. The crowd went crazy again as the favorite house DJ took his place in the booth.

Will turned his head once to make sure Blow was behind him, then moved along the fringes of the crowd, looped around to the back, pushed the doors open, and entered the kitchen.

The kitchen was in chaos. Orders were shouted, cooking oil sizzled, pans clashed against the burners, dishes clattered in the large sinks. The rear doors were propped open to vent the hot air outside.

No one looked at them as Will and Blow made a swift exit through the kitchen and out to San Bruno Avenue. There was a gap in a fence leading to an area just under the freeway overpass, where it was dark and noisy.

Blow was saying, "Man, you're too paranoid. I could sell you this shit inside a police station and there's nothing anyone could do about it."

"I like privacy," Will said.

"To each his own," said Stevie Blow. "Anyway, you're gonna love this stuff."

He was sorting out his packets when Will took his gun from his waistband. He held the gun by the grip, stuck the barrel into an ordinary plastic shopping bag, a plastic sleeve that would contain the shell casings and GSR.

Will aimed and then fired twice.

The sound was muffled by the suppressor; two little puffs, like popcorn kernels exploding in an air popper.

Stevie Blow dropped his merchandise, flattened his palms to his chest.

He looked at the blood on his hands, then brought his eyes to Will. He said, "Whaaa?"

"You're guilty and you're dead, that's what. I feel bad for your parents, though. I'm sorry for them."

Will put a shot into Stevie's forehead, watched him fall, then dragged the body over to the wall and propped it in a sitting position between piles of bagged garbage.

As he headed toward his wife's car, Will felt no sadness for Stevie Blow. He was thinking about his own boy, how in twenty minutes he'd be turning off Link's TV and then getting into bed beside his dear wife.

He wasn't going to lose any sleep tonight.

Chapter 88

I heard a phone ringing from far, far away, then someone was shaking my arm, saying, "Lindsay, wake up."

I was jerked out of a deep well of sleep.

"What's up?"

I was in the passenger seat of the unmarked car two hundred yards from Will Randall's yellow house. The house was dark and Randall's SUV was still in his driveway.

"What time is it?"

"Just after one thirty," Conklin said. "Brady called. There's been a shooting in the alley behind Zeus. A drug dealer took some shots to the head and chest."

"Randall couldn't have done it. Could he?"

Conklin repeated what Brady had told him: a busboy had seen two men pass through the kitchen. The one identified as the victim was known to the busboy as a dealer. The second man was six feet tall, dark-haired, and looked like the narc who'd busted the busboy's cousin five years before.

"The busboy was shown a photo array," Conklin told me, "and tentatively identified Randall. He couldn't be a hundred percent sure."

William Randall was dark-haired, six one, and had spent five years in Narcotics—but I was staring at his car. It hadn't moved.

Randall must have left the house by the back door, taken some other vehicle to Zeus, and shot the dealer while I was taking a snooze. It was quite possible.

We had agreed not to use the radio, so I called Brady on his cell, told him I wanted to go into Randall's house, see if our man was missing or if he was asleep in his bed.

Brady said, "If Randall is home, treat him with all due respect. He's Meile's pet."

What if William Randall was home and *had* committed tonight's shooting? That meant he had most likely committed all of the shootings we attributed to Revenge.

The Randall house was full of kids.

What if Randall took his children hostage?

What if he decided to make a stand?

If I had been wearing boots, I would have been shaking in them, thinking about all of the truly bad things that could happen if we went into Randall's house. But I saw no choice. If he knew he was being watched, there was no telling what he would do. We had to get him away from his children.

"Screw Meile's pet. Send backup," I told Brady. "Send everything you've got. If I'm right, I don't want to play pattycake with this guy. If I'm wrong, I'll apologize to him. Profusely."

Two unmarked cars arrived within

minutes. I told the officers to park on Golden Gate, then proceed to the back of the Randall house on foot and cover the exit. And I told them that the suspect was a cop.

"If you encounter him, he could be wearing a uniform or he could ID himself as a cop. Treat him as you would any suspect who is armed and dangerous."

More cars streamed silently onto Elm, their sirens and headlights off. I briefed six more unis, told them that we had a murder suspect inside the house, that he was armed and dangerous, that there were five children and at least two other adults inside.

I sketched out a plan, and then Conklin and I went up the long flight of outdoor steps that led to the front door. Conklin stood back with his gun drawn.

I rang the bell and then knocked, calling out, "Sergeant Randall. This is the police."

I prayed that we could reason with William Randall.

I prayed that bullets weren't going to come flying through the door.

Chapter 89

A hall light blazed inside the house, then the main floor lit up. Someone peeked through the fan light in the door. The door opened and a woman in a thin yellow robe, her face lined with sleep, asked, "Can I help you?"

I showed her my shield and introduced Conklin, who holstered his weapon. I asked the woman if she was Becky Randall and she said that she was. I told her in a few words that we were investigating a shooting that had taken place in the last hour.

"I don't see how I can help," she said,

"but my husband is on the force. William Randall. He's with Vice."

"Where is your husband now, Mrs. Randall?" Conklin asked.

"He's upstairs, sound asleep."

"We have to talk to him."

"Sure. Please stay here. Lots of sleeping kids and I want them to stay that way. I'll go and wake Will up."

More squad cars were streaming onto the block from both directions. Becky Randall understood suddenly that we weren't conducting a routine canvass.

She said, "What's going on?"

"Please come with me, Mrs. Randall," I said. I took her arm and guided her firmly onto the outside landing, after which Conklin put his big foot between the woman and her front door.

I said, "An officer will stay with you until we've spoken with your husband."

I walked the loudly protesting Becky Randall down the steps and turned her over to Officer Cora. I used the time to get myself together.

It didn't matter how many people were going through Randall's front door. We were all at risk: my baby, my partner, the Randall kids, and the guys who were taking orders from me.

I followed Conklin across the threshold with my gun in hand, switching on lights as we went through the house. I signaled to the uniforms to fan out on the second floor, and after the main floor was cleared and contained with a cop standing outside every bedroom door, Conklin and I proceeded upstairs to the attic.

As I had thought, there were two rooms on the attic floor. One of the bedroom doors was open. I could see the entire room from the hallway: there was a young man lying in a hospital bed, a mobile of mirrored stars gently swaying above him.

He turned his eyes to me, said, "Ahh."

I threw on the lights, searched the room, then waggled my fingers at the boy and shut the door.

The door to the second room was closed.

Conklin and I flanked the door and then I knocked.

"Sergeant Randall? This is Sergeant Lindsay Boxer, SFPD. Don't be alarmed.

We just have some questions for you. Please come to the door and open it, slowly. Then step back and put your hands on your head."

He said, "*Who* is it?"

I repeated my name, heard floorboards creaking, and then the voice came through the door again.

"I'm not armed," he said. "Don't shoot."

The door swung open, and standing a few feet inside the doorway was William Randall. He was wearing blue boxers and his hands were folded on top of his dark hair.

There was a tattoo on his chest, an eagle with wings spread and two-inch-high letters inked under that emblem. I knew the words, of course. It was the motto of the City of San Francisco, and also of the SFPD.

Oro en paz. Fierro en guerra.

Gold in peace. Iron in war.

Apparently it was William Randall's motto too.

Chapter 90

It was a grim scene in the squad room that night.

Randall's superiors, past and present, stamped their feet and yelled at Brady for the way Conklin and I had extracted Randall from his home.

Brady shouted back, "If he's the doer, he's killed six people this week. Do you get that?"

Brady defended us and said that we had done the job right.

But I was starting to wonder.

While we were walking Randall out of his house, the busboy had retracted his tentative ID, saying he wasn't sure he'd picked the right guy out of the six-pack. So while the busboy's memory was still fresh, Brady called for a lineup.

Conklin fit Randall's general description so he was drafted to stand with Randall. Four random justice department workers filled in the ranks.

I stood behind the glass with the busboy as six men filed across the room and took their places at the height board. Each man stepped forward, turned left, turned right, and stepped back.

I held my breath as the busboy asked for Randall to step forward again. The busboy ID'd him—then when Meile said, "Are you absolutely sure?" the kid changed his mind and positively ID'd Morris Greene, an assistant DA who'd been pulling an all-nighter before we'd drafted him for the lineup.

What now?

Brady's expression was resolute.

He said to me, "Pretend he's David Berkowitz. Pretend he's Lee Harvey Oswald."

The observation room behind the two-way mirror was packed with brass: Brady, Meile, and Penny were there, and a few guys from the top floor I didn't know.

I brought coffee for three into the interrogation room, apologized again to Randall for the one-thirty wakeup call with drawn guns as well as the solitary two-hour wait in the box.

He said, "Look. I'm innocent of any crime. Do your job, but let's speed it up, okay? My wife and kids are in hell right now. And I'm about two minutes away from turning in my badge and telling all of you to take a flying leap."

What had we done by bringing Randall in?

What could we possibly accomplish?

We had no witness, no evidence, just a career cop who'd been asleep in his undershorts when we crashed into his house.

Had Sergeant William Randall killed six people in seven days? Did we have a committed spree killer under lock and key? No pressure at all. With the top floor watching from behind the glass, Conklin and I had to ask the right questions and either clear Randall—or get him to confess.

Chapter 91

Randall looked tired and irritated. Conklin and I pulled out chairs and sat across from a man who might have set a new record for murders by a cop.

I pushed a container of coffee toward him, waited for him to stir in his sugar, then said, "The more you cooperate, the faster this will go, Sergeant. Where were you for the last eight hours?"

"I arrived home after my shift at approximately six o'clock p.m. I was home all night, as my wife told you."

"Do you have another car, Sergeant Randall?"

"No. My wife has a car."

"Do you have a gun?"

"Department issue only. I don't want guns in a house with kids and a father-in-law who has no short-term memory."

"Did you drive your wife's car or any car between the hours of six last night and one this morning?"

"No, I did not."

"Did you fire a weapon in the last week?"

"I like how you ask me that with a straight face."

"Did you?"

"Hell no. You tested my hands, Sergeant. Negative for GSR."

That was true.

Randall's hands had been negative for gunshot residue, although he could have washed up and probably had. We had had no warrant to search his house or bring in his clothes for analysis. I got up, walked around the room, came back to my chair, and leaned across the table.

"We have a witness who saw you at Zeus."

"I guess he failed to identify me in the lineup."

"Others may come forward. When the ME does her post on the body, when CSU finishes processing the alley, we're going to find physical evidence. You can count on that."

"Knock yourself out, Sergeant. I'm not worried."

Conklin took his turn.

"Sergeant. Will. I don't have to remind you, now is the time to tell us the truth. We're going to be sympathetic. We're going to go out of our way to help you. Your victims are criminals. You've got friends in high places."

"I didn't do it."

I sighed, said, "Any idea who the shooter might be?"

"No idea in the world, but I admire the work he's doing. He's cutting through the red tape and putting the scumbags down."

Randall looked at me as though daring me to confuse his attitude with an actual confession.

He said, "I've got nothing for you, Sergeant. My kids are scared. My wife is going crazy. Lock me up or let me go."

We kept at it for another hour, Conklin and I taking turns, drilling down on his activities of the week before, going back over the same ground, but never tripping him up. Randall was smart and had as much interrogation experience as I had.

We'd done a good job and so had Randall. He hadn't given us a crumb and I couldn't think of anything else to ask him.

"You're free to go," I said. "Thanks for your cooperation."

Randall stood up and put on his nylon windbreaker.

"I need a lift."

Then, as an afterthought, he said, "You should be careful, Sergeant Boxer. You don't want to take chances with your baby."

I took it as a sincere remark.

Conklin walked Randall out, and when he came back, I was still in the interrogation room. I hadn't moved.

"Did he do it?" I asked.

"I can't tell."

"You know what, Rich? I kind of like the son of a bitch."

"He's a hard-ass," Conklin said. "Kind of reminds me of you."

Chapter 92

I brought Martha with me to breakfast at a great neighborhood bistro out in Cole Valley called Zazie. Zazie had scrumptious food and a patio garden out back. We came through the front door and the hostess told me she was sorry, but dogs weren't allowed.

"Martha is a police dog," I said.

"Is she really?"

The hostess held on tight to her menus, looked down at my small, shaggy border collie, and showed by her dubious expression that she couldn't believe Martha was in the K-9 Corps.

I've got to hand it to Martha. She looked up, made direct eye contact with the hostess, and conveyed professionalism and sharp canine wisdom with her deep brown eyes.

I backed her up.

"See?" I said, holding up my badge. "I'm a cop. She's my deputy dog."

"Okay. She's a drug sniffer, I guess. I shouldn't touch her, right? Kinda cute, isn't she? Should I bring her some water? Sparkling or flat?"

I had my first grin of the week, then had another when I saw Claire waiting for me at a table at the back of the long, narrow garden enclosed by ivy-covered walls.

I hugged her. She hugged me. I just couldn't get enough of that hug. When we finally broke apart, Claire bent and kissed Martha on the nose, making my little pal all waggle-tailed and squirmy. Martha really hearts Claire.

We sat at the nice long table in the corner of the patio, and Claire moved her newspapers out of the way—but not quick enough.

"Hey, let me see those."

I read the headlines.

The *Post:* "Another revenge killing at Zeus," by Jason Blayney.

The *Chronicle:* "Suspect held in House of Heads mystery," by Cindy Thomas.

"It's true: you can run but you can't hide." I handed the papers back to Claire, who said, "So what's the latest with you and Joe?"

"You go first, butterfly. I can't talk until after I've had hot chocolate and gingerbread pancakes."

"I haven't been to bed," Claire said. "Can you tell?" Now that she mentioned it, I realized that she was wearing scrubs.

I said, "Tell me what's going on."

"Where should I start? Yesterday, seven p.m. We've got a full house, of course. Among my other patients, I've got a seventeen-year-old boy on the table. Contact muzzle stamp on his temple and soot in the entrance wound. It's a clear suicide, but his parents aren't accepting it. Everything I say, they come back with 'No, Davey would never do that.'"

"The doors show any signs of a break-in?"

"I asked the same thing. They said, 'No, but maybe someone came in through the window.' He's got GSR on his hands, Lindsay. I took a sample for testing, just to be safe, but the windows are locked from the *inside*. It's obvious and it's heartbreaking—and then, here comes Mr. Dickenson.

"He's got a history of high blood pressure; he starts to feel lethargic and blacks out. His wife gets him to the hospital, and he's two minutes from a CT scan, which would confirm he's having a stroke, but no, he codes in the hallway.

"So now Mr. Dickenson is coming in through the back door of the morgue and I have to do an autopsy he wouldn't have needed if he'd coded two minutes later. Meanwhile, Davey's family won't leave, still insisting that their son was murdered."

We took a time-out to order breakfast from our waitress, then Claire picked up where she'd left off.

"So, I do Mr. Dickenson's post. I can find nothing wrong with his brain. Hey, where's the stroke? So I keep going. He didn't get hit with a stroke. I find a dissecting aortic aneurysm. See, I learned something. Again. Never jump to conclusions.

"About then, midnight or so, Edmund calls. Rosie is running a really high fever. I say, 'Take her to the hospital. Go. Now,' and before I hang up with him, here come new patients through the ambulance bay. Two cars in a head-on collision on Henry, both drivers are DOA."

Claire's phone buzzed on the table and spun like a june bug on its back. She looked at the faceplate, shut off the ringer.

"How's Rosie?" I asked as the waitress brought our coffee.

"She's fine. Temperature back to normal. Edmund said she's sleeping now. Both of us panicked, and that's what you do when you have a little one—as you are about to find out, girlfriend. After the check, I'm outta here, and I'm not going back to work anytime soon. Swear to God. Now, sweetie. Talk to me about Joe."

I put down my coffee cup, said to my

friend, "He's called me a hundred times and apparently he's sleeping in his car, sometimes right outside the apartment. I haven't said a word to him since I found out about his girlfriend. Not one fucking word."

Book Four

IN FROM THE COLD

Chapter 93

I'd just hung Martha's leash on the coat-rack and kicked off my shoes when the intercom buzzed. I looked at the video screen showing the foyer and saw T. Lawrence Oliver downstairs in the entranceway looking into the camera's eye.

I was expecting him, but he was early.

"Be right down," I said into the speaker.

A shiny black BMW was at the curb, and Oliver was holding open the back door. Harry Chandler dipped his head so that he could see me, said, "Please get in, Lindsay."

I got in and Harry told Tommy Oliver

to step out and take a long walk around the block, give the two of us a chance to talk.

I leaned back in the leather seat and said, "Thanks for coming, Harry."

"It's okay. I wanted to tell you about Connie Kerr in person. I don't know if I should put up bail for her or not," he said.

"Bail isn't an issue—yet. Connie isn't under arrest. We're holding her as a material witness and if we can't file charges against her by tomorrow afternoon, she walks. Do you want to file any charges?"

"No. I can't do that to her. I spent eighteen months in the clink while awaiting trial. Incarceration made a deep impression on me."

Chandler told me about his long-ago short-term romance with Connie and said that she had always seemed fragile to him. Crazy—maybe. A killer—no, he didn't see it. I told Chandler that I appreciated his help, said good-bye, and got out of the car as Tommy Oliver got back into the driver's seat.

I was deep in thought and had just put my key into the downstairs lock when I felt a hand on my shoulder. I whipped around, ready to throw a punch or lash out with a kick to the knee.

It was Joe.

I stared at Joe; no mugger could have made my heart beat faster. My brain was instantly thrown into shock and confusion. I saw Joe, my husband, the man I love.

And I was simultaneously hit with a current of revulsion.

I know I looked as though I could kill, and that must have been why Joe said, "Lindsay, it's me, it's me. Take it easy. Let's talk, okay?"

"I have nothing to say to you."

"I have plenty to say to you, damn it. You're all wrong about this, Linds, and you have to stop shutting me out."

I was flooded with images of June Freundorfer looking into Joe's face, and I felt deeply wounded all over again. I had trusted Joe with everything. I was having his baby. I was making a family with him for keeps—and then this. I had never felt so betrayed by anyone in my life. I had to get away from him. I couldn't stand to look at him for another moment.

I put both my hands out and shoved him away. He took a step back; I turned the key and opened the door slightly. I wedged myself through the narrow space and slammed the door shut.

I darted for the elevator, and before the doors even closed, my phone started ringing. I ignored my cell and I ignored the landline that was ringing when I walked into the apartment.

Both phones went quiet, then the landline rang again, and I checked the caller ID.

I picked up the phone in the kitchen, said hello to my partner.

"Sure, Richie. I'll meet you there."

Chapter 94

Constance Kerr sat with Conklin and me in a very small room at County Jail Number 2 on Seventh Street, only a couple of blocks from the Hall. Connie looked pitiful in her orange jumpsuit, her blondish-gray hair frizzed around her head like Frankenstein's bride's.

"This is a terrible place," she said. "Horrid. The screaming. The language. It's too much."

I felt bad for her. I really did.

"What did you want to tell me?" Conklin asked her.

"I have to get out of here," she said to

my partner. "Tell me what I have to say to get out of here."

"Tell us what you know about those heads, Connie, and this time let's get on the path to truth. I'll get you started," I said. She switched her eyes to me as though she'd just realized I was there.

"I've spoken to Harry Chandler."

"Yes? How is Harry?"

"He says you were never his girl-friend."

Her laugh was the small feeble cousin of the long guffaws she'd let out previously.

"He says you stalked him, Connie, stalked him for years."

"No."

"So he can't be a character reference for you, I'm sorry, and he said he wouldn't be surprised if you'd killed his wife."

"Oh, no, no, he can't be serious."

"It's all serious. This is a *homicide* investigation."

I had her attention now, and I knew when to shut up.

I folded my hands and watched Connie Kerr think it all through, how she could go from being a trespasser to being a murder suspect with a movie star willing to testify against her.

"I *did* see someone in the garden," she blurted out.

"Don't make anything up," Conklin said.

"It's true. I spied on the garden. It's black as a damned soul in there at night, but every once in a silver moon, I'd see someone doing nighttime gardening—with a shovel. It looked more like a shadow than an actual person. The shadow would bury something, then put down a rock to mark the spot."

Tears spurted, made tracks down her cheeks.

"I did suspect foul play, but I couldn't tell anyone. I was afraid Harry would put me out on the street. Although I did want to know what was buried under those stones.

"That's why I did what I did."

"What did you do exactly?" Conklin asked.

"One night, when the lights were out in the house . . . Excuse me, I need to blow my nose."

I had a packet of tissues in my jacket pocket; I gave them to Connie, waited for her to speak again.

"I took my hammer and went around to the front gate and I broke the lock," she said. "Mercy. That's breaking and entering."

Conklin and I just kept up a steady gaze.

"I knew where the gardener kept his tools," Connie said. "So I went around back to where the walls meet and there's the toolshed. It wasn't locked."

"Okay."

"I borrowed a shovel and gardening gloves and went to one of the stones— and I dug a hole. I didn't have to go very deep.

"I found that old skull, and when I brushed it off, an idea came to me. That's how it happens when you write, you know. Sometimes an idea just arrives fully dressed when you didn't even know it was there."

Connie Kerr seemed sane to me. Cracked, yes; loony enough to dig up skulls in a garden while thinking she was creating fiction. But I wasn't picking up stark raving cuckoo. And I wasn't feeling her as a murderer.

"What happened after you dug up that skull, Connie?"

"Well. I dug up another one."

Chapter 95

Connie dabbed at her eyes with a wad of tissues and continued her story.

"The second head was bad," she said. "I wasn't expecting it to be—to have—hell. I didn't expect it to be so disgusting. I was coming up with my plan, though, and I just told myself to have courage. I thought of it as forensic archaeology."

"Appropriate term," I said.

"You think so?"

I said, "Yes," not adding that in this situation, the correct term for her activity was *evidence tampering.*

Connie went on to say that she'd placed the "horrid remains" on the patio, returned to get the first skull, and then the idea took full form.

"I went back to my place and got a pair of index cards. I had a cool idea, very dramatic, but I was scared going back to the garden," she said.

"I was thinking that I was now wandering into the area of premeditation. But I couldn't stop. I was on a roll. The chrysanthemums were so *white*. So I plucked some and I made a wreath. I laid it around the heads," Connie Kerr said, making a wide circle with her arms. "It looked very good. After I finished the wreath, I started to feel better. In fact, I felt elated."

"You were excited."

"Yes, that's it. I was excited and my wheels were turning. I wanted to draw attention to the victims, you see. I wrote numbers on the index cards. I knew the numbers would make these heads into a big story. And I did a clever thing."

"Those numbers are a code."

"You're warm." Coy smile from Connie.

"Numerology," I said. "The number six."

"Aren't you smart!" she said. She clapped her hands together, and for a moment the woman who had pirouetted around her small apartment was back.

"So you wanted the police to find you?"

"Yes! I wanted the police to find the killer and I wanted to be the heroine who helped solve the case. I wanted good realistic details for my book. I'm calling it *Eleventh Hour,* because the crime is solved at the last moment. But I never expected to be charged."

"So that's your story, Connie? You did forensic archaeology, left some false clues for the police that led to your door."

"I've committed crimes, haven't I?"

I nodded. I wanted her to be afraid, but truthfully she wasn't guilty of much. Trespassing. Falsifying evidence. It wasn't illegal not to call the police to report a crime.

"See, I am cooperating," she said. "I didn't even get a lawyer. Can't you help me, please?"

"Who was the so-called night gardener?" Conklin asked.

"I don't know. I was peeking through a curtain sixty feet above the ground. It was always dark. I would tell you if I could."

"How do you get your food?" I asked.

"Nicole leaves it for me on the back steps. She's that lovely girl who lives next door."

"I'll look into getting you released," Conklin said. "But if we can do it, you can't leave your house."

"Don't worry. I'm quite the homebody," Constance Kerr said, "and, you know, I've got a lot of writing to do."

Chapter 96

Will Randall sat on the side of his bed
and sent a text message to Jimmy
Lesko. He used a disposable phone and
identified himself as Buck Barry, one of
Lesko's private customers, a cautious
man with an impressive drug habit.

The confirmation from Lesko came
rocketing back, and the meeting was
set for eleven that night; a transfer of
cash for coke on a dodgy street in the
Lower Haight.

It wouldn't be the transfer Jimmy
Lesko was expecting.

Will closed the phone, leaned over,

and kissed Becky. He whispered that he loved her, left an envelope on the night table describing Chaz Smith's double-dealing drug operation and how Smith had profited from being a cop. Then Will turned off the light.

He went to Link's room and stood over the bed watching his son's jerking, restless sleep.

His sweet boy.

Link should have been at Notre Dame now, on a scholarship. Should have been going out with girls. Should have been a lot of things he wasn't and would never be, in a world of things he would never do.

Will kissed Link's forehead, then went downstairs to the main floor and opened the door to the girls' room. There were handmade quilts on the beds and a mural of a pastoral countryside painted on the cream-colored walls.

He picked stuffed animals off the floor, tucked them into Mandy's bed, kissed her, then kissed her twin, Sara. Sara stirred and opened her eyes.

"I was flying, Daddy."

"Like a bird? Or like a plane?"

"Like a *rock-et.*"

"Was it fun?"

"So fun. I'm going to go back now . . ."

Will covered Sara's shoulders with her quilt, said, "Have a safe flight, sweetheart," then went to the boys' room across the hall.

The hamster was running on the endless track of his wheel. The two goldfish stared at him, almost motionless in the stream of bubbles coming up from the little ceramic diver at the bottom of the bowl.

Willie was asleep on his stomach, but Sam was awake and he grabbed Will's hand and wouldn't let go.

Will smiled at his boy, sat down on the bed beside him.

"What, son? What can I do for you?"

"Are you going out?"

"Yeah, the car's gas tank is empty and I don't want to stop tomorrow when I'm on the way to work. Rush hour, you know?"

"Will you get me something?"

"If I can."

"A motorcycle. A Harley. Black one."

"No problem."

"Really?"

"What about a peanut butter granola bar instead?"

"Sure," said Sam. "That'll be okay."

The kid was a born negotiator.

"Go to sleep now," Will said to his boy. "It's late."

Will kissed his youngest son, went down the hallway, and stopped to speak with Charlie, who was in his La-Z-Boy watching the news.

"Is that you, Hiram?"

"It's Will, Charlie. Becky's husband. I want to give you something."

"Sure, what is it?"

"You need a good shake."

"Ahhh-hah-hah." Charlie laughed as Will leaned in and grabbed his father-in-law by both shoulders and shook him gently. Will said, "You're a good man, Charlie Bean. I'll see you later."

"That's fine, Hiram. I'll wait up for you."

Taking the stairs down to the garage, Will thought about what was coming that night. He took his jacket off the hook, put it on, then got the gun out of a toolbox near the pyramid of paint cans. He wrapped the gun in a plastic bag, stuck it inside his jacket pocket. Then he grabbed a flashlight and left the house by the back door.

Will knew cops would be watching Becky's car on Golden Gate Avenue so he stayed on the deeply shadowed side of the street. There was an unmarked car at the corner of Scott, two guys in the front seat.

Will kept his head down and walked past it, kept going south another couple of blocks until he saw the silver Chevy Impala, probably a 2006 model.

The door was unlocked and Will got in, shutting off the dome light. It took him about five minutes by flashlight to remove the ignition plate and hot-wire the car, but the engine started right up and there was fuel in the tank.

The risk was building. But Will had already passed the point of no return.

Tonight was the night he'd been working toward for the last three months, the night when he would take his most personal revenge. He pulled the Impala out onto the street and headed for the Lower Haight.

Chapter 97

Jimmy Lesko had been in bed when he'd gotten a text message from Buck Barry, who was desperate to make a buy. It was a pain in the butt, but Lesko needed the extra cash.

He parked his sparkling new Escalade on Haight, a two-way commercial corridor, crowded in on both sides by peeling Victorian houses. All of them were shades of gray at this time of night, mashed together with single-story concrete utility buildings and bars and shops and more residences after that.

Sitting in the driver's seat, Lesko

watched the entrance to Finnerty's, a bar between Steiner and Fillmore known for its cheap suds and oversize burgers. Buck would be waiting for him in the men's room in about five minutes.

A UCLA film-school dropout, former up-and-coming protégé of the late Chaz Smith, Lesko traded in good-quality dope, had protection from the cops, and sometimes, like now, could make good money.

Lesko anticipated a quick transaction and an equally quick return to his house and the delicious young medical student who was asleep in his bed. He looked at the time again and got out of the car, then locked it with his remote.

He was crossing the street when someone called his name.

He turned and saw a man coming up Haight on Finnerty's side of the block. The guy was dark-haired, about forty, looked happy to see him.

"Jimmy. Jimmy Lesko."

Lesko waited on the sidewalk for the guy to reach him, then said, "Do I know you?"

"I'm William Randall," the guy said.

Lesko searched for some recognition. The name. The face. An association. Something. Nothing came up. Lesko had a good memory—but he didn't know the guy.

"What's this about?" he said.

"I want you to see this."

The guy took his hand out of his pocket. He was holding something weird. It was a plastic bag covering what looked to be a gun.

Shit. A gun.

This was not happening. This was just not *on*.

Jimmy jerked back, but he was hemmed in by the clots of boozed-up pedestrians on the sidewalk and cars at the curb. He went for his gun, stuck into the waistband at the back of his pants. But this fucking asshole Randall had pushed him back onto a car and pinned him there. He put the gun right up to his forehead.

Lesko threw his hands up. Dropped his keys. Wet his pants.

What was this? What the hell was this?

Didn't anybody see what was happening?

Lesko screamed, "What do you want? What do you want? Tell me what you want, for Christ's sake!"

"I'm Link Randall's father," the guy said. "Any idea who that is? Doesn't matter. You ruined my son's life. And now I'm going to ruin you. Totally."

Chapter 98

As Will Randall pulled the trigger, he was jostled by a lurching bum in a woman's coat who grabbed on to his arm to steady himself, saying, "Whooaaa."

Will's shot went wild, and Lesko took the split second of confusion to get away.

Will stiff-armed the bum and knocked him aside, then he aimed at Lesko. Jimmy was now a moving target in the dark, running like he was carrying a football under his arm, smashing into a couple of kids holding hands, ramming into a homeless grandma with a shopping cart. He knocked both the cart and grandma to the sidewalk, and she lay there with her limbs splayed out, her cart's wheels spinning, garbage everywhere.

Forward motion blocked, Lesko took the clearest path, bounding up steps that led to the front deck of a house.

Will fired at Lesko's back—and missed. And now Lesko crouched on the deck one story above him and shot at Will through the wrought-iron railing.

Will took to the street, then popped out from behind a van and got off six shots. But Lesko returned fire and Randall realized he had to corner this bastard and kill him at close range.

Pedestrians screamed and fled as Will charged toward the stairs, and then tires squealed and voices came from behind him.

"Freeze. Randall, put down your *gun*. Drop your gun *now*."

Will turned his head. He saw cops—cops that he *knew*. The blond guy with the ponytail—Brady. And the other two. Conklin and Boxer, who had brought him into the Hall.

How had they found him?

They'd been inside the unmarked car on Golden Gate Avenue and had seen him, followed him, that was how.

There was screaming on both sides of the street, Lesko yelling for help, pedestrians freaking, cops shouting, "Drop your gun! Hands in the air!"

Will turned toward the cops, waved his gun, and shouted, *"I know what I'm doing. Clear out of here. Don't make me shoot."*

A cop yelled, "Drop your gun now!"

And then the cops fired at him.

He felt a shot hit his left shoulder and it enraged him. Adrenaline surged. He was right. They were wrong. He had told them to *leave.*

He fired toward the cops, watched them duck and cover.

Someone shouted, *"Officer down. Officer down."*

Cops were down.

It was happening so fast. The blood left Will's head as he realized, with an almost calming clarity, that he wasn't going to leave this street alive. But he still had to do what he had come to do.

Lesko was pulling the trigger on his empty gun. He pulled again and again, looked at the gun, swore, then dropped it.

Will took the stairs and advanced on Lesko, the good-looking kid with blood staining his expensive clothes, blood dripping down his pants. He had his hands in the air, was backing up against the side of the house.

Lesko shouted at Will, veins popping in his neck and forehead, *"You've got the wrong person! I'm Jimmy Lesko. I don't know you. I don't know you."*

Will said, "I feel sorry for your father. That's all."

He fired two shots into Lesko's chest, then turned with his gun still in his hand. He felt the blow of a shot to his gut. His legs folded.

Will was on his belly, fading out of consciousness.

Lights flashed. Images swam. Voices swirled around him.

He got Jimmy Lesko.

He was sure. Almost sure. That he'd got him.

Chapter 99

Cindy was at the half-moon table in the corner of the living room, what she liked to call her home office, when the phone rang. She glanced at the clock in the corner of her laptop screen, then snatched up the phone.

"Ms. Thomas? This is Inspector May Hess, from radio communications. I have a message for you from Sergeant Boxer. There's been a shooting. Go to Metro Hospital now."

"Oh my God. Is it Richard Conklin? Has he been shot? Tell me it's not Rich. Please tell me."

"I just have the message for you."

"You must know. Is Inspector Conklin—"

"Ma'am, I'm just supposed to deliver the message. I've told you everything I know."

Cindy's mind slipped and spun, then she got herself together. She phoned for a cab, put a coat on over her sweatpants and T-shirt, stepped into a pair of loafers, and headed downstairs.

She paced in front of her apartment building, calling Richie's phone, leaving messages when the call went to voicemail, then calling him again.

The cab came after five minutes that seemed like five hours. Cindy shouted through the cabbie's window, "Metropolitan Hospital. This is an emergency," then threw herself back into the seat.

She was trying to remember the last thing she'd said to Richie. Oh God, it was something like *Not now, honey, I'm working.*

What the hell was wrong with her? What the hell?

Her body was running hot and cold as she thought about Richie, about him being paralyzed or in pain or dying. God, she couldn't lose him.

Cindy didn't pray often, but she did now.

Please, God, let Richie be okay.

The cabdriver was quiet and knew his way. He took Judah Street past UCSF Medical Center, made turns through the Castro and across Market, all the way to Valencia.

Cindy was lost in her thoughts, came back to the present only when the cab pulled up to a side entrance of the hospital.

"Faster for you if I drop you here," the driver said. "Twenty-Second is jammed."

That's when Cindy found that she didn't have her purse, her wallet, had nothing but her phone.

"Tell me your name. I'll send you a check and a really good tip, I promise that I will."

"That's great," the driver said, meaning the opposite. "No, listen. Forget it. Don't worry about it. Good luck."

Cindy had been to this hospital many times before. She walked through the lobby, passed the elevator bank, and headed down the long hallway, past radiology and the cafeteria; she followed the arrows pointing toward the ER.

The waiting room outside the ER was dirty beige and crowded with people with all kinds of injuries. She found Yuki balled up in a chair in the corner of the room. Cindy called out to her, and Yuki stood up and flung herself into Cindy's open arms.

Yuki was sobbing and Cindy just held on to her, dying inside because she couldn't make out anything Yuki was saying.

"Yuki, what happened? Is Richie okay? Is he *okay*?"

Chapter 100

It had been a night like no other I'd ever experienced. It felt like a military firestorm, gunshots cracking, bullets flying in all directions.

A sixty-year-old shop owner fell at my feet; never said a word, just died.

A drug dealer had been shot dead at point-blank range by an active cop who'd gone completely fucking rogue, and then there were other cops, my friends and my partner, who'd been injured in the line of duty.

I'd fired my gun, shooting to kill.

Maybe I was the one who brought Randall down.

I came out of the ER and found Cindy, Claire, and Yuki huddled together in the small, crowded waiting room. Cindy looked stunned. Yuki had been crying and now seemed distracted, as if she'd turned entirely inward.

Claire had the worn-down look of a person who hadn't slept in twenty-four hours and had not yet gotten a second wind.

My clothing was blood soaked. I wasn't injured, but I was scared, and I'm pretty sure I'd never looked worse.

When Yuki saw me, she jumped out of her chair and asked, "What did they tell you?"

Brady had caught a bullet in his lung and had taken another through his inner thigh. That shot had hit an artery, and thank God the EMTs had arrived as fast as they had. Still, Brady's condition was grave. He'd lost a lot of blood.

"He's in surgery," I told Yuki. "Claire, you know Dr. Miller."

"Boyd Miller?"

"That's him."

Claire said to Yuki, "Miller is a fantastic surgeon, Yuki. The best of the best."

Yuki said to me, "They told me that it's touch and go. Touch and *go!*"

"He's strong, Yuki. He's young," Claire was saying.

Conklin came into the waiting room from the hallway. His left arm was in a sling. He opened his right arm to Cindy, who threw herself at him. He hugged her hard, kissed the top of her head as she wept, then said to me, "I put Randall's wife in the chapel."

I left the waiting room and went down the corridor to the chapel, a sad-looking place that tried to give solace on a financially strapped city hospital's budget. An ecumenical altar was backlit with subdued lights, and comforting sayings had been written in script along the walls.

Becky Randall sat in a pew with a little girl in her lap, three other kids hanging on to her arms, waist, and legs. She disentangled herself from her children, stood up, and said, "Willie, you're in charge."

She and I walked together into the hallway.

"No one will tell me anything," she said. "Please, Sergeant. What happened? Tell me everything."

Tell her everything?

I didn't know everything yet myself, and considering what I did know, I had to edit my comments with compassion.

Could I tell Becky Randall that it looked like her husband had shot several people before he shot Chaz Smith dead in the men's room of a school with a hundred kids all around? Could I tell her that following the shooting of Chaz Smith, her husband had shot and killed even more people and that because of him my lieutenant might lose his life?

Could I tell her that some of the five bullets inside her husband's body had probably come from my gun?

Will Randall was alive, but he was on a ventilator and going into surgery. If he survived, he was looking at multiple charges of murder in the first degree.

Even if he lived, life as he had known it was over.

"Your husband shot a drug dealer tonight, Becky. The man's name was Jimmy Lesko. Does the name mean anything to you?"

"No," she said. "Why did he shoot him? It must have been in self-defense."

An hour later, all I knew from Becky Randall was that she had no idea about her husband's secret life and in fact denied that he had one. What was it Joe had said?

Do we ever really know anyone?

I'll never forget that hour in the corridor outside the chapel. Kids skated on the linoleum hallway on socked feet, asked for quarters for the vending machines, fooled around with wheelchairs while Becky sat in shock, denial, disbelief.

"Will is a wonderful, decent man," Becky told me. "What's going to happen if my husband dies?"

Chapter 101

The TV was on in the waiting room.

Jason Blayney was on the screen, standing outside Metropolitan Hospital in a smart jacket and tie, telling the network news what had gone down on Haight Street.

He looked and sounded authoritative, as if he knew what he was talking about. But Blayney was doing what he always did. He didn't know what happened, so he made up the facts.

As Blayney told it, the cops had come onto Haight Street and started firing.

"William Randall, a ten-year veteran in

Vice, was pursuing a drug dealer named Jimmy Lesko," Blayney said. "Lesko was a small-time drug dealer, and according to witnesses, Lesko was unarmed. Randall fired at Lesko without provocation, kept firing until Lesko was dead.

"Homicide detectives were alerted to the shooting and tore onto Haight Street, where they began firing at anything that moved.

"Sergeant Randall was seriously wounded and is now in surgery at Metropolitan Hospital, fighting for his life.

"Nicholas Kiernan, age sixty-two, was a resident of the Lower Haight, an innocent bystander who stepped outside his home and was caught in the cross fire," Blayney went on. "Mr. Kiernan, father of three, died at the scene.

"Two other police officers were shot in the blistering hail of gunfire. Lieutenant Jackson Brady, head of the Southern District Homicide Division, and Inspector Richard Conklin are in surgery right now, their lives hanging by threads.

"This is a shameful night for the San Francisco Police Department, which can truly be described as the gang who couldn't shoot straight."

It was a nasty story, the worst of Blayney. There was no mention of Randall's being a bona fide rogue cop, no hint that the SFPD had warned Randall to drop his weapon, no indication that the police had fired on him only when he refused to drop his gun. And Blayney's biased reporting was now flashing around the world as truth.

I grabbed the remote control and turned off the set.

Randall was still in surgery, and from what I'd been told, the odds were against his coming out of the OR alive. Brady was also fighting terrible odds. As he was being cut and stitched, a whole lot of prayers came his way from the waiting room.

At around two in the morning, Cindy took Richie home to bed, and Claire let me walk her out to the parking lot. She made me promise to call her when Brady was out of surgery.

After that, Yuki and I sat together surrounded by Homicide cops who had come to show support for Brady. Lieutenant Meile arrived in street clothes and apologized to me in front of a packed waiting room.

"I'm sorry for the things I said to you, Sergeant. And I'm sorry for a few things you didn't hear me say. I'm a dumbass, but I believed in Will Randall's innocence. He'd better not die before he tells me what the hell he was thinking. Damn him. I have to know."

Chapter 102

I wasn't thinking about Randall.

I sat close to Yuki, thought about Brady, and revisited some pretty deep memories of the months I'd known him.

The first time I saw Brady was his first day with Homicide. I'd noticed the hard-eyed, suntanned looker who was sitting in a folding chair at the back of the squad room.

I got up and gave an update on a case I was working. It was a bad one: a madman had just shot a mother and her little kid and had left a cryptic message behind.

I was almost nowhere on the case, but I presented what I had with confidence.

When the meeting was over, Brady introduced himself, said he was transferring to our squad from Miami PD. Then he told me that what impressed him about my presentation was that I was sucking swamp water.

His blunt assessment didn't endear him to me, but days later, there was a standoff in front of the madman's house. A bomb went off, a diversion, and the madman made it to his car. Brady stepped in front of the car and emptied his gun into the windshield in an attempt to bring the bad guy down.

I had been impressed with his bravery.

But I still didn't like him.

When Brady started dating Yuki, I was shocked and I was worried. Yuki's a fighter, don't get me wrong, but she's got terrible judgment when it comes to men, and I couldn't see her with a badass cop like Brady.

I thought he would hurt her; I really did.

Then I saw them together.

I pictured them now at a lawn party, first tossing footballs, then Brady carrying Yuki around slung over his shoulder. He was sweet with her. And she made him laugh. They brought out the best in each other and that counted in his favor.

I hadn't forgotten that he was only legally separated from his wife, who still lived in the Sunshine State. I hadn't forgotten that he was my superior officer or that I didn't like his rough management style.

And I certainly hadn't forgotten that he'd accused Warren Jacobi of being Revenge. He was going to have to take that back for sure. I hoped to hell he lived to do it.

I looked up when Dr. Boyd Miller came into the hallway outside the waiting room. He was thirty, bald, thin-lipped. He did not look warm and fuzzy. He did not look like he was bringing good news.

"Is Mrs. Brady here?" he asked.

"I'm his girlfriend," Yuki said. "He's with me."

"He's my commanding officer," I said.

"I was on the scene when he was shot. What's his condition?"

I expected that Miller was going to say that he could speak only to Brady's immediate family. I didn't think either Yuki or I could handle that.

"We successfully repaired the damage to his femoral artery," he said. "His lung is going to be fine. He has two broken ribs and there's not much we can do about that. He's on his way to the ICU now. I'm optimistic," Dr. Miller said. "But officially his condition is guarded."

"Can I see him?" Yuki asked. "I have to see him."

"Not yet. I'll let you know when it's okay."

It was just about five in the morning when Yuki was told she could look at Brady through the glass.

When she came back to the waiting room, her expression was soft. She sat down next to me, squeezed my hand.

"He's going to be all right," Yuki said. "My mom told me that he's going to be fine. And she likes him now. She said, 'Brady very good man.'"

I nodded, said, "That's great."

I had to accept that Yuki thought that her dead mother spoke to her. Maybe she did.

"I think your mom is usually right," I said.

"Good, because she also said that you should go home now, Lindsay, and get some sleep."

Chapter 103

Claire turned her car into the lot on Harriet Street, parked in the space with her name stenciled on the asphalt. It was after ten in the morning, the first time in a year that she'd been late for work.

The reception room of the Medical Examiner's Office was churning; the new girl with big brown eyes was at the desk juggling the constantly ringing phones. Messengers came and went. Cops milled around, waiting for bullets and other forensic material to take out to the lab.

Claire waved at the receptionist, went through the glass door to her office, hung her coat and voluminous bag on a rack in the corner, and sat down at her desk.

She was dialing Lindsay when the brown-eyed girl knocked on the door and opened it. She came toward Claire with a flat package in her hands.

"This just came, Dr. Washburn. It's marked *urgent.*"

Claire took the package, looked at the return address. It was from Ann Perlmutter, the forensic anthropologist at UC Santa Cruz.

Claire sliced open the package with a scalpel and found six disks, each in its own case. And there was a letter from Dr. Perlmutter.

Sorry this took so long, Claire.
Call me if you have questions.
   Ann

Claire inserted one of the disks into her computer's DVD drive. A picture of a woman appeared on the screen, so lifelike it could have been a photo-graph—but it was a computer-gener-ated 3D facial reconstruction of one of the skulls from the Ellsworth compound case.

This 3D-imaging technique was a kind of miracle, and Claire knew how much time, skill, and artistry had gone into creating this likeness.

A 3D representation had been made of each skull by a laser scanner that uti-lized light, mirrors, and sensors to cap-ture the image and generate a wire-frame matrix. Information from CT scans of living persons was added, and the sophisticated software program dis-torted reference points on the 3D skull to correspond with points on a refer-ence CT scan, creating a facial shape for each skull.

The six bare skulls that had been ex-humed from the Ellsworth garden had faces now. These representations could not be 100 percent accurate—but they would be close.

The face on Claire's screen had been labeled JANE DOE EC 1. The woman had rounded eyes, a wide forehead, a small nose, and long, wavy hair.

In real life, Jane Doe EC 1 had had a family, and soon, Claire hoped, she would have a name.

Chapter 104

Dr. Andrea Shaw came to the waiting room just before the sun came up. She was a small woman with a sweet expression and wavy silver hair.

She said to Yuki, "Jackson is going to be okay. He's asking for you."

Yuki's face brightened. It was as if all the stars had come out at once and the sun and moon had done the tango together just for her.

She hugged the doctor almost off her feet, then she hugged me, making tears jump out of my eyes.

"Go to him. Go," I said.

A few hours and a change of clothes later, I was at my desk in the Homicide squad room. I would be subbing for Brady until he was back on the job. All the phone lines were ringing at once, but when I saw Claire's name come up on the caller ID, I stabbed the button, didn't wait for her to say hello.

"Brady's condition is stable," I told her. "Randall is still critical. No change."

"Man, that's great news about Brady. Listen, I've got something for you, girl-friend. I've got *faces* on those heads from the trophy garden."

The wind went right out of me.

I blinked stupidly long enough for Claire to repeat herself, and then I got it. Ann Perlmutter had done the facial re-constructions. With faces, we might be able to ID the Ellsworth compound skulls.

"Have you run the images through missing persons?"

"There are six heads here, Lindsay. And I've got only one pair of eyes, one pair of hands."

"I'm on it."

Within an hour, Cindy, Yuki, Claire,

and I each had at least one Jane Doe disk. Cindy was at home; Yuki worked from her laptop inside Brady's hospital room. Claire was downstairs at her desk, and I was at mine. The Women's Murder Club was connected by a mission and our shared network.

I booted up the disk and stared at Jane Doe EC 2 as she came on my screen. She was pretty, with short, dark hair, arched brows, and full lips. I pressed Next and saw that Dr. Perlmutter had provided variations on this depiction of my Jane Doe to account for the artistry and guesswork that had gone into creating the image.

She'd made it easy for us.

But matching virtual images to real people was still an enormous job with plenty of room for error.

We ran the 3D images through NamUs, the Doe Network, the SF missing-persons databases, and the FBI criminal database. Matches came up.

It was amazing, almost magical.

Claire got the first hit: Jane Doe EC 1 was Lina Rupert from Sioux Falls, South Dakota. Cindy's match was to Margaret

Shubert from Toronto. The other four victims appeared to be missing persons from Chicago, New York, Omaha, and Tokyo.

We four shared the pictures in a Windows Cloud and chatted together in a dialogue box on the screen. Comparing notes took very little time. The victims were of all ages, the youngest only eighteen, the oldest forty-eight.

The victims weren't criminals, and none of them was local.

Apart from their burial ground, what did these six women have in common? What had brought them together in a homemade boneyard in Pacific Heights?

Chapter 105

Yuki was sitting in the enormous chair in Brady's hospital room. He had woken up for a moment, long enough to give her a lazy "Hiiii . . . Yu . . . ki."

He told her he was enjoying the drugs and then fell asleep again.

The phone rang after that. It was a woman who said she was Jennifer Brady, Jackson's wife.

"Who is this?" she'd asked.

Yuki considered telling the woman that she was a nurse but went with the truth.

"I'm Yuki Castellano. I'm with Jackson."

"With him? What do you mean?"

"We're significant lovers," Yuki said.

The long silence was underscored by Brady's loud breathing.

Yuki said, "He's doing well, Jennifer. He's sleeping, but he's going to be okay. I'll tell him that you called."

Yuki dropped the receiver into the cradle, looked at it for a moment as if it were a porcupine. Then she upended it and turned off the ringer.

She said hello to the actual nurse who came in to attend to Brady, and then Yuki went back to her laptop and her Jane Doe EC 5, a young woman Yuki had identified as Hoshi Yamaguchi.

Yuki had already begun her research on Hoshi; she'd learned that she had been twenty years old when last seen. She had been going to school in Tokyo, was a student of history and fine art, and she disappeared while on vacation to the USA four years ago.

A family member had put up a website for Hoshi. There was a large portrait of Hoshi on the page. The next photo was of Hoshi ice-skating with her sister. The two were wearing leggings and matching blue puffy jackets, and they were holding hands.

Yuki could read some Japanese and was able to translate the caption under the photo.

Have you seen my sister?

Yuki opened a link and found messages from Hoshi's friends listed in chronological order. The first notes were to Hoshi, asking her to write. Subsequent messages pleaded for anyone who had seen Hoshi to respond.

There was a link to the police reports and reward postings, and there was a section devoted to more pictures of Hoshi.

What had happened to this lovely young woman? Why had she been killed? And damn it, how had her head come to be buried in San Francisco?

Yuki was about to send a message to the girls when she noticed a link at the bottom of the photo section. It was marked, in Japanese, *Last message from Hoshi*.

Yuki clicked on the link and a video

window opened on her computer. A young woman's voice narrated in English as the camera panned Vallejo Street.

"Kendra, this is a very old street in San Francisco and this is the Ellsworth compound, one of the first houses built here," the voice said. "Sometime you have to come from New York and see it because you would love it. This house survived the great fire of San Francisco and I've been told it holds many secrets."

The picture jiggled, as if the camera was changing hands, and then the narrator came into focus; she was posing in front of a brick wall with a wrought-iron gate.

The speaker was Hoshi Yamaguchi, there was no doubt in Yuki's mind.

Hoshi spoke to the camera using a playful entertainment-TV voice.

"The famous movie star Harry Chandler lived here for ten years and has been accused of murdering his wife. I've been told that he didn't do it. And I believe it, because you know I love Mr. Chandler."

The very cute Hoshi hugged herself and mugged for the camera. Then she said, "I'm going to take pictures of his house before I send this to you. Hold on, Kendra."

Then Hoshi said, "Thank you," and reached out and took back her camera. Whoever had been holding it ducked and put a hand up to block the picture. There was a break in the video. Apparently, the camera had been shut off.

Then the video continued with more of Hoshi's narrative and pictures of the outside of the house as seen through the iron gate. Hoshi said, "Bye for now, Kendra. See you online."

And the film was over.

Yuki hit the Replay button and watched the video once more, this time knowing that Hoshi had never seen her friend Kendra again, either online or in person. Yuki was pretty sure that Hoshi Yamaguchi had visited the Ellsworth compound on the last day of her life.

Chapter 106

Yuki posted the video of Hoshi Yama-guchi and I watched it run. There was the girl standing in front of the brick wall on Vallejo Street, a flash of a red tour bus at the curb.

One of the victims had been alive and present at the scene of the crime. As I watched the little homemade movie, my eyes teared up and my heart went gid-dyap.

Yeah. I was having some kind of heart attack, but it wasn't fatal. I felt maybe, just maybe, this freaking case was go-ing to break.

Graceland, I typed into the dialogue box. *Neverland.*

Yuki typed back, *Wut do u mean?*

I wrote, *Did all the victims go on the historic-house tour?*

Yuki replied, *I'll call the tour company now.*

Claire wrote: *Questions. If Hoshi was killed at the compound, were all of the women killed there? Where did the killings happen? Where are the bodies?*

I watched the video again, this time pausing at the frames where Hoshi's camera changed hands. There was a close-up of Hoshi's neck and I saw that she was wearing a necklace with an amethyst pendant. The stone was set in a gold bezel. I wanted to yell, *Rich! Look at* this. *I've seen this necklace. We have it in evidence. It was buried with one of the heads.*

My partner wasn't there.

I sent him an e-mail to keep him in the loop, then dropped an imaginary glass dome over my desk so no one in the squad room would interrupt me.

Shooting a video of Hoshi Yamaguchi didn't make anyone a killer. Assuming that the victims had all been tourists, assuming they'd all been killed at the compound, Claire's questions were good ones. Where had the murders taken place? Where were the bodies?

I opened my browser and searched for architectural plans of the Ellsworth compound. I found what I was looking for in the San Francisco Historical Society archives.

There were reams of old drawings on file, drafts of blueprints and renderings of the house in progress: all of its floors, the basement, the garden, and the plans for the row of servants' quarters on Ellsworth Place.

I put the drawings up for my group to examine, and while Yuki researched the Historic House Tour bus company, Cindy, Claire, and I studied the plans for the house that had been designed by Drake Ellsworth and his architect back in 1893.

Claire put her cursor on the drawing of the basement, a large room that ran under the entire main house.

You could kill cattle in a room this big, she wrote.

I had been in that basement with Charlie Clapper. There were several generations of boilers and pumps in that vast space, devices replaced by successive pieces of modern machinery but not removed.

We'd looked in the small rooms off the basement. One was filled with furniture. Another had once been a pantry.

Clapper's team had been all over that underground warren with cutting-edge equipment and had found no blood, no tools, no evidence of a chop shop.

Now I needed CSU to go over the whole house again.

Chapter 107

While Brady recovered from his injuries, I was in charge of the Homicide squad, so I mustered a caravan of law enforcement officers and called in the CSU.

Conklin flatly refused to stay in his bed when *this* was going down. I picked him up on the corner of Kirkham and Funston, then drove to the Ellsworth compound with my injured partner in the seat beside me.

I pulled up to the iron gate, and Clapper's van arrived and parked right behind me. I ordered cruisers to close off the triangle of streets surrounding the compound, then six of us mounted the wide front steps to the main house.

I dropped the brass knocker on the strike plate, and Janet Worley opened the door and saw half a dozen cops and the dapper Clapper standing in front of her. She gripped the collar of her starched white shirt, fear flashing across her face.

"We're executing a search warrant, Mrs. Worley," I said, handing it to her.

"You've already searched—"

"We're doing it again."

"All right, then. Come in."

"We need to see your husband," Conklin said.

"He's working upstairs. He *was* in a good mood."

Conklin, Clapper, three crime scene investigators, and I walked through the front entrance and, under Charlie's direction, filed through the enormous old house.

I was standing in the middle of the large foyer with Janet when Nigel Worley came down the stairs with his fulminating anger. He scowled at me and asked, "What's this about?"

"It's about premeditated murder, Mr. Worley. Inspector Conklin will keep you and your wife company in the kitchen."

"Bugger that. I've got work to do."

"Thank you. We appreciate your co-operation."

Conklin corralled the Worleys and I headed down to the basement, where I found Clapper and a couple of techs opening their scene kits, getting to work.

The overhead lights were on, but they weren't bright enough to illuminate all the corners of this vast space.

Still, neither clutter nor gloom deterred us.

We worked the room going from east to west, parallel to Vallejo Street, doing an eyeball search and using ALS wands to pick up signs of organic trace. CSU techs who had been deployed upstairs trickled down to the basement and joined us in the subterranean vault as the hours unfurled behind us like the cars of a night train.

I was wondering if we had been wrong in assuming that this basement was the scene of multiple homicides when, at around five in the evening, we reached the southernmost basement wall. Cartons of books and crates of empty wine bottles were stacked to the ceiling against the brick and timber.

I was behind Clapper when he shouted, "Awww, shit. How did I miss this?"

I stepped to Clapper's side and saw that the ceiling-high crates only *appeared* to be touching the wall; it was clever fakery. There was a narrow gap behind the cartons, and an old sliding door on an overhead track was mounted on the actual wall.

Clapper gave the door a shove and it slid open, revealing the entrance to another basement room, this one running southwest to northeast, parallel to Ellsworth Place.

There was free access between the basement of the main house and the one in 2 Ellsworth Place.

A person could move from one to the other without being seen.

Chapter 108

I hit the light switch in the connecting basement room and took in the surroundings as CSIs shot pictures.

The basement under number 2 was about forty feet across, thirty feet deep, with a dirt floor and a brick ceiling. To my immediate left was a large, sunken cistern about ten feet wide, no doubt used by previous owners of this house to collect rainwater through downspouts from the roof.

To my right was the furnace and the pump, and on the far side of the room, against the eastern wall, were modern appliances: a freezer, a washer, and a clothes dryer. Shelving banked the walls and held a typical assortment of basement junk, paint cans, and tools.

Charlie Clapper examined the cistern and after a moment said, "There's a ladder going down about seven feet and there's a drain in the bottom of this thing. Turn off the lights, if you would, Lindsay."

I flipped the switch and Clapper sprayed the inside of the cistern with luminol, then turned on his ALS wand.

He whistled through his teeth and said, "You should see this."

When Charlie said you should see something, it usually meant *You should see something awful*.

The interior of the cistern was bright with a phosphorescent glow, the effect of black light on blood. A great amount of blood had been spilled in that well, probably washed down with the hose hanging over the lip of the cistern. But the evidence of a bloodbath remained high on the walls and ringed the bottom drain.

Images came to me, the faces of the

seven women who might have been murdered and dismembered in this vat.

I turned to Clapper, but he had started working the walls, spraying luminol as his assistant followed him with the ALS wand. There was so much blood evidence, spatter and splash and handprints on everything.

Clapper turned the lights back on and as I looked around, I saw something on one of the shelves that dropped another piece of the puzzle into place.

I crossed the floor and took a good close look at a cordless ripsaw resting next to a carton of old medicine bottles. I called to the CSI with a camera and asked him to take shots of the saw.

Claire had told me that the victims had been decapitated with a ripsaw, and it wasn't much of a stretch to think the saw on the shelf had been used in those procedures. No black light was needed. I could see darkened blood on the blade and reddish smears on the handle.

Clapper rummaged in the box of medicine bottles.

"Lindsay, here's something you should see."

Another something I should see. I felt the floor roll. Clapper said, "You okay?"

I was okay. But my baby onboard was having some trouble with this crime scene.

"What have you got?"

He called over the tech to shoot pictures of the contents of the box, then pulled out two items that were photographed as well.

The first item was a stun gun.

The second was a sixteen-ounce brown bottle labeled SODIUM PENTOBARBITAL.

"This is a barbiturate," he said. "Vets use it to euthanize large animals."

I grabbed Clapper's arm to steady myself.

The vivacious and compassionate Nicole Worley worked with wildlife rescue. She could have swiped a bottle of this stuff if she wanted to. And I was pretty sure she'd know how to put animals down.

Chapter 109

I called Conklin and filled him in as I raced up the stairs to the main floor of the house. I found my partner sitting with Janet Worley at the round table in the kitchen, empty teacups and a plate of crumbs in front of them. Janet's face was pale and pinched.

Nigel Worley was missing.

"Nigel took a swing at me. Any other day, I would have clocked him," Conklin said.

"He's under arrest?"

"For his own good."

I said to Janet, "Where's Nicole?"

"You don't have the *right*—"

"I don't need your permission, Mrs. Worley. Where is she?"

Conklin and I followed Janet up the main stairs of the house, boards creaking under our feet. I was thinking about Nicole Worley, the self-possessed young woman who worked for the good of animals and lectured to tourists about the history of the Ellsworth compound.

When we reached the sixth floor, Janet opened the first door on the left, the door closest to the back of the house.

The room smelled of floral sachet, an old-lady smell. I flipped on the light switches, expecting to see Nicole in the bed or in a chair. But the room was empty, and it looked like it had been empty for years. The bed was crisply made. There were no personal items on the dresser or on the nightstand.

"What's this room, Janet?"

"Follow me. It's this way," she said, throwing a lightning bolt of a stare in my direction.

She turned and headed toward a small closet door in the corner of the bedroom where the ceiling slanted under the eaves. Janet opened the door, pushed aside clothing on a rod, then stooped to enter a hidden Alice-in-Wonderland doorway.

The door led to a tunnel that ran under the eaves. I turned on my flashlight and continued behind Janet Worley's crouched form until the tunnel opened into another hallway, one with a staircase leading down and three doors off the landing.

I knew where we were.

This was the top floor of 2 Ellsworth Place, another concealed access point between the main house and the servants' quarters around the corner.

Janet pointed to the door and said, "This is Nicole's room. I doubt that she's here."

I pulled my gun as Janet knocked.

"Nicole. Are you here, darling?"

No sound came from within.

I reached around Janet Worley and tried the knob. The door was locked from the inside. I said, "Rich. Give it a try."

I pulled Janet Worley aside and said, "Stay here in the hallway."

Then Conklin kicked in the door.

Chapter 110

Nicole was wearing black up to her chin.

She had wedged herself between her bed and the window, propped her elbows up on the mattress, and was holding a large kitchen knife in front of her with both hands.

She was pointing that knife at us.

Her heart-shaped face no longer looked angelic. Her features were locked in a crazy stare and her hair was damp with sweat. Her green eyes were blank as stagnant pools.

She looked absolutely feral.

Nicole was twenty-six, but her room

had gotten stuck in a teen-theme time warp. The walls were painted with vertical stripes in three shades of green. The spread and curtains were the same colors in a polka-dot print.

There were pictures of Harry Chandler all around the room, including a life-size cutout on the wall and a black-and-white headshot on the dresser mirror inscribed *To Nicole, XOXO, Harry.*

Nicole said in a deep voice, almost a growl, "Don't come any closer, you bitches. I'm not afraid to use *this*. And I'm not afraid *to jump*."

The room had two exits: the door behind me and the window behind Nicole. From what I could see, Nicole didn't have a direct view of the house and garden. But the oblique view took in the back of the Ellsworth house, the brick patio, and a wedge of the garden where heads had been buried.

My eyes went back to Nicole, who was still facing us down from behind her mattress. She seemed irrational. And I didn't like the options she had given us.

My partner stepped forward.

He wasn't holding a weapon and his

left arm was strapped across his chest. If there'd ever been a time for the Conklin charm factor, this was it.

"Nobody wants to hurt you, Nicole. We don't want any trouble. None at all."

"I'm in charge here," Nicole said. "I make all the decisions."

"You're only in charge of what *you* do," Conklin said. "So I want you to move very slowly. Put the knife down."

She laughed, a hysterical yip.

"So you can do what? Shoot me. I'll put the knife down when you back out of my room."

With that, Nicole lunged.

Conklin sidestepped and stood between me and Nicole. I didn't have a shot. *I didn't have a shot.*

Conklin reached across the bed and grabbed Nicole by her thick dark hair; he pulled her across the bed and onto the floor. He stepped on her right hand and yelled, "Drop it!" until the knife was lying on the ground.

He kicked the knife away, and then, Nicole's hair still wrapped around his hand, he forced the woman to her feet.

Janet was screaming, "Stop! Nicole

didn't do anything. It was me. I killed all those women. It was me. It was me."

The shrieking was about to take off the top of my head. I cuffed Nicole as her mother pleaded, "You have got this *wrong.* I'm the one. It's *me.*"

Nicole was regaining her equanimity. She said, "Mom, stop the hysterics. They've got nothing on you, and they've got nothing on me."

I said, "Nicole Worley, you're under arrest on suspicion of murder."

I stepped behind Janet, told her to put her hands behind her back. I cuffed and arrested her too, read both of them their rights.

I said, "Mrs. Worley, we've got plenty of murder charges to go around. So no fighting for credit, okay?"

Nicole was laughing, but I didn't find her amusing. She was one of the scariest people I'd met in my life.

Conklin took charge of Janet, and I gave Nicole a shove toward the door.

I was desperate to get her alone in the box.

Chapter 111

Claire was in the basement of number 2, standing with Clapper in front of the chest-type freezer. They'd been staring at it for at least a full minute. She said, "What are you waiting for, Charlie? Christmas?"

"It was Christmas for someone. See how nicely the presents are wrapped?"

When the condensation blew off, Claire could clearly see that the freezer was packed to the brim with body parts. There was no order, no organization. Parts had been loaded into the chest helter-skelter, all loosely wrapped in plastic.

Clapper said, "I'm going to be the first to state the obvious. This killer had no respect for the dead."

"What brass to leave all of this right here in an unlocked chest. I just hope we've got proof positive of whodunit in here. I'm praying."

"We're going over this freezer for prints as soon as you're done here. There *will* be prints. I can almost see them with my naked eyes. We'll swab for DNA too.

"And listen, Claire," Clapper added, "you're not going to like this, but we need to know how many bodies we've got here. So can you go through it here? Count the pieces?"

It was better to load the freezer onto a flatbed truck and then take it and its contents back to the lab. But if counting pieces was a priority, it had to be done.

Claire turned to her assistant and said, "Bunny. We're going to do a five hundred series."

"Like this was a plane crash or something like that," Bunny said.

"Right. Disaster numbering system. You know how it goes?"

"Sequential numbers from five hundred up."

"Right. So that all of these individual parts are logged in one file."

Bunny laid a sheet down on the floor. It was blindingly bright in the gloom. Clapper placed a wrapped body part on the sheet, and Claire took photos.

Bunny unwrapped the plastic, tagged the arm with the number 501, and Claire put it back on the sheet; she took a couple of pictures before she wrapped the sheet around the limb. A CSI zipped the arm into a body bag.

A new sheet went down and Clapper lifted another part out of the freezer, and once again they tagged and bagged. There were dozens of parts, and Claire saw that processing this chop shop would take many long hours; first here, then a repeat of every step in the lab.

Clapper lowered a body part to the sheet. It was half a chest, sawed lengthwise between the breasts.

Bunny moaned.

"I'm going to pass out," she said. "Excuse me."

"No, no, don't—"

But the girl scrambled to her feet, found a corner of the basement, and heaved.

And then she started to cry.

Claire went over and put her arm around her assistant. "It's okay, Bunny."

"No, it's not. I contaminated the crime scene."

"Everyone does it at one time or another. I threw up *on* a body once. Go upstairs. Take a break."

"I'm okay," Bunny said. "I'm here for the duration."

"That's good, because I need you. Go upstairs and wash your face. Then please call our husbands. We're not going home tonight."

Chapter 112

Nicole Worley and I were facing off in Interview 1 while Conklin interviewed Janet in the room next door.

Our suspects were in custody and our forensic team was awash in grisly artifacts, but we were still waiting for solid evidence that conclusively tied Janet or Nicole to the human remains.

Nicole hadn't asked for a lawyer, but psychopathic serial murderers don't always want lawyers. Some like to talk to the police for days on end, a cat-and-mouse game in which they believe themselves to be the cats.

I wasn't sure what Nicole was up to, but I was willing to play along. A CSI was dusting surfaces, searching her room for evidence. And for the past couple of hours, Claire had been processing body parts taken from the basement freezer.

Nicole denied any knowledge of murders at the Ellsworth compound other than what she had learned since the police answered her mother's 911 call.

But she did like to talk about Harry Chandler.

She told me how she'd seen all of Harry's pictures dozens of times. How people she knew couldn't believe that she knew him personally. That he had been a friend of her childhood. She knew special things about him, what he liked to eat, funny things he had said.

Nicole Worley was just wild about Harry.

Or you could say she was obsessed with him.

It was time to get to the point.

"We opened the freezer," I said.

"What? The one in my basement? I

haven't used that freezer in years. I can't remember the last time."

"We lifted fingerprints from the inside of the lid," I lied. "And as we speak, body parts are being cataloged."

"That's terrible. Just terrible," she said with a tone and an expression that showed me that she didn't care at all.

I said, "I'm going to check on how things are going at the morgue."

I called Claire and she picked up on the first ring. I said, "Have you got a progress report?"

Then I turned to Nicole and said, "Sit tight. I'll be back in a while."

"I've got a headache," she said.

I left Nicole in handcuffs and went down the stairs to the lobby and out the back door, then took a brisk and chilly walk to the Medical Examiner's Office.

Claire came to the door and I followed her through to the autopsy suite.

Claire had a chunk of meat on the table in front of her. She pulled down her mask, said to me, "See, I've got to treat each part like an individual specimen. I'm x-raying each part, looking for anything that will help ID this person. Metal plates or bullets or old fractures."

"Have you found anything like that?" I asked.

The chunk of meat looked like a haunch that had belonged to a small white person, probably female.

Claire was saying, "I've got to use a clean scalpel for each part, do a unique description of each part, weigh each, look for GSR and wounds. I've taken fingerprints from a couple of hands, found one that matches our girl Marilyn Varick."

"Got anything solid that connects body parts to our killer?"

"I pulled blood whenever I could. And I made some muscle-tissue samples for DNA testing . . ."

"Claire. Claire. Have you got something for me? I've got two suspects in custody. Give me something."

Claire picked up the block of flesh on the table and turned it around. She pointed to a bloody line. I followed her finger as she showed me several other identical lines.

"See these knife wounds? Could be

they're going to match that knife of Nicole's. And look at this," Claire said.

She took a sheet off the top of a metal basin, showed me the section of shoulder in there.

She said, "Consistent with stun-gun burns. I'm guessing that's how she knocked her victims down."

"I need pictures," I said.

Chapter 113

It was two in the morning when I got back upstairs to Homicide. Conklin met me in the squad room. He said, "Harry Chandler is in Brady's office. He's waiting for you."

"Good. I asked him to come down. We can use his help. Where's Janet?"

"She's in a holding cell. I'm not getting anything believable out of her. I'll try her again in the morning."

I went into Brady's office, said hello to Harry Chandler, and thanked him for coming in at that hour.

"Happy to do it," he said. "Have you

learned anything about what happened to Cecily?"

"Janet is taking responsibility for the seven women whose heads were buried in the garden, but she can't give us any details on the murders. Nicole maintains that she's innocent. So far, nothing about your wife."

Harry nodded, then said, "Has Janet or Nicole asked for a lawyer?"

"No."

"Lindsay, I need to know what happened to Cecily. Ten years after her death, even after I was acquitted, the public still believes I killed my wife. And now people are coming up to me in restaurants calling me a murderer. They think I killed those other women too.

"I can't keep living this way. I've got an offer for Janet or Nicole, whichever one of them can name the killer and give you enough evidence to prove it."

Chandler and I discussed his offer for another minute or two, and then I asked him to stand by.

Conklin and I found Nicole napping in the interview room, cheek down on the old gray metal table. I kicked the chair and it scraped across the floor. She lifted her head and Conklin and I took chairs on either side of her.

"How's it going, Nicole?" the good cop asked her.

"It's late. I want to go home now."

I slapped morgue photos down on the table one after the other, close-up shots of arms, legs, thighs, buttocks with knife wounds, and a right shoulder blemished by burns from a stun gun.

"Do you recognize these body parts, Nicole?"

"Oh. Gross."

I pointed to the knife cuts in the quartered haunch of human flesh.

"See these? These are stab wounds. And I'm betting they're going to perfectly match the knife you were waving around a few hours ago. The lab is doing the workup now."

"Well, you gotta do what you gotta do," Nicole said.

Her words were flippant, but her expression had changed. She was starting to believe that we had evidence to indict and convict. Her eyes flicked from the photos to me and then back.

"We're only hours away from nailing you to the wall, Nicole. But if you confess before we lock this case up, you could avoid the death penalty."

"Really."

Her voice was resigned. She twisted up her hair, kept her hands on her head, leaned back in the chair, and looked at the ceiling. She was beat. And so were we.

I got up, righted Nicole's chair so that the force of the legs hitting the floor made her head jounce. I sat back down across from her.

"Look at me, Nicole."

She shook her head.

"Then listen to me. Harry Chandler wants to know what happened to his wife and to the seven other women you killed. He'll pay your attorney's fees if you confess to all of it. There is no limit to how much he'll spend on an attorney to represent you."

I got up, opened the door, and Harry Chandler came in. He was big, imposing, and he looked straight at Nicole.

He said, "It's a good deal and it's your choice. Top-dog attorney, top-drawer law firm to negotiate your sentence—or you can deny everything and get whatever kind of lawyer you can afford."

Nicole said, "Do you care about me, Harry?" She lifted her arms up to Chandler, but he backed away and left the room, closing the door behind him.

Nicole wailed, a wordless, keening cry.

Then she wiped her face with the sleeves of her turtleneck and said in an uninflected voice, "I need aspirin. I want to make a statement."

Chapter 114

It was a new day, a Friday to be exact, and Yuki, Claire, Cindy, and I were all gathered in Jackson Brady's office.

Cindy plugged in her laptop, checked the power light, got ready for her just deserts.

"Start talking, Lindsay," she said as she opened a new file. "What happened after Nicole spoke to Harry Chandler?"

"Well, she got a great lawyer, Francine Bloom, beautiful woman. Wore a three-thousand-dollar Armani suit, Ferragamos—"

"Lindsay! Stop fooling around."

Claire, Yuki, and I laughed. It was a nervous, almost giddy reaction to enormous relief.

The bloody fingerprints under the freezer lid had been smudged. The stab wounds in the body parts and the stungun wounds were inconclusive. And Janet Worley wouldn't turn on her daughter.

Maybe Nicole would have been convicted anyway, but it wouldn't have been a sure thing. Nicole's confession slammed the house-of-heads case closed.

Yuki and Claire knew it all, and now Cindy deserved the whole scoop and nothing but the scoop.

I told Cindy that we weren't laughing at her; we were just relieved. "Nicole confessed to killing the seven women whose heads were buried at the Ellsworth compound. And she confessed to killing Cecily Chandler too."

"Oh. My. God. But why?"

"Because Harry Chandler gave her a good deal. And because she believed we had incontrovertible evidence."

Cindy said, "I meant why did she kill *Cecily?*"

"This is Nicole's story, you understand. She was only sixteen when Janet and Harry got involved. Harry dumped Janet, and Nicole wanted to avenge her mother. Her idea of justice was to strangle Cecily one dark night in the garden. Take *that,* Harry."

"And what did she do with the body?"

"Dragged Cecily into the basement and then went to her mother for help."

"So Janet was part of this?" Cindy asked, fingers doing the cha-cha on her keyboard.

"Janet and Nicole sawed Cecily's body into pieces, bagged and froze the parts. Then they drove up north to Modoc National Forest."

"That's, what? A six-hour drive? They buried her body in the wilderness?"

"Nicole says that they put the wrapped parts in the backseat under a tarp. When they got to a good deserted section of road, they stopped the car every hundred yards and walked into the woods with a package for the animals to eat," I told my friend. "So Janet *was* involved in covering up Cecily's murder. She did it for Nicole, but actually she was protecting her entire family.

"According to Nicole, that was the only time she involved her mother."

"Meanwhile, Harry went on trial for Cecily's murder," Yuki said.

"Right," I said, "and with the spotlight on him and her own involvement in this crime Harry didn't commit, Nicole fixated on Harry.

"Janet and Nigel stayed on as caretakers and lived in the main house 'so the place wouldn't go cold,' as Janet said, and Nicole eventually took up residence in number two.

"By then, she had a degree in biology, a driver's license, unrequited love for Harry, and recurring fantasies about killing again."

Cindy told me to hang on a minute, which I did, and then she said, "So, the victims come from many parts of the world. They were all on a house tour, maybe self-guided tours."

"Exactly. Every now and then a tourist, a Harry Chandler fan, presented Nicole with an opportunity to relive her first murder," I said. "She knew which ones were unlikely to be reported missing right away, and Nicole told us that she liked petite dark-haired women who reminded her of Cecily."

Claire said, "What she'd do is take them down to the basement on a pretext of showing them some of Harry's personal trophies, and they were easy enough to kill. A zap with a stun gun from behind, then a knife across the throat."

Yuki said, "She got the disposal part down to near perfection. Then, thank God, she got lazy."

"Lazy, but not crazy," I said. "Nicole knows right from wrong. You know what she said to me when I took her to jail? 'Tell my mom to be happy for me. I retired at the top of my game.'"

Chapter 115

The Women's Murder Club was going for a ride in my Explorer on our way to a long overdue reckoning. I was behind the wheel and Cindy was behind me, leaning over the seat divider, breathing down my neck.

We headed up Seventh at a good clip, crossed Market, passed the Civic Center BART, then turned left on McAllister.

I slowed the car and stopped at the light. There was a pack of unmarked cars parked in front of the Asian Art Museum, across the street from the Abby Hotel. Just as promised.

The Abby Hotel was a peach-colored six-story Victorian building with white trim, a brown awning over the entrance, and a fire escape zigzagging up the front of the building.

It stood in all its shabby elegance across the street from the Asian Art Museum, two blocks from City Hall. The homeless roamed this part of McAllister freely, but it was also the hub of government and legal activity.

Now, at noon, the streets and sidewalks were filled with suited men and women from the courts carrying briefcases or pulling luggage trolleys, their heads bent to their iPhones.

I parked in front of the hotel, and the girls and I got out of my car. I showed my badge to the doorman, a gnarled-looking boozer somewhere between his late fifties and early seventies. It looked to me as though the last time he'd had his uniform cleaned was—never.

Then I bent at the window of an unmarked car to talk to Lieutenant Meile from Vice. He was working off his guilty conscience by giving us a tip and following up by providing all hands on deck.

He gave me a room number, said, "History tells us he'll be in there for another twenty minutes."

Two cops from Vice, Billy Fried and Johnny Rizzo, got out of the unmarked and joined me and the girls on the sidewalk.

The six of us entered the Abby's scruffy, mildewed lobby; we passed on the rickety metal elevator car and instead took the fire stairs to the third floor.

Vice took the lead. Fried rapped on the door while Rizzo took a stance on the other side of the doorway, holding his gun in a two-fisted grip.

Fried said, "Open the door. This is the SFPD."

There was a scuffle inside, two alarmed voices, and then the sound of something crashing.

Fried turned the knob, saw the chain, and applied the force of his foot to break in the door. He stepped in and said, "Hands up, Blayney. Everyone, freeze."

I headed into the room and saw Jason Blayney raise his hands, dropping the stained sheet he'd been holding in front of his privates. Jewel Bling, a low-rent call girl, was still in the bed. She drew a ratty blanket up to her chest. A lamp had been shattered during Blayney's overheated rush to get dressed and lay on the carpet of this beyond horrific maroon-and-gray-appointed room.

"I'm researching a story on prostitution," Blayney yelled. A bulb hanging from a cord above him swayed, casting a harsh, unflattering light on his blanched face and naked body.

"Research?" The hooker hooted. "What kind of research? How many times you can get your pipes cleaned for thirty dollars?"

Cindy stepped forward with her camera and shot a lot of pictures of Blayney trying to cover himself with his hands.

"I want to make a deal," said Jewel Bling.

"Shut up!" Blayney bellowed.

He grabbed the sheet off the floor and turned a pitiful face to Cindy. His eyes were squinched up, and he cried out, "Cindy, please. Let this go and I promise I'll make it up to you."

I was stunned.

This was the bastard who wrote lies and leaked information for the pure glory of getting his name on the front page. Now he was begging for mercy.

"My wife will leave me if she sees those pictures," he said. "She'll take the kids. They're all still young. I won't be able to explain this to them."

I couldn't take it anymore.

"You're a hypocrite, Blayney. This is part of the SFPD's crackdown on crime. He's your collar, Billy."

Billy Fried walked to Blayney, dragged the reporter's hands behind his back, and cuffed him.

"You're under arrest for pandering, buddy. Don't worry. The penalty is just going to be a fine."

Cindy fired off a few more shots with her Nikon, then said, "I think I've got your best angle, Jason. And don't worry. I will spell your name right. You don't have to worry about *that*."

Chapter 116

Rich Conklin was dragged away from a deep place of no pain.

He'd been sleeping when Cindy squeezed his good shoulder, called his name. He opened his eyes and saw the tops of her breasts showing in the neckline of her loose pink top.

"If you don't get up, you won't be able to sleep tonight," she said.

He loved looking at her sweet face. Her rhinestone clip sparkled in her blond curls. Rhinestones looked like diamonds on Cindy. Still, he wanted to get her actual diamonds someday.

"Come to bed," he said. He took her hand, tugged on it.

She frowned, said, "No. You have to get up. Come on." She left the room.

"What's wrong, Cin?"

"You said you wanted to talk," she called.

"I said that? Oh, last week? When you were steaming toward a deadline and said you couldn't be disturbed?"

Rich heard her choking on a laugh in the next room.

He swung his legs over the side of the bed, looked at the clock on the nightstand. It was almost six. Jeez. He'd been sleeping all day.

He shuffled into the living room in his T-shirt, sling, boxers.

The table was set and champagne was open, standing in a flowerpot full of ice. Cindy bent over the table and lit some candles.

"Sit here, honey," she said, patting the back of the chair.

He did what she told him to do, then watched her pour champagne into the two flutes they had gotten at a flea market six months ago.

"What's the occasion?" he asked.

"It's a new tradition," Cindy told him.

Now he smelled the aroma of herbs and spices coming from the kitchen. He hadn't eaten anything in twelve hours.

"What are we calling this tradition?" he asked.

"It's the first-day-of-the-month dinner, Richie. And I propose that we do this every month, no matter what. No matter what case. No matter what deadline. We need to shut everything off for an hour and just be together."

"Sure, Cindy. It's a good idea. Why do you look so sad?"

"I have to apologize."

"For?"

"I've been straying in my mind."

"Some other guy?"

"No, not that."

Cindy explained to him that she'd been in a panic about committing to marriage and motherhood, had worried about losing her place as a journalist, being marginalized as a part-time writer.

"I've been keeping part of myself out of our relationship."

"Okay, stop beating yourself up now."

He got up from his seat and hugged Cindy with his good arm. "I want you to be happy, Cindy. I know you're ambitious and I love that about you. Plus, I'm a boring guy without you."

"I was so scared when you got shot."

"I know."

"It got me focused on the right stuff."

"Did you make beef stew?"

"For instance, that you're just the best man in the world."

"Do you love me?"

"Yes, Richie. I do."

"Did you make your deadline today?"

"Uh-huh."

"Are you pregnant?"

"Nope."

"We won't have babies until you say so. *If* you say so."

"You still want to marry me?"

"Feed me our new traditional first-day-of-the-month dinner, Cindy. Please?"

"You betcha. I might have burned it though."

"Kiss me."

"Okay. Here. Here. And here."

"After we eat, let's go to bed."

Chapter 117

Jacobi and I were having dinner at Aziza, a Moroccan restaurant; aromatic, homey, decorated in deep, earthy tones, and fragrant with all the spices of Arabia.

Jacobi's color was good and he was wearing a blue sweater that made him look years younger than his age. Better than he'd looked in a long time.

"William Randall died without gaining consciousness," Jacobi told me. "Good side of that is that he wasn't convicted of anything. His widow will still get his pension."

"You think Randall knew that Chaz Smith was a dirty cop?"

Jacobi shrugged. "He could have known. It's very possible. Ah. I got back the ballistics, Lindsay."

"Are you going to tell me something bad, Jacobi? Because I just want to catch up and have dinner."

"The shot to Randall's kidney came from Brady's gun. That was the kill shot, and since Brady's going to be on leave for a while, it won't matter if he has to be without his gun and badge while we prove he fired on Randall in self-defense."

"Don't tell me I have to keep running the squad, Jacobi. I really don't want to do it."

"I'm going to be running the squad. Me."

"Yeah?" I grinned. I liked what Jacobi was saying. A lot.

"Until Brady returns and I can move back upstairs to my nice office with its beautiful view of Bryant Street."

I slapped his hand above the plate of couscous, lifted my virgin mojito, and said, "Here's to having you back in the corner office."

Jacobi grinned and clinked his glass against mine, and then he laughed.

"I'm not going to let you cowboy around while I'm running the squad."

"Oh, like you can change me. Don't get your hopes up."

"You've got a baby in the oven, Boxer—"

"I think that's 'bun in the oven'—"

"And I'm part of your family. Don't forget that I walked you down the aisle on the happiest day of your life."

"I haven't forgotten."

I hadn't forgotten a minute of that day. Me on Jacobi's arm. Walking on rose petals. Seeing my husband-to-be waiting for me in the gazebo overlooking the sea.

I put my hand on my tummy, stared off into space, then came back to the moment when I realized that Jacobi was staring at me.

"Is something wrong, Boxer?"

I touched his hand. "You were terrific that day. Standing up for me."

"It was a great honor."

His eyes showed me what I already knew. How much he cared. How close we had been and would always be.

"I'm going to get sloppy," I said. "Brace yourself."

"No, no, please don't do that," he joked.

I got up and went around the table and he stood up, and I hugged him really hard. I said into his ear, "I missed you, Warren. I'm so glad you're coming back."

Chapter 118

It was a pretty Sunday morning and I was at Mountain Lake Park, herding children.

Well, *Martha* was herding children and I was blowing the whistle and giving commands. Martha was a little older than the kids, who were about six or seven, three girls and a boy.

I held Martha by the scruff of her neck, said, "Get 'em," let her go, and she loped over to the little squealers and ran circles around them. I said, "Come," blew on the whistle—high-low-high—and Martha ran back to me, wagging her tail, happy lights sparkling in her eyes.

I asked her to cut between the little kids, separate the tallest little girl from the rest. The kids and their nannies laughed and more people gathered.

Other dogs saw that a good time was going on and wanted to get in on it. And so barking and yapping added volume and range to the giddiness.

Bystanders called out asking for more tricks, and volunteers stepped forward to be herded. Martha showed off and we got rounds of applause.

Oh, man, I had to do this more often.

And that's when I felt a pain in my gut.

I bent over, grabbed my knees, and Martha broke ranks and licked my face. I was hit with another cramp, and this time, I thought the worst.

I was about to miscarry in my second trimester. How could this happen? *Please, God. Don't let me lose my baby.*

I leashed Martha, summoned a smile for the children, waved good-bye, and found a bench at the edge of the park.

My cell phone wasn't charged to the

limit, but I had enough juice to call police dispatch, then my doctor, and then Joe. I was able to reach only the police.

A squad car pulled up. Tom Ferrino jumped out.

I said, "Take me to the hospital, Tommy. I'm going to give you my keys so you can bring Martha home afterward."

"What's wrong, Sergeant? Are you in pain?"

He helped me and Martha into the back of the car.

"Put on the siren," I said. "Drive as fast as you can."

My phone rang as we rounded the corner from Arguello Boulevard to Sacramento Street and were in sight of the hospital. I looked at my phone. The caller was Joe.

"Where are you?" I asked him.

"I'm at the airport. My flight leaves in fifteen minutes. What's happening?"

"You're going back to DC?" I asked.

I'd lost him. I'd lost Joe to that woman in DC. I'd shut him out, locked my door, refused phone calls. What in God's name could I expect? I bit my lip and held on to the armrest as the cramps hit me again.

Joe said, "I'm told that I'm the best border security guy around. I'm in demand." He laughed. "Lindsay? I can't hear you. Wait until the sirens blow past you."

I shouted, "I'm going to Metro Hospital. I need you, Joe. I need you to come right now. The sirens are with *me*."

Chapter 119

I was home in bed, under the covers and with orders to rest. The cramping had turned out to be nothing more than ligaments stretching to support my growing womb.

But with the pain and my stress level, which was off the charts, I panicked.

Joe had canceled his flight and was sitting in the chair next to the bed with his shoes off, his feet on the mattress. My fingers crawled over to his toes and held them.

Joe was saying, "She had been my partner. When I was a Fed."

"June Freundorfer."

"We had a thing after my divorce."

"A thing."

"A fling."

"Did you love her?"

"Maybe. Once. But then I wanted to move on. I said so and June took our breakup hard. I started seeing *you*. I fell in love with *you*."

I felt tears welling up, but I was determined not to cry.

"I fell in love with my honey-blond honey Lindsay Boxer, Sergeant Superwoman, SFPD. June asked about you and I told her."

"Uh-huh."

"She called me a lot. Sometimes I talked to her. She got promoted. After that, she called me less. A couple of years passed and I assumed she was over me. I had lunch with her a few times, as friends. And yes, I went with her to that charity dinner. I should have told you, but I thought the explanation was going to make it seem like more than it was. It was easier just to take her to the dinner and then fly home.

"Then Jason Blayney came across the photo. Don't ask me how."

"So why did June tell me that you two were still involved?"

"She lied, Lindsay. She lied her face off. I can't know what she was thinking, but I'm guessing she was trying to drive a wedge between us. She hasn't given up."

I looked into Joe's eyes. I like to think that I'm very good at telling when a person is lying. Joe's eyes didn't shift to either side. He kept a soft and steady gaze, put his hand on my cheek. I moved the blanket aside.

Patted the bed next to me.

Joe sighed happily, undid his belt, shucked his clothes, and came into the bed. I rolled toward him, put my hand on his chest. It was a gentle, even tentative touch.

I had to get used to being with him again.

Joe put his arms around me and pulled me close. He wasn't tentative at all.

"I'm two hundred percent yours, blondie. I'm sorry this happened."

"I'm sorry I didn't believe you, Joe."

"It takes a while to make a marriage. We're new at this. We're still working out the kinks."

I nodded, held on tight to my husband, my baby's wonderful dad. I fell asleep. When my eyes opened again, Joe was still there, his arms around me and our baby.

I woke my husband up so that I could kiss him and tell him how much I loved him. I truly did.

Acknowledgments

Our thanks and gratitude to these top professionals who were so generous with their time and expertise: Captain Richard Conklin, Stamford, Connecticut, Police Department; Dr. Humphrey Germaniuk, medical examiner and coroner, Trumbull County, Ohio; attorneys Philip R. Hoffman and Steven M. Rabinowitz, New York City; Chuck Hanni, IAAI-CFI; and forensic science consultant Elaine M. Pagliaro, MS, JD.

Thanks too to our talented researchers Ingrid Taylar and Lynn Colomello, and to Mary Jordan, aka the Control Tower.

About the Authors

JAMES PATTERSON has had more *New York Times* bestsellers than any other writer ever, according to *Guinness World Records*. Since his first novel won the Edgar Award, in 1977, James Patterson's books have sold more than 240 million copies. He is the author of the Alex Cross novels, the most popular detective series of the past twenty-five years, including *Kiss the Girls* and *Along Came a Spider*. Mr. Patterson also writes the bestselling Women's Murder Club novels, set in San Francisco, and the top-selling New York detective series of all time, featuring Detective Michael Bennett.

James Patterson also writes books for young readers, including the Maximum Ride, Daniel X, Witch & Wizard, and Middle School series. In total, these books have spent more than 230 weeks on national bestseller lists.

His lifelong passion for books and reading led James Patterson to launch the website ReadKiddoRead.com to give adults an easy way to locate the very best books for kids. He writes full-time and lives in Florida with his family.

MAXINE PAETRO is the author of three novels and two works of nonfiction, and she is the coauthor of several books with James Patterson. She lives in New York with her husband.

Books by James Patterson

FEATURING ALEX CROSS

Kill Alex Cross • *Cross Fire* • *I, Alex Cross* • *Alex Cross's* Trial (with Richard DiLallo) • *Cross Country* • *Double Cross* • *Cross* • *Mary, Mary* • *London Bridges* • *The Big Bad Wolf* • *Four Blind Mice* • *Violets Are Blue* • *Roses Are Red* • *Pop Goes the Weasel* • *Cat & Mouse* • *Jack & Jill* • *Kiss the Girls* • *Along Came a Spider*

THE WOMEN'S MURDER CLUB

11th Hour (with Maxine Paetro) • *10th Anniversary* (with Maxine Paetro) • *The 9th Judgment* (with Maxine Paetro) • *The 8th Confession* (with Maxine Paetro) • *7th Heaven* (with Maxine Paetro) • *The 6th Target* (with Maxine Paetro) • *The 5th Horseman* (with Maxine Paetro) • *4th of July* (with Maxine Paetro) • *3rd Degree* (with Andrew Gross) • *2nd Chance* (with Andrew Gross) • *1st to Die*

FEATURING MICHAEL BENNETT

Tick Tock (with Michael Ledwidge) •
Worst Case (with Michael Ledwidge) •
Run for Your Life (with Michael Ledwidge)
• *Step on a Crack* (with Michael Ledwidge)

THE PRIVATE NOVELS

Private Games (with Mark Sullivan) •
Private: #1 Suspect (with Maxine Paetro) •
Private (with Maxine Paetro)

OTHER BOOKS

Guilty Wives (with David Ellis) •
The Christmas Wedding (with Richard
DiLallo) • *Kill Me If You Can* (with Marshall
Karp) • *Now You See Her* (with Michael
Ledwidge) • *Toys* (with Neil McMahon) •
Don't Blink (with Howard Roughan) •
The Postcard Killers (with Liza Marklund) •
The Murder of King Tut (with Martin
Dugard) • *Swimsuit* (with Maxine Paetro) •
Against Medical Advice (with Hal Friedman)
• *Sail* (with Howard Roughan) • *Sundays at
Tiffany's* (with Gabrielle Charbonnet) •
You've Been Warned (with Howard

Roughan) • *The Quickie* (with Michael Ledwidge) • *Judge & Jury* (with Andrew Gross) • *Beach Road* (with Peter de Jonge) • *Lifeguard* (with Andrew Gross) • *Honeymoon* (with Howard Roughan) • *Sam's Letters to Jennifer* • *The Lake House* • *The Jester* (with Andrew Gross) • *The Beach House* (with Peter de Jonge) • *Suzanne's Diary for Nicholas* • *Cradle and All* • *When the Wind Blows* • *Miracle on the 17th Green* (with Peter de Jonge) • *Hide & Seek* • *The Midnight Club* • *Black Friday* (originally published as *Black Market*) • *See How They Run* (originally published as *The Jericho Commandment*) • *Season of the Machete* • *The Thomas Berryman Number*

FOR READERS OF ALL AGES

Middle School: Get Me Out of Here (with Chris Tebbetts, illustrated by Laura Park) • *Maximum Ride: The Manga, Vol. 5* (with NaRae Lee) • *Witch & Wizard: The Fire* (with Jill Dembowski) • *Witch & Wizard: The Manga, Vol. 1* (with Gabrielle Charbonnet, illustrated by Svetlana Chmakova) • *Daniel X: Game Over* (with

Ned Rust) • *Daniel X: The Manga, Vol. 2* (with Ned Rust, illustrated by SeungHui Kye) • *Middle School: The Worst Years of My Life* (with Chris Tebbetts, illustrated by Laura Park) • *Maximum Ride: The Manga, Vol. 4* (with NaRae Lee) • *ANGEL: A Maximum Ride Novel* • *Witch & Wizard: The Gift* (with Ned Rust) • *Daniel X: The Manga, Vol. 1* (with Michael Ledwidge, illustrated by SeungHui Kye) • *Maximum Ride: The Manga, Vol. 3* (with NaRae Lee) • *Daniel X: Demons and Druids* (with Adam Sadler) • *Med Head [Against Medical Advice* teen edition] (with Hal Friedman) • *FANG: A Maximum Ride Novel* • *Witch & Wizard* (with Gabrielle Charbonnet) • *Maximum Ride: The Manga, Vol. 2* (with NaRae Lee) • *Daniel X: Watch the Skies* (with Ned Rust) • *MAX: A Maximum Ride Novel* • *Maximum Ride: The Manga, Vol. 1* (with NaRae Lee) • *Daniel X: Alien Hunter* (graphic novel; with Leopoldo Gout) • *The Dangerous Days of Daniel X* (with Michael Ledwidge) • *Maximum Ride: The Final Warning* • *Maximum Ride: Saving the World and Other Extreme Sports* • *Maximum Ride:*

School's Out—Forever • *Maximum Ride:*
The Angel Experiment • *santaKid*

For previews and information about the
author, visit JamesPatterson.com or find
him on Facebook or at your app store.